THE TRAVELS OF MAUDIE TIPSTAFF

Plagued by a roisterous husband, strait-laced, outspoken, domineering, Maudie Tipstaff has been invited by her two daughters and her son to spend four months with each of them. It is almost the first time she has ever left Glasgow. This is the story of these remarkable visits, by the author of *Georgy Girl*.

MARGARET FORSTER

The Travels
of Maudie Tipstaff

WORLD BOOKS : LONDON

First published in England 1967
This edition published 1969 by
World Books, 9 Grape Street, London W.C.2.
By arrangement with Martin Secker & Warburg Limited

Printed in Great Britain by Richard Clay (The Chaucer Press), Ltd.,
Bungay, Suffolk

For
JAKE
who sat through this with me

PROLOGUE

Maudie inspected the room and kitchen for the last time. At ten o'clock, Mrs McAllister from the shop was coming to collect the key, the front door Yale key and the big, heavy back door key. Every week she would come in and give the place a bit of a dust and pay the rent on a Friday dinner-time. Maudie could have paid the rent in advance for a year, she had the money. But she didn't want it that way. She wanted it paid every Friday dinner-time, just as usual, for one week only.

There wasn't a speck of dirt anywhere. Maudie could see a hundred and one things that still ought to have been done, so she cursed and swore and got ready to protest to Mrs McAllister that she was leaving her place like a pigsty. She knew, of course, that in fact hers was the cleanest room and kitchen in the whole of the building. Indeed, when MacPhail collected the rent he said, week in and week out, that she had the cleanest, brightest wee place in the whole of Glasgow.

Maudie hesitated in front of the clock. It was a grandmother clock, hanging in the recess between the bed-in-the-wall and the clothes press. It was inlaid with mother of pearl and had been presented to Maudie's father by all the other butchers in Glasgow in recognition for his services to their new union. Maudie's dilemma was whether to stop it herself, or let it run down. On the one hand, it was tidier to stop it. She would be able to visualise the time it showed on its handsome face when she was imagining all her other possessions in the positions she had left them. But on the other hand, it would be comforting to think of some sound in her home when she had gone and left it for the first time in fifty-one years.

She decided to leave it. Walking over to the sideboard, she

7

checked again that all the doors were locked and the drawers firmly shut. There were two dozen lace tablecloths inside, some almost new, and even the very old and worn so exquisitely darned that the darn was like an addition to the pattern. Her best china, her silver teapot, her bone-handled Sheffield cutlery and her embroidered napkins, were all in there too. Mrs McAllister was to check them every other week. The big gate-legged table was covered with a dark green cloth and the leather-seated chairs were pushed together so that they touched each other underneath. The sofa had a freshly laundered but second-best cover on it, and so had the two easy chairs. The curtains of the bed-in-the-wall were drawn together, with the bed inside stripped and shrouded in a cotton counterpane.

Now for the vital jobs. Turn the gas knobs even harder to the right, see that the main tap beside the meter was at the black OFF. Push the electricity handle up, so that it was off too. See that the light switches were up—one never knew with electricity: the main might be off but sometimes funny things happened and Maudie didn't want any of her lights shining out for all Glasgow to see in the middle of the day. She had already been outside to see that the water was off. The taps inside had been twisted till they ached. The plug was in the sink, the overflow was clear, and to make doubly sure Maudie had put a big tin tub underneath. Lastly, the curtains. There was an in-between way that the whole building adopted when they went out. The curtains were pulled together until they were a foot apart and that signified neither being permanently drawn, as at night or for a funeral, nor properly open as during the day. The half net curtains stayed as they were, successfully blocking any view in or out.

These things done, Maudie put on her gloves, took hold of her umbrella in one hand and her handbag in the other and stood waiting in the middle of the room. She couldn't sit down because that meant disturbing something and that she wasn't going to do just for the sake of an idle five minutes. So she stood still, with her feet slightly outturned and leaning a little

8

forward, which was how she had been led to believe that the Royal family were trained to stand for long periods. She could not help but look at herself in the mantel mirror, though it was a practice the minister quite rightly disapproved of. But it wasn't as though she was doing it for reasons of vanity. At sixty-eight she had no notions of fancying herself like some. As long as her face was clean and her hat proper, that was all she wished to see.

She wished Mrs McAllister would come. She could go to the shop and give her the keys, but there were burglars everywhere noticing things like that. Besides, it wouldn't do. The handing over of her keys was ceremonial. It had to take place right here in her room or she wouldn't leave happy.

It wasn't that the waiting made her nervous so much as miserable. Even at this late, irrevocable hour she was still not sure that she was doing the *right* thing. It was certainly the obvious, even the natural thing to do. Nobody could blame her for going to live with her own children now that Joseph had gone. They all had homes, they had all written and pressed her to come and live with them for good, never mind just for four months each. Many would have given up their room and kitchen and gone to live with one or other forever. But Maudie remained unconvinced that she was doing the right thing, right for herself and right for her children. She was used to being independent. She'd had her own home and her own ways for too long to relish being in someone else's house. And then she hadn't really tasted her freedom. It was barely four months since Joseph had gone and there had been so much to do that she hadn't had time to feel lonely.

Sighing, Maudie shifted her weight again. It might work, standing like that, if you were trained as a child, but it didn't seem to work for her. Then her eye caught just a slight flash of blue through the net curtain and she cheered up as she realised it was Mrs McAllister's hat passing her window. Relieved, she took the keys from her bag. What was done, was done, that was what she must remember. She had decided to go and see them

9

all, therefore she must want to and it was perfectly right. If it wasn't, she could come straight back.

Mrs McAllister panted up the steps and hammered on the door. Maudie maintained she was a little deaf, though she had a keen enough ear for gossip as everyone knew fine well, and Mrs McAllister didn't want her not to hear and then accuse her of being late. She was early. Ten had been the time and it was only three minutes to, but Maudie had a habit of treating everyone who wasn't half an hour early as late. Like everyone else, Mrs McAllister was afraid of Maudie Tipstaff, even though she was counted as one of her closest friends. She was afraid of her tongue and her wrath. Being Maudie's friend was one of the most exacting roles life could call upon one to fill. It required depths of loyalty known only to the slaves of Eastern despots. Maudie could not stand lying, unpunctuality, deceit, hypocrisy or any lack of gratitude. She was particularly strong on this latter requirement. Everyone had cause to be grateful to God, Queen and Maudie and let not him or her forget it.

'I thought you were never coming,' snapped Maudie. She eyed the breathless Mrs McAllister with doubt. She had perhaps misplaced her trust. Annie McAllister had a scattiness in her that only the most firm handling could control, and God only knew what would happen now that that hand was to be removed. But she lived near and for one reason and another was the best choice of an ungrateful bunch.

'You said ten,' said Mrs McAllister, 'and it's only after being three minutes to.'

'I didn't say you were late,' said Maudie. 'I know I said ten. But I thought you were never coming.'

'I left John Graham slicing his own bacon,' said Mrs McAllister.

'That's nothing to do with me,' said Maudie. 'You should get yourself better organised. Now, step inside.'

Mrs McAllister stepped, and Maudie held out her hands, a key in each hand.

'That,' she said sternly, moving the right one, 'is a Yale key,

Annie. It's for my front door. You mustn't use it at all. You'll keep it in this little bag on the string I've made for you and it can hang round your neck. Nobody will see it, and if Alan says anything you can tell him it's my key. But you are never to use it. I'm giving it to you for safe keeping only. Is that understood?'

'Yes,' said Mrs McAllister. She had been through all this before and had debated with herself the wisdom of asking Maudie why she didn't take the key with her. But there was bound to be a reason, and she would just make herself look ungrateful.

'And this,' said Maudie, 'is the back door key. You'll get in and out with this. You're not to leave it with yours above your back door, for that's a sinful temptation to thieves. You're to keep it in your purse and never let it out of your sight. You're only to use it to get in and out of here on a Friday forenoon. Is that understood? Were you listening, Annie McAllister?'

'Yes, Maudie. That's the front key that I'm not to use and that's the back that I'm to get in by and keep in my purse.'

Reluctantly, Maudie gave her the keys. Promptly, Mrs McAllister hung the one round her neck like an albatross and put the other in her leather purse that stayed in her pinafore pocket.

'Now,' said Maudie, 'if there's any trouble, what are you to do?'

'Tell the minister.'

'Right. And he'll inform me. He's got all my addresses. You're to pick the rent up from his house every Friday morning. He'll draw it every Thursday afternoon, and we'll just have to hope that the manse is safe overnight. Now, if I'm coming back, I'll let him know and he'll tell you and you'll come and light a fire. That's all, I don't want you doing anything else and muddling everything up. Just light a fire.'

'Yes, Maudie.'

'Well, I'd better be going.' Maudie ushered Mrs McAllister out, and with a brief glance round, locked the door with the spare key she was taking with her. It was done. Feeling a little choked and stuffed up with emotion, but determined that Mrs McAllister should not see this, she held on to the iron rail and walked firmly down the steps. She knew folk would be looking out of their windows—they all knew about her travels. But she had bid her goodbyes to those who deserved them and she wasn't going to start again with a lot of waving.

'I hope you enjoy yourself, Maudie,' said Mrs McAllister when they got past the buildings and out on to the street where her shop was.

'I'm not going to enjoy myself,' said Maudie sternly. 'I'm going because it's my duty.'

'You're lucky having children and grandchildren that are longing to meet and love you,' said Mrs McAllister, unforgivably carried away.

'Don't start that,' rebuked Maudie. 'Luck doesn't come into it and I've told you that before.'

'I was only wishing I was off to see my children and grandchildren that I haven't got,' said Mrs McAllister.

'Don't talk so silly,' said Maudie. 'Get yourself back in that shop.'

She knew Annie dearly wanted her to cry. Well, she wasn't going to. There was nothing to cry about. Not even bothering to see if her final command had been obeyed, she walked to the bus stop, and when the bus came, got on, settled herself comfortably and refused to look at her room window as they re-passed it.

The night before, John Mackey had taken her cases down to the station for her. He was an obliging man, even if he had been a friend of Joseph's, and he had a car so she hadn't felt it was taking advantage of him. He had given her the left luggage tickets within the hour and refused to take any money. Maudie had felt that wasn't right, but he had a will to match her own. He had offered to take her to the station and see her on the bus but Maudie had said she wasn't incapable, yet. She was glad, however, now that it came to the bit, that he had taken the cases. There was a lot to be done. She had her ticket, but she must get a porter, however much she despised such a thing, and find the bus and a seat and get all her things together. She needed all the rest she could get before this ordeal, or she would find herself having to take a pill.

Furtively, Maudie felt for the box. The white cardboard cube felt fragile to her touch. She ought to have put it inside a tin box. Vexed, she half drew it out of her bag and peeping inside saw the red pills, tiny and uncrushed. They were for her pain. Before Joseph went, in the middle of all the heartbreak and tears, she had had a sudden and violent pain across her chest. She got over it each time and stopped eating hot scones for a while, but then it happened in front of the doctor and he had forced her to let him examine her. She had been furious when he told her to rest or she would kill herself. He had given her the pills and said when she felt a pain she must swallow one and then tell him. Maudie had no intention of doing either, but she had remembered them when she knew she was to set off on her travels and had brought them.

The bus rattled over the last remaining cobbles in Glasgow and Maudie was glad that the long distance bus had a lavatory. She wouldn't have any trouble with her bowels because she'd taken her Sennacot tablets last night and they had worked perfectly this morning. But she would want to spend a penny at least once during the day and it would have been a dreadful worry trying to gauge all the stops so that she wouldn't be caught short in between. There was, however, a proper lavatory. The booking clerk had been quite adamant about that. So Maudie had written to Jean and told her she was definitely coming by bus at a saving of £4 10s. on the rail fare.

There had been endless letters about this. Jean had written that they were paying her fare and wanted her to come in seven hours, not fifteen. Maudie had said that if it took seven hours it might as well take fifteen. Jean said Edward would be furious if she came by bus. She was too old for such a journey and anyway it would look bad. Maudie sent back the cheque he had enclosed and the time of her arrival at Victoria Coach Station. To her, it was quite simple: you could pay £4 10s. or you could pay £8 10s. to go to the same place. Money was money. If the bus had had no lavatory the reckoning would have been slightly different, but even so the bus would have won.

Maudie got off one bus and went in search of the other. She was panting ever so slightly with the excitement and her cheeks were flushed. She pursed her lips and strove to keep calm and be businesslike. First, she found the luggage office and got her cases, and then she looked around for someone to carry them. She was perfectly prepared to give the right man a shilling. But there didn't seem to be any porters. She tested the weight of one case and knew it was too much for her. Perhaps she could find the bus and the driver might help, but then someone might steal her cases while she was gone. The dilemma brought two bright red spots of colour to her already pink cheeks.

'What's the matter, mother?' said the left luggage man, who had eyed her all along with amusement.

'I'll need to have these cases carried to the bus,' said Maudie.

'Which bus?' the man said.

Maudie almost said the one with the lavatory. 'To London. The 11 a.m. to London.'

The man turned to the boy helping him. 'Take these along for grandma,' he said, and smiled at Maudie, who felt compelled to smile back. 'She's going to see the Queen, aren't you, darling?' Maudie stiffened. Familiarity was never to be tolerated, whatever the circumstances. Luckily, the boy had already gone with the case so she could afford to walk stiffly away. She could hear the man laughing.

Choosing a seat was a dreadful responsibility. She knew all about being in the middle of trains in case they crashed but wasn't sure if the same rule applied for buses. She didn't want to sit near the door and get the draught, or over a wheel and

14

get the vibration, or near the engine and get the fumes. The back part bounced and the front part shook. She sat in five seats in rapid succession, changing her mind each time she was settled. When at last she had decided on a right hand gangway seat midway between door and driver, she sighed with satisfaction. Hardly had she taken her heavy overcoat off before she felt the twinge of a new doubt: which way would the sun be? But she shook that one off and stayed put.

There was still half an hour to go and no one else in the bus. Maudie marvelled at how late people could leave it to catch vital buses. She watched the latecomers taking their places, hugging to herself the folly of their choices. When the bus was ready to go, it seemed two people still had not arrived. The bus waited a few minutes and Maudie seethed. It was disgraceful. A timetable was a timetable. They knew full well what time the bus was to leave. If they weren't on it, that was their fault. The driver had no business to keep punctual people waiting. She longed to shout 'Start the bus!' When, as the driver revved the engine, a young couple hurled themselves on to the bus, laughing and giggling in a thoroughly disgusting manner, Maudie almost burst a blood vessel. If they'd had the decency to look ashamed, if it was obvious they'd been held up by an accident or a bereavement, if they'd got on in a proper way and apologised to the rest of the passengers, but to laugh and carry on like that...

It took Maudie to Hamilton Cross before she had calmed down sufficiently to arrange herself for the journey. She had brought some knitting with her to while away the time, and the parish magazine which she had kept for three days unread, and the children's latest letters. They had all written to her to catch her before she left. Jean had written only a short note. Maudie examined the postmark carefully before taking the single sheet of blue paper out. Seven-fifteen was a funny time to have posted a letter. She knew, of course, that this was the collection time, but even so it must have been posted very late at night or it would have had the 10 p.m. stamp.

15

Jean said she hoped the journey wouldn't be too exhausting but that she could in any case sleep all the next day if she wanted. Maudie snorted. Sleeping during the day was a purely heathen habit. They were all looking forward to seeing her. That was all, but then it was understandable, Maudie allowed that. Jean wasn't a good correspondent but this time she had an excuse.

Sally had sent a letter card. If Jean didn't write much or often, Sally was worse. A letter card was good for her. Usually it was a plain postcard with about five words on it. She said have a good time at Jean's and hurry on to us, the wee ones are longing for their grannie. Then the rest was full of things that had gone wrong on their farm. Maudie grew impatient over the endless accounts of potatoes and cows and pigs. She didn't know how Sally could be bothered. She wasn't even sure if she wanted to hurry on to the big, cold farmhouse full of howls and screaming and fights.

Putting the girls' brief messages away, Maudie unfolded the airmail letter from Robert. There were six, large, single space typewritten pages, all full of love and concern for Maudie and accounts of the island and how happy they would be when Maudie got there. Maudie read all Robert's letters several times a day on the days after they arrived, and she hardly seemed to have fully drunk in the last one before another arrived. Maudie never gave up exclaiming that such a son could have come from such a father. The warmth and openness of his letters shocked as well as secretly delighted her. She had never nurtured such demonstrativeness. She couldn't remember even having kissed Robert after he was a baby, and not much then, and yet he wrote as though they had been, and still were, close and intimate. It overwhelmed her. She was almost afraid to meet him again, but then letters were one thing and real life behaviour another. And the letters were all she had had for so many years from him. Once he had gone abroad, first America, then Europe, he had never had the money to come back, and she had never been able to go to him, until

16

now. It was because she wanted to be with Robert the most that she had left him to the last, just as she ate the best bits of meat on her plate after the fatty bits and the vegetables. Always take the worst first, then you've the best to look forward to.

Briskly, Maudie checked herself for such wandering thoughts. She must keep occupied. It did her no good at all to indulge in such daydreaming. All the way to Carlisle, she knitted fiercely and almost finished the sleeve of Nicholas's pullover. She was sure he didn't need a pullover, but it seemed only proper to knit a garment for someone in the household she was visiting, even though Sally's brood clearly needed her services more. At Carlisle, there was a stop. Maudie didn't want to leave the bus in case anyone stole her tweed coat, but she didn't want to wear it for it was really a very warm day. She compromised by standing on the steps and looking across at a bakery where there were some delicious pies. From Carlisle to Scotch Corner she read the magazine, and thought contemptuously of whoever did the home hints. Fancy telling anyone it was a good tip to use half marge, half butter in a Dundee cake. It didn't matter two hoots. The only sure way of making a good Dundee cake was to put two tablespoons of water in at the egg mixing stage. Now that was a tip. Through Yorkshire, Maudie dozed, though it would have been hard to prove this conclusively. Her eyes remained open, as did the magazine, but her head lolled forward suspiciously and her mouth hung open. The afternoon sun made the bus hot and stuffy and most people were sleeping with their seats tipped back.

At Doncaster, Maudie came to with a dreadful taste in her mouth and feeling very uncomfortable and cross. She took a wet face flannel from her bag and wiped her brow and hands, and then cleaned her glasses and very surreptitiously combed her hair and re-set her hat. Then she poured herself a cup of tea without spilling a drop, and after drinking this felt a little better. She then took a mint from her pocket, and sucking it

17

vigorously got out a pencil and her notebook. She had her accounts to do next.

Maudie had always recorded everything. At thirteen she had gone as a maid to the local big house and the lady of the house, who had fancied herself as an educator of the poor, had told her to always keep herself clean, aloof and to write everything down that she earned and spent. The lady had made the latter very easy by providing Maudie with her keep and a shilling a week. Nevertheless, she graciously doled out beautiful red shiny pocket books and Maudie had been thrilled to write down her meagre expenditure. She had always kept this up. The first pocket book had lasted her until she was nineteen and lady's maid to the original lady's daughter. Then she had met and married Joseph Tipstaff and used up four pocket books in one year.

She could remember clearly at a distance of fifty years four months Joseph's screams of laughter when she had produced her pocket book for the first time. They were at Luss, on Loch Lomond, where he had taken her for a day out. She had imagined splendid things and instead had spent the whole afternoon fighting him off in a field near the water's edge. He was wild and noisy and she hardly knew why she had walked out with him.

'Then I'll have to marry you,' he said. He laughed loudly all the time and his face was perpetually red.

'That's up to you,' she had said primly. He roared and lunged for her. She knew she looked neat in her sky blue dress. 'Well,' she said, taking out her pocket book, 'can you afford to get married and keep a wife?'

'What's that?' he said. 'Dear Jesus, you're not wanting it in writing?'

'It's my accounts book,' she said. 'Where's yours? What's your income and what's your expenditure? What's outstanding credit and debit?'

'Holy God,' Joseph said, and sank back in the grass.

She married him six months later. He hadn't an accounts

18

book, so she did the figures for him in hers and very rosy they looked. Joseph was a bookie's runner and a part-time barman. He said he didn't know how much he made, so every day for a month Maudie made him tell her how much he had made that day. It averaged out at the astonishing sum of nine pounds a week, which completely stunned Joseph. Maudie had it all in her book, neatly added up. Joseph had four and elevenpence in his pocket.

'Dear Mother of God,' he said, 'how can I make that much a week and have only this?'

'Expenditure almost exceeds income,' Maudie said.

'And what may that mean, you witch?' Joseph asked.

'You've spent it all on drinks and bets,' said Maudie, 'you who could be rich.'

It was still under the spell of this magic realisation that Joseph had married her. He told everyone he was marrying a bloody genius. Every other girl he had ever had had spent his money too quickly to stop to find out how much he had. Maudie didn't want anything spent on her. Dumbly, he handed over the pound notes and she transformed them into a grand room and kitchen in the best part of Glasgow. She took the shillings and they had a leather armchair and carpets and china. On the day he married her they were the best set up young couple in Scotland, and all on six months' money. They even had a few pounds in the post office when everything was paid for. And Maudie had gone through two pocket books and four thick lead pencils.

Maudie worked away slowly, writing everything very neatly in spite of the movement of the bus. You might as well not do accounts if you weren't going to do them neatly, that was her honest opinion. She knew Jean kept hers beautifully, even now when there was no strict need to, though Maudie thought they were as well kept however rich you were. There was more muddle possible with a lot of money. Robert had never kept any on paper. He said he kept them in his head, and sure enough when Maudie tried to test him in the old days he rattled off lists of figures that seemed to add up. Sally was the hopeless one, just like her father. She never knew what she had coming in or going out and that witless Willie of hers was no better. They and the six wee bairns would come to a bad end.

The sums were soon done, and everything neatly balanced. As yet, she didn't need money from anyone. She could manage fine on the little she had coming in and her savings and now the income from the lump sum that she had wisely invested under the minister's guidance. It worried Maudie to think she was making money out of money, sheer idle profit it was, but it was the best thing to do. That way, she could manage for a good few years yet and wouldn't need Jean or Robert's charity. There would never be any forthcoming from Sally.

Fifty miles from London, Maudie started collecting her things together. She didn't want to be taken by surprise. They would be there to meet her and she only hoped she would recognise them all, though it was a shameful thing to have to admit there was some doubt. It was seven years since she had seen Jean. She had only met Edward, her son-in-law, twice in the twenty-five years he'd been married to her daughter, and her grandson, at fifteen, was a total stranger to her. She couldn't count the glimpse she'd had of Nicholas at six weeks when they'd passed through Glasgow on the way to Ullapool and hadn't had the decency to stay long enough for the kettle to boil. It was all a dreadful way to carry on and Maudie considered they had a lot to answer for.

As the bus entered the outskirts of London, Maudie struggled with herself to put all evil thoughts out of her mind. No matter how ungrateful she thought they had been, she would have to make a great effort to forget and start afresh. What was done, was done. They had invited her to come and live with them, or at least stay as long as she wanted, and that showed they were aware of what they owed her and wanted to make amends. She must be Christian and go half way to meet them. And yet, at the back of her mind, rebellious thoughts pricked her conscience. What would they have done if she had said yes, she would come and live with them? Hadn't they worked it out before they asked that she would refuse? If they cared about her at all, why hadn't they come up to fetch her? They had a big car. Edward was his own boss.

Maudie decided all over again to stop thinking like that, though it was too much to ask herself to stop disliking Edward. That she couldn't do. Until Edward came along, Jean had been a good and loving daughter, knowing where her duty lay and doing it accordingly. She had brought her pay packet home and given seven-tenths to her mother and one-tenth to the church and kept a fifth for herself, which was as it should be. She had stayed in four nights a week, worn grey or brown or other proper colours, and gone on holiday with her family once a year. Maudie had been able to rely on her. She was a help with her father when he was at his worst and never flinched when Maudie called upon her assistance. There had been every prospect that she would continue on the path to salvation until Edward Drobny had picked her up.

Maudie still burned at that recollection. To have had a daughter of twenty-four, a properly brought up young lady in the full old-fashioned meaning of the phrase, actually allowing herself to be picked up. No matter how much Jean had pleaded the violence of the rain and the respectable appearance of Edward, Maudie could not forgive her getting into a car with the first strange man who had offered her a lift. It was mortal sin from the start of the engine. And then the deceitful way she had kept all this to herself, only revealing the whole liaison when, with chittering teeth, she had said she was going to be married—married to a man whose name Maudie had never until that minute heard, whose face she had never seen, whose foot had never crossed her threshold. Not a single rite of courtship had been observed. Nothing, until the announcement that she was going to be married.

Time and questions revealed that there were excellent reasons for suspecting that this Edward was as vile as his

21

manners implied. Maudie had him into her room for five minutes and her worst suspicions were instantly confirmed. The man was a foreigner. One look at his greasy black hair, and that narrow dark face, and the very smallness and thinness of him and Maudie knew he was no Scotsman, or even Englishman for that matter. However much he might protest that his father was from Selkirk and his mother from Liverpool, Maudie could see there was more than a touch of the tarbrush there. Jean might have black babies by him. Then he hadn't been a soldier, or served his King in any way. He said he was rejected on medical grounds, which brought Maudie to point three. He was a weakling, a wreck. His shoulders were round and he was pigeon-toed. He coughed and tried to say it was a tickle in his throat. His complexion was dreadful and Maudie knew without asking that he must suffer from boils.

She had told Jean point blank that her Edward was the worst specimen of manhood she had ever seen. She would regret marrying him for the rest of her life. Surprisingly Jean hadn't cried. She'd let Maudie rant and rave and not said a word, until the final 'Why do you want to marry something like him?' and then she had said 'I love him'. Maudie had fainted with fury and horror. That her daughter could be taken in by some romantic rubbish was past her comprehension. It hadn't been possible that Jean should not know about marriage and all the disgusting and horrible things it meant for a woman, not with her father being as he was. Yet there she stood, blathering about *love* as though she had lived with her eyes shut all her life, her ears and her eyes tightly shut.

They had got married. Maudie said they needn't tell her the time or place, she wasn't interested. She didn't want to see her daughter going to such a fate after all she had done for her. Then there had been a long silence of five years. Secretly, Maudie waited for a card announcing the birth of a baby, but none came, and she began to wonder if on top of everything else that Edward couldn't even give her Jean a wee baby. When Edward wrote and said Jean was in hospital and their baby, their third baby, was dead and Jean very ill and wanting to see her, Maudie had instantly forgiven her. The score was paid. Jean had sinned against her mother and the good Lord had punished her. Full of compassion, she had gone to Carlisle, where they were living at the time, and Jean had wept on her shoulder and Maudie had nursed her slowly back to health, all without having much to do with Edward. Then she had gone home and prayed for another baby, and at last, after another long five years and a bedridden pregnancy Jean had had Nicholas. The last time Maudie had seen them all she had thought the breach was healed and the visits would be many. She let it be known she was willing, for Jean and the baby's sake, to receive Edward.

Shaking her head over her wandering, Maudie sat up straight and tried to think only about Nicholas. For a start, she didn't like his name. The first boy ought always to be named after the paternal grandfather which in this case was Hamish. Hamish was a perfectly good name, but even if it hadn't been, the boy still ought to have been called Hamish, just as if it had been a girl Maudie would have fully expected a little Maud. Jean ought to have known better, with her history of babies, than to fly in the face of providence like that. Maudie had pointed this out, only to be told that Edward didn't want his son to be called after anyone. He was to have a completely new name. There was nothing Maudie could do, except wait for disaster to strike. It didn't however. She was left to follow Nicholas's—the name stuck in her throat—progress through Jean's letters. There were many things Maudie disapproved of. For example, Jean fed him with a bottle which was a device of the devil to entice lazy mothers from their bounden duty. She didn't even show him a pot until he was two years old, in spite of Maudie asking every letter if he was pot trained. His baby-hood and infancy were full of such unorthodox ways.

Maudie didn't know what to expect. She had had a regular two letters a year from Nicholas for the last ten or so years, thanking her for birthday and Christmas gifts. They told her nothing, except that Nicholas was no great hand at letter-writing. But that might be his schooling. He had gone to some school a long way from his home which Maudie knew could not possibly do any child any good. He was still at this unnatural establishment that took people's children away from them, and Maudie would only see him for a short time because his holiday was nearly over. She hoped he knew his catechism or she would have to spend all that precious short time teaching him.

Maudie had no idea where exactly they were, but from her watch they had only three quarters of an hour to go. She felt it was time to remind the driver that she wanted to be let off at Golders Green, wherever that was. Jean had said it would save half an hour. Getting up, Maudie stood for a minute trying to stretch her muscles. She was afraid that if she set off down the gangway the minute she was on her feet, she might find herself seized with cramp in the middle of the bus. Satisfied that everything was in working order, she walked down the gangway, passing both hands from one seat back to another. The driver looked at her through his mirror, and smiled.

'I'm come to remind you about Golders Green,' Maudie said.

'What about it?' the driver shouted.

'You're to let me off there,' Maudie said. 'My daughter's to pick me up there.'

'Sorry, grandma, but I can't. Not tonight. We're behind schedule, see. Only stop out of town if we're ahead of schedule.'

'You're to let me off at Golders Green, young man,' snapped Maudie.

The driver shook his head, still smiling. Maudie began to tremble. 'I want off at Golders Green,' she said. 'Do you hear?'

'Now don't get in a paddy,' the driver shouted. 'Victoria will have to do you and it's no good arguing. It'll be all right. They'll tell your daughter and she'll go on to Victoria. There's nothing to get excited about.'

To finish the conversation, he revved the engine harder and

24

the bus shot forward even faster. Maudie was caught slightly off balance and would have fallen if the man on her right had not put out a hand to steady her.

'It's disgraceful,' Maudie said, 'I'll report him. I'd never have come if they'd said they might not let me off at Golders Green.'

The man smiled. 'Not to worry,' he said, and patted her arm kindly. 'Best get back to your seat, love.'

Maudie could hardly get back to her seat for suppressed fury. Her hands shook and missed the seat backs that had steadied her on the way down. It wasn't so much the driver's casual attitude, or even the way everyone treated her as a dothery old fool, it was the upsetting of her plans. Those plans had been laid in detail this last three months. They had been transmitted to Jean as irrevocable, and now, because the bus had got behind, they were shattered in a minute.

She reached her seat and sat down. The worry started with a headache, and soon it was seeping through her, bringing out all the rheumatism and arthritis and lumbago that was always there waiting for just such aggravation. Jean and Edward would never be told what had happened. She would arrive at the centre of terrifying London all alone. She would have to get off the bus. She would have to claim her cases. She would have to phone Jean, but Jean wouldn't be there and there would be no way of getting a message to her. It would be hours before they thought of trying Victoria and by that time the natives would have robbed her of every stitch she possessed and every penny would have been filched from her. She would have nowhere to wait. There were places where you could have tea, but she had heard about them. Tea alone, in a cracked cup with no sugar and lipstick stains round the edge, was 1s. 3d. a time, and that a pale watery beverage liable to give her diarrhoea. Coffee might be cheaper but it was American, so no thank you. As for food—the mere sight of the tasteless sliced bread they used in such establishments was enough to put her off. She would just have to sit tight on a bench, her cases at her feet, and reply to nobody. If morning came and she still hadn't been found, the dear Lord alone knew what she would do.

Instantly, Maudie tried to imagine what indeed the dear Lord would do. She could see herself so clearly, frozen and stiff, fainting from hunger, at six a.m. Simple solutions never occurred to her—they were not as interesting, nor in Maudie's lifetime of experience, as likely. The worst always happened. She should never have inwardly congratulated herself on catching the bus so easily. She should never have relaxed when she got such a comfortable seat. They had seen and prepared this as revenge as they always did. Let them know you were even passing happy, and like lightning they would strike.

It was an omen. She should never have set off on her travels. She should have stayed quietly at home, minding her own business, and depended only on herself. She had been a fool, throwing herself into other people's hands like this. It would be like this all the time—other people's mistakes spoiling her own carefully planned timetables. This was only a beginning. She would never be able to do what she wanted when she wanted as long as she was away from home. Everyone would trade on her physical weaknesses and her age and her good nature and she would have a dreadful time of it.

Maudie was crying. Surreptitiously, because it was the most dreadful thing in the world to do. She knew other people did it all the time—and laughed loud, too—but such violent emotions were things for the privacy of one's own room. Crying at all was a sinful weakness. There should never be any need for tears. Crying in public was immoral. It flaunted grief in front of others and forced them to share it. It was as bad as taking all your clothes off like a wanton woman and saying enjoy me. But she couldn't help it. She knew with increasing anger that it was a sign of age. She had so little control over herself these days. First her bowels, now her tears. She was being robbed of her pride year by year. Her one comfort was that, though she was crying, no one would know. She made no noise. She delicately edged a handkerchief towards her eyes and pretended she had caught something in one of them. Look, she was saying, as she pulled an eyelid down and cunningly trapped the tears, look, I'm trying to get a piece of dirt out of my eye.

Finally, her tears were got rid of. It was over. Weak, she folded her hands and stared out of the window. She was lost. Her check on the time meant nothing now. They might be anywhere. She wouldn't know when to stand up and put her big coat on, when to suck the last peppermint. She would have to suffer the ignominy of actually being driven into the bus station without a decent preparation made.

It was getting dark. Her own reflection bounced back at her through the window, hat, nose, glasses sharply and unattractively silhouetted. At least—though Maudie was not given to comforting at leasts—at least she would not be pounced upon for other, more awful reasons. She was not young and pretty, with a handsome figure. There would be no danger from that sort of man. Maudie almost regretted it, for she had always been adept at dealing with that. Her hand slapped fingers straying towards her knee long before they reached their destination. She could turn a cool head at just the right moment, and twist her shoulders haughtily out of reach of any hug that threatened. Her contempt had always seared the most persistent of beasts. Except Joseph, and that was because she hadn't tried.

The lights were switched on in the bus and her shadow disappeared. It was light outside, too, for now they were in city and everywhere the shops glared with neon brilliance. There were rows and rows of them, a flashing cavalcade of clothes and furniture, so many that one could never imagine there would be half enough buyers. And the people and cars, hundreds of them, all away from home and with unfathomable reasons for being so. She dared say they were even passing famous buildings, but she wouldn't know them. Only at Buckingham Palace might she hazard a guess, but the dark night deluded her even there. Jean had promised her endless tours of 'the sights' and she had been furious that she should have been ranked as a common sightseer when her travels had such purpose.

Then Maudie clearly saw the sign—GOLDERS GREEN. She half rose in her seat, and as if sensing her agitation, the driver accelerated and swept round the corner and the sign disappeared. Trembling again, Maudie sank down. She felt like someone who had been kidnapped and had foolishly missed their opportunity to catch public attention. She should have rapped with her spectacle frame on the window. She should have thrown something out with her name on. Oh, there were umpteen things she ought to have done and hadn't.

Her fate was now settled. Heroically, she tried to organise herself. There was no doubt that they were not far from the terminus so at least she could prepare herself for the ordeal ahead. She arranged all the objects that had come out of her bag in the course of the journey on her knee and began systematically to pack them away. Her sandwiches were only half eaten. She folded the remaining two rounds in tinfoil paper and put them into their Tupperware container. The Lord provided for those who provided for themselves. Even if all went well, God willing, those good meat sandwiches were fit to grace the proudest supper table. Her flask was unfortunately quite empty, and also the aspirin bottle of milk and the Sellotape tin of sugar. All her tea, her life's blood, was gone. There was never a flask big enough yet neat enough for her needs and she was always doomed to stretches of agonising drought on her rare journeys. She put the empty vessel horizontally at the bottom of her bag. Wherever she spent that night, it must be washed out thoroughly or the taste of stale tea would ruin the countless other brews yet to be enjoyed from it. The rest of her bits and pieces went in easily. She left her knitting on the top. As well as staving off idleness, it passed through her mind that a knitting needle could be a dangerous weapon.

Maudie was left to put on her top coat without disturbing her neighbour. Her neighbour was a woman who had got on at Wetherby. She smelled. Maudie detected the stink immediately this person wearing a red coat had got on the bus and she had inwardly recoiled from any contact. When the stink drew level with her and actually asked if the seat was vacant, Maudie had only been able to purse her lips and reluctantly shake her head, such was her nausea. The woman had duly settled down. She had taken the red coat off to reveal a dress of even more outrageous vulgarity, and had crossed her knees showing a black suspender, and then had lit a cigarette. Maudie was beside herself with this wanton exhibition of selfishness. She longed for the woman to try to be friendly so that she could snub her scathingly, but the offender never said a word. She got on with stinking and smoking and reading revolting *comics*, that was all Maudie could call them. Having put up with this for so many hours and never once acknowledged her presence, Maudie did not want to lose out at the last minute by knocking her companion and having to suffer the humiliation of apologising.

Gently, she edged on one sleeve and then the other, and with a little hitch got the shoulders on. By leaning forward slightly, she was able to let the coat drop down, and the rest was simple. Then, as she buttoned the buttons from neck to knee, the woman moved. She bent down, hitting Maudie's foot, never saying anything about being sorry, and brought up a small zipped bag. She took out bottles and tins and tubes, and on the ledge in front of her set up a small mirror and then she began. She opened the evil smelling containers and daubed liquids and powders over her horrible face with little wadges of cotton wool. The reek was unbelievable. Maudie turned away and ostentatiously buried her nose in a clean, fresh air scented handkerchief. But she could not keep her eyes away. It was like being present at some awful witches' rite. She simply could not conceive what the smelly woman thought she was about. She just made herself odious.

Maudie had known for a long time that she was alone in this opinion. The minister's wife wore lipstick, old crones like Annie McAllister threw the powder on, making themselves look ridiculous, and every young girl from the most Christian and irreproachable downwards seemed to have mastered the entire art. Maudie had, of course, never touched the stuff. She hated the smell, she hated the feel, she hated above all the deception it was bringing about. It wasn't that she thought it wicked so much as both dishonest and ugly.

She hoped Jean would not be too plastered with the stuff. Surely to meet her own mother she would have the decency to turn up with a clean, scrubbed face and a healthy sweet smelling body. It would be a dreadful thing to have to shy away from her embrace because, like this woman beside her, she stank, or to have to shrink from touching her face because it was corroded with filth. By now, at her age, she would probably be on to wearing powder and not be content with the lipstick she had used so furtively in the early days. Maudie could remember first detecting the poisonous thing on Jean's lips. She had come in rubbing at them hastily and guilty with her glove, and still, when she had lowered the glove, her lips were luridly red. Jean had said they were faintly pink. Maudie had said God had given her faintly pink lips and He knew what faintly pink was and dared she look in the mirror and say again that hers were still faintly pink? Maudie had secured the lipstick itself, cheap and nasty in its gold case, with the disgusting and silly name 'Heavenly Rose' stamped on the top. It had gone in the dustbin, and Maudie never knew it was extracted and hidden before collection day to be kept at work and thoroughly removed after each wearing in the public lavatory at the town hall on the way home. It became the sign of liberation, so that whenever Jean escaped from home she thought first of her lipstick and how she would put it on thickly and blatantly and wet her lips and think how she was fooling her mother. But Maudie knew she was being fooled, in every possible way. She had steadily felt, in some indefinable way, Jean's growth outside her grasp. It was to her the most bitter failure of all, and it was none the less hard to bear at a distance of thirty years on the way to her home and a supposed welcome.

Maudie struggled not to give way again to that sort of

mental behaviour. She gave herself a last reminder that there were to be no faults on her side. She was to be kind, patient, honest, long-suffering. She would turn the other cheek at every insult. She would look to the present and the future only. Whatever went wrong would be their fault, and that must be plain for the world to see.

The bus slowed down. Feverishly, Maudie peered again out of the window. They were passing rows of other buses. More were nosing their way out of sheds. Obviously, they were nearly there. She did not know whether to be first off the bus or last. By being first she would avoid the rush and put herself out of her misery quicker. But by being last, she would remain calmer and give herself plenty of time to get off with dignity. She decided to remain to the last. She had been first on, so it was fitting that the first should be last.

The bus trundled into the station, into the huge covered-in area that seemed to belong neither to inside nor outside but to be an in-between world of draughts and dim light and echoes. The driver drew up at one of the concrete stands, and turned off his engine. He stood and yawned and stretched, and after a casual look around the bus, took down his newspaper and bait box and overcoat and got off, his cap tilted on the back of his head.

The noise had gone. Inside the bus, the murmurs and rustlings as people got their things together seemed hushed and soothing. Very slowly, the first passengers went down the steps and gradually the aisle filled as others waited. Maudie stayed in her seat, by a tremendous effort of will. The bus was securely stationary. She trusted it for the first time since she had got on. With that press of folk in the doorway, it was unlikely that even the most impetuous of drivers could change his mind and leaping aboard race back again into the night before Maudie had a chance to get off. As she sat there, she felt weak and tired. Travelling was an exhausting business. All that sitting and thinking and worrying when really one should always keep on the move. Be busy, and there is no time for brooding. Maudie had trained herself over the years to seize a brush and give the carpet a going over every time the tears threatened. The polish and a rag were always handy to put paid to daydreams, and imagination was easily drowned in a sea of soap suds.

She closed her eyes, just for a second, and in spite of her wrought state, she felt herself slipping away and struggled to open them quickly. She would have to stand up. She stood, half crouching in the confined space, and began edging her way towards the aisle. The last few ahead of her seemed to run off the bus. There she was, alone, and the whole aisle stretching empty ahead. She stepped out firmly, but her legs were as weak as when she'd had the flu. She had to propel herself from seat to seat and the last steep steps were difficult to negotiate.

Outside, she paused to fasten the top press stud of her coat. Everyone seemed to have gone very quickly. She walked anxiously to the back of the bus to get her case, not knowing how she was to have it carried with no one about. The boot was closed. She took hold of the handle and pulled it, but it didn't budge. She turned and twisted and shook it, and still the gleaming chrome remained tightly shut. Maudie looked around, her heart beginning to flutter and dance around her rib cage. 'Oh dear God' she found herself saying, over and over again, 'Oh dear, dear God.' There were her cases, her big one and her small one, locked in there forever and now she was more in trouble than she had ever imagined. Never, never would she be last off anything again.

She could hardly bring herself to leave the boot handle at all, but the sight of her driver coming out of the men's lavatory across the way sent her scurrying that way.

'My cases,' she said, 'oh, dear God, my cases.' She laid an arm on his sleeve and gasped and sobbed.

The driver gently shook her off and called her mother and asked her what all the fuss was about, and between exclamations and sighs she told him. He said there was nothing in the boot, that was why he had locked it. Nothing at all left in it,

she could be sure. Maudie's shrieks drowned any further pro-
testations. She clung to him again and called on dear God to
witness that her cases had been put in there before her very
eyes at Glasgow bus station, and he must open the boot again
immediately. Shrugging, the driver crossed with her to the bus.
He whistled as he selected the right key, and smiled down at
Maudie, who was nearer a stroke than she had ever been, as he
turned it in the handle. The large rounded lid swung back
and down, revealing an empty, petrol-smelling cavern behind
it. Quite empty. Absolutely, irrevocably empty. Maudie
fainted.

They carried her into the nearest cafeteria and laid her
gently on three chairs. All concern, a little embarrassed and
guilty, the driver got her some tea and with the help of his
mates propped her into a sitting position and tried hard to get
some of the thick, sweet tea between her lips. The cafeteria
lady clucked around and gave her opinion who should be sent
for as Maudie showed the first signs of reviving.

'Oh, dear God,' she said, and the tea rushed, scalding hot,
into her suddenly opened mouth. Spluttering and coughing,
she fought to swallow it. The driver told her to take it easy and
not to worry. Maudie closed her lips again, but she sat up and
struggled to control herself. She was one big shake. She shook
with fear of what she was going to do, she shook with anger at
herself for giving way so disgustingly, she shook with the sheer
physical shock of seeing that empty boot. Her thin chest
heaved as she tried to tighten her mind and her muscles.
At last, she felt she could move. She sat up very straight,
clutched her bag which was still, mercy be, hanging on her
wrist, and looked with cold distaste at all the robbers about
her.

'I've been robbed,' she said firmly. 'I want the police.'

'Heh, now,' said the driver, glad to be amused again, 'heh,
now, mother.'

'I am not your mother,' Maudie snapped, 'and if I was, I'd
teach you to respect your elders. I have been robbed of my

cases. I saw them put in the boot at Glasgow and they are not there now. I've been robbed. I demand the police.'

'Let's get the cases first,' said the driver. 'They're probably in the second bus.'

'They were in that bus,' Maudie said.

'Yeh, but we transferred some of them—mine was too full. They'll be coming in on the second bus. If you'd given me time I'd have told you not to worry,' the driver said. He lit a cigarette, smiling again, and offered Maudie one. She knocked the cigarette flying from his cheeky lips.

Thereafter, she was on her own. She was no longer a sweet little old lady they felt they had to help. The group split up and went away and she was left on her own under the reproving eye of the cafeteria lady who saw no call for such uncharitable behaviour. Maudie liked it better that way. She knew now who her enemies were. Courage came the minute she raised her hand, and now that she had acted she was ready to take on all comers. She was besieged in this loathsome place by grasping, dishonest bus-drivers who were at this very moment probably sharing out the contents of her cases. She did not believe their story for one minute, and even if it were true, it showed the most dreadful effrontery and nerve. Nobody had asked if they might move her cases, nobody had mentioned anything about the boot being full, and in any case she had been first there and her cases were the most likely to have been safely and inextricably buried beneath the rest. It was inconceivable that she had travelled all that way with her body in one bus and her cases in the other. They were all liars.

Maudie became businesslike, even in these strange and awesome surroundings. She managed to find an inquiry office, and found out where the next bus would come in. They said it was probably in already, the two travelled really as one. Maudie set briskly off, head held high, and there under a notice saying RELIEF BUSES she saw a bus identical to her own with 'Glasgow–London' written on it. There were folk still in it. Charging up to the driver, Maudie demanded to know if he'd taken her

34

cases. This driver was not a smiler. He gestured glumly towards the open boot, where there was still a dozen or so cases left, and invited her to take her pick. Almost disappointed, Maudie saw her two, neatly stacked side by side at the very front. She took a deep breath and told the driver exactly what she would be suing him for. The driver yawned, yanked her cases out on to the ground and turned to the next traveller.

Sitting on the bigger case, a stalwart article not far removed from a tin trunk, Maudie reflected that she was now in a very serious position, cases found or not. She had offended half the bus station. Nobody was going to help her carry her luggage to a waiting-room. Nobody was going to help her find Jean. And yet she felt exhilarated. She was proud she'd shown them her mettle. She felt her gesture had made up for her unwonted hysteria and feebleness, and that she had shown them she wasn't so old after all, not so old that she had to put up with impertinence and condescension.

She sniffed and put her feet more firmly together against the smaller case. Something would have to be done. Her sharp little eyes darted around the bus station, hostile and penetrating, looking for a way out of seeking help. Then she saw, not far away, a small trolley, a miniature version of the railway kind. She calculated it would be easy to push. She could commandeer it and push herself out of this den of iniquity and find a policeman. She got up, and with a deal of complicated manoeuvring in order to keep her eye constantly on the cases, she reached the trolley. It moved at a touch. Delighted, she trundled it forwards and levering her cases on to it, set off for the main exit. People looked vacantly at her. Nobody tried to stop her, though she longed for them to try. Panting a little, she got the trolley to the big gap opening on to the street, and humped her cases on to the pavement. She was out, at last, free of that crowd.

And there she was, sitting hunched up on her cases, her head high and a funny little smile on her face, as Edward and Jean parked their car across the way. Jean jumped out, relieved beyond belief, and began waving wildly as she tried to cross the road. But her mother ignored her. She sat holding her handbag as though it were a weapon, and staring ahead as though she was having a vision.

PART ONE

JEAN

CHAPTER ONE

Over the whole household there had lain a feeling of misery and gloom. It extended even to Kipper, the dog, who was suddenly hurled into a period of intensive good manners training, which had never been tried in anything but jest before. No one thought for one minute that Grandmother's visit was going to be enjoyable. They all knew they had a duty to try to make it so, but at the back of everyone's minds was the fear that they might unwittingly succeed and she would stay forever and they might as well all die.

Yet no one questioned that she must be asked to stay. They were proud that they had got the letter off welcoming her the very day hers had arrived with the news about Grandfather. As Jean repeatedly told her friends, Edward hadn't hesitated. He had said immediately that they must have the old horror—the latter bit affectionately, of course. Even Nicholas hadn't moaned about his privacy being invaded as he tended to do at any mention of visitors during the holidays. They had been united. Their instincts were in the right places. The old horror must come.

When Grandmother replied and said she would come, there had been an instant, well suppressed feeling of depression. They had all worked hard at being realistic.

'She can have her life,' Edward said, 'and we can have ours.'

'Oh Edward,' Jean said.

'We'll make her as comfortable as possible but she's not going to spoil our lives,' Edward said. 'She must fit in with everything we do. We're making no special concessions.'

'What do you mean?' Jean said.

'Well,' Edward said. 'She won't like having her breakfast at nine instead of seven, will she? And rolls and coffee will be no substitute for porridge and kippers.'

'The poor soul can surely have those,' Jean said, 'and if she cares to get up quietly at seven . . .'

'Your mother doesn't get up quietly,' Edward said. 'No. No concessions. We'll make her comfortable but I will not have everything changed for her.'

Jean bit her lip and sighed. It wouldn't be like that at all. She could hear herself explaining to her mother that Edward didn't want her to get up till nine because he didn't. Even Edward wouldn't dare tell her, in spite of his firm tone now. Mother would get up at seven. Gradually, they would all get up at seven and that would be that. They would quarrel over it in bed at night, keeping their voices very low, and nobody would say anything at all to Mother.

They talked of nothing else but the approaching visit. Whatever topic came up, at mealtimes especially, which was when Edward seemed to suffer most from forebodings, it was soon dropped. Every detail of the arrangements to be made obsessed them.

'Where,' said Edward, 'are you going to put her for a start?'

'The spare room, I suppose,' Jean said.

'No,' Edward said, 'not next to us. You know what *that* would mean,' with a significant look at Nicholas. 'Oh no, not next to our room.'

'Where, then?' said Jean.

'The attic,' Edward said, munching the French bread he could see he wasn't going to enjoy for much longer.

'Oh Edward, really,' Jean said. 'That's the most dreadful thing you've said yet. You'll be suggesting the garage next.'

'Not a bad idea,' Edward said. 'Would there be room for a bed beside the car? She could clean it at night when she has one of her wakeful bouts.'

'I think you're mean and awful,' Jean said, 'and if you're

going to joke about her like a bad music hall comedian then she needn't come at all.'

'All right,' Edward said, 'she needn't come.'

'You know we've got to have her. You said so yourself.'

'I must have been mad. I can't think now of one reason why we should.'

'I owe her a lot,' Jean said.

'You owe her bloody nothing.'

'She's had a hard life and——'

'Entirely her own making. I'm not surprised your father was driven to——'

He stopped of his own accord as Nicholas raised his head from his coffee and looked intrigued.

'Anyway,' he said, 'it was a serious suggestion.'

'What? The attic?'

'Yes. It's ideal——'

'It's cold and bare and utterly horrible. And it's full of cases and rubbish.'

'But it could be very nice,' Edward said, 'if it was converted. We'd clear it out, have it decorated and furnished, extend the central heating and put in a washbasin and some sort of cooking facilities. It's a big place—extends right across the top of the house, don't forget. Then when she'd gone, we could let it.'

'But I suggested that years ago,' Jean said.

'Alright, well now I'm agreeing.'

'You said it would be a ridiculous, unjustifiable expense.'

'So it would, darling, but now I happen to think it would be worth it.'

Jean had never seen her husband show such enthusiasm and persistence. Usually, nothing was ever done in the house because at the first obstacle to a project he gave in and said forget it. Before, if builders had said they couldn't start for three months and most of what they wanted was impossible anyway, then he would have put the phone down and lost interest. All that changed. He personally went round builder after builder

41

until he got one willing to start the next week. Nothing daunted him. He didn't mind having to pick up radiators himself, or ferrying Jean to and from shops to choose paper and paint. He was determined to get that beautifully self-contained room ready for his mother-in-law's arrival. He dreamed that he had her in there, then nailed up the door and they lived happily ever after.

The room took shape quickly and dramatically. The minute the lumber was cleared out, it looked almost habitable. They liked the tall, sloping rafters overhead but they knew Maudie wouldn't, so they put a false ceiling in, easily detachable later. The view over the rooftops from the dormer window was lovely, but Jean willingly shrouded it in thick white net. Furnishing it, because it had a future beyond her mother, she couldn't quite give in to Maudie's well known prejudices. In fear and trembling, she chose a self-coloured deep rose carpet, and striped cotton curtains and a dark grey cover for the divan bed. They got a heavy Chinese screen to hide the basin and the small electric cooker, and Edward made a long unit of shelves and cupboards along one wall from plain pine wood, untouched by paint or varnish. It all looked very attractive, especially the white walls with the pink carpet. It all looked very nice, and they both knew Maudie would hate it.

'To hell,' Edward said, viciously. 'We've spent hundreds on it. She's a bloody lucky woman.'

'It's the idea of it,' Jean said. 'She'll think we don't want her—Oh, don't say she'll be right. I do want her. I really do. I want her to be happy and us to be happy.'

'Yes, well, exactly,' Edward said, heavily. 'There you have it. She's incapable of being happy, for a start. She doesn't believe in happiness.'

'Because she's never had any.'

'Oh, for God's sake!'

'Has she? Tell me one time when she's had any happiness—go on, just tell me.'

'I'm not saying things haven't been difficult for her,' Edward said, 'but it's a matter of temperament. Other women have just such a hard time but they don't turn out old moans like her.'

'Don't insult her before she even gets here.'

'Better than waiting till she does.'

'Better not at all.'

It was all such a fuss, Jean thought, when it ought to have been the most natural and joyous of events. It shocked her to think of all the weeks of special preparations necessary before her own mother came to stay. Why couldn't they just open the door, and kiss her, and say it's lovely to see you? They had worried and schemed over every facet of her visit. It was disgraceful.

Nicholas was the only one who retained any dignity, she felt. He was largely unbothered, at least at first, by his grandmother coming. In fact, he looked forward to it in the early weeks.

'Why haven't I seen her?' he asked.

'She lives a long way away,' Jean said.

'Oh for heaven's sake, Mum, she only lives in Glasgow. Last year we went to Greece and that's about sixteen million times as far. Why haven't I seen her? Don't you get on?'

'No,' Edward said.

'That's untrue,' Jean said furiously, 'that's prejudicing him most unfairly against Mother.'

'It's answering him truthfully,' Edward snapped. 'What other explanation would you suggest? He's fifteen. As he's pointed out, Glasgow isn't far.'

'You've always said it was,' Jean said. 'Every time I wanted to go——'

'You never really wanted to,' Edward said.

'I *beg* your pardon?'

'So you don't get on,' Nicholas said quickly. 'Why? Why, Mum?'

'Your father can answer that,' Jean said. 'As far as I'm concerned we get on perfectly well, as well as any other mother and daughter.'

'Oh ho, what cowardice,' Edward said.

'Why don't you get on, Dad?' Nicholas shouted.

'The reasons will soon be evident, my son, so contain thy patience and give thanks for being spared up to now.'

'Why?' Nicholas said.

'You ought to have been out of the why stage long ago,' Edward said.

'No, but really why? I'm not just saying it pointlessly. I really want to know.'

'It would annoy your mother,' Edward said.

'Oh, come on,' Nicholas said.

But they were silent. They talked of nothing else but his grandmother, yet they would tell him nothing about her. His father grew more cross and irritable every day, and his mother had a permanent frown. He was glad to get back to school. Then all term they wrote dreary letters about what he would and would not have to do in the holidays when Grandmother came, until she became a kind of ogre. They were so obviously scared of her.

'One simple question,' he said, resignedly, a few days before she came, 'it won't kill you to answer this. Why exactly is she coming now, after all these years? I mean, is it asking too much to know that?'

'Your grandmother won't like that impertinent tone,' Edward said, 'she dislikes sarcasm.'

'Oh, honestly, for heaven's sake——'

'Or blasphemy.'

'That wasn't blasphemy.'

'Your grandmother would have called it that.'

'You're sidetracking me,' Nicholas accused. 'Can't I know why she's coming?'

'Because Grandfather's gone,' Jean said abruptly.

'Gone where? Do you mean he's dead?'

'No.' Jean stopped, and looked appealingly at Edward.

'All yours,' Edward said sweetly. 'I wouldn't like to say the wrong thing again.'

44

'It just so happens she's on her own now,' Jean said, diffidently.

'I don't want to make you scream,' Nicholas said, 'but why is
she suddenly on her own? Is he in prison?'

'No certainly not,' Jean said.

'Well, where is he, then?'

'He's gone on a holiday,' Jean said lamely. Edward laughed
loudly. 'What's the matter? Why are you laughing?' she said
angrily. 'You just never help, do you?'

So Grandfather, too, was a mystery. It at least added a little
romance to the family tree which up to now had been yawn-
ingly plain and simple. He had one known set of grandparents,
fat and clueless, who lived in Bradford and came for Christmas
every year; three aunts, four uncles and eight cousins, none of
whom he had ever seen. And on top of it all, he was an only
child. He understood about that—his mother just wasn't made
right for having children, as his father put it. He was quite
impressed by the oft-told struggle to have him. It was nice to
think one's creation and bearing had acquired such importance through the effort needed. But he had never understood
why he was shut off from all the kith and kin. He would've
thought they would've been keen for him to see his cousins, to
make up for not having brothers and sisters. He hoped his
grandmother might throw some light on that, if she wasn't so
awful that you couldn't ask her things like that. Until he got
the chance, Nicholas contented himself with saying at intervals
'I don't know why you think it's going to be so dreadful' and
'What difference will she make anyway?'

It was hard to answer. Particularly in the last few days before her mother arrived, Jean kept trying to rationalise the
whole business. Their worry and hysteria was so very silly.
Nicholas was right. They shouldn't find that Maudie would
make any difference at all. Their daily life was set in a hard
and fast routine that not even she could change, except in the
most trivial of details. Edward worked in his surgery all day. In
the evening, they had a meal and read the paper and watched

television. Two nights a week, Edward went out on his own, one night they both went out, to the golf club. They rarely entertained. They were quiet and peaceful and contented. It wasn't a contentment anyone would find easy to shatter, because they had passed through all the dangerous phases of their marriage. It wasn't even a contentment so private and sacred that they couldn't bear intrusion. Jean often longed for an intruder, someone to shake them out of their calm, just for a little while, and then go away again to leave them appreciative of the monotony. But not her mother.

It was almost, she decided, that they were ashamed of their life. She felt so much *acting* would be necessary, such keeping up of appearances. She would never dare stay in bed all morning and be fed up. She would have to leap around and be cheerful and above all, busy. Otherwise, Maudie would pounce and gloat and insist there was something horribly wrong and what was it.

Now and again, it did enter her head that her mother might have changed. It was, after all, fifteen years since she had lived in the same house. She herself had changed drastically in fifteen years. Why not Maudie? She was now old and perhaps softened. She could never have retained exactly the same edge and drive and ruthless determination. The very fact that she was coming to them at all was surely an indication that the famous implacable will was weakening. There might be coming into their house the sweet, gentle, rather dothery grandmother that Nicholas seemed to have fixed in his mind. Jean felt quite weepy at the thought.

But that phase passed. The day before Maudie came, Jean sat alone in the flat they had prepared, and thought 'I am afraid of my mother.' No sooner had she thought that, and acknowledged it as absolutely true, than she also thought 'I do not know her, I have no contact with her,' and that too was true. Her mother was a terrifying stranger, bound to her by the mere fact of relationship. For that one fact, she would have to suffer everything. She could not escape the unwanted responsibilities and closeness that it implied. At the end of fifteen years' virtual separation it seemed a kind of twisted miracle that, to her, blood remained blood. She had not the coldness to say 'I do not want you, I do not like you, I owe you nothing.' She was frightened to be a person who could say that.

For Edward, moving between drill and chair all day with studied gloom, the problem was much simpler. It didn't perplex him. His mother-in-law was the incarnation of all music hall jokes. She was a nasty minded bitch, and to feel sorry for her was an unwarrantable weakness it was unwise to indulge in. He was under no illusions as to why she was coming: she was coming to claim her pound of flesh. Not to have completely ground out all initiative in her daughter Jean was an omission she would always have vowed to put right one day. That day had now arrived. She would stay until Jean had not only sunk back into her yes-mother stage of twenty odd years ago, but had also gone beyond and surrendered completely to her mother.

He would, of course, stand no nonsense. About that he was quite determined. He wasn't the worried, nervous, inescapably guilty young man of the years of Jean's miscarriages. Then, when Maudie had arrived, triumphantly sent for, he had felt miserably aware of his own inadequacy. Jean had wanted her mother. God knew why, but she had wanted her, and not him. He had never seemed to be able to do anything to help her. He could neither comfort her, nor restore her confidence, and Maudie had inexplicably been able to do both, and then miraculously left before carrying her conversation a stage further. He had quailed before her and meekly carried out all her injunctions to do this and that and the other. He had been glad to take a background seat.

Let her just try it now. He realised that already he was longing for a scene, and thought how vindictive middle age was making him. All he wanted was a chance to make her suffer for her rejection of him in the very early days. He was childishly pleased that she would be forced to admit he had

47

done very well indeed. He could see her glinting little eyes flickering over the large house and car, taking in the opulent furnishings, silently noting their high standards of living. With a little care, she would also get the opportunity to size up his bank balance and the list of his shares, and she could not fail to be impressed by the extent and nature of his private practice. She would note, for dear Maudie missed nothing, his standing in the neighbourhood. He would display their invitation cards on the mantelpiece, and leave his club cards lying around. But more important still, she would see what sort of life Jean had—the gadgets, the home help, her own money, her clothes and car. What else could she ever have wanted for her daughter but those things he had given her? He almost hoped Maudie would be driven to jealousy. He waited grimly for her to find an apparent flaw in his perfection as a husband and provider, ready to leap upon it and show her it was no flaw at all and that she would have to admit the no-good whipper-snapper had proved more than worthy of her daughter.

They had dinner that night instead of high tea. They didn't know quite why. Edward said, as he sometimes did as a special occasion approached, 'It would be nice to have dinner on Tuesday evening' and Jean agreed. They sat at the dark, polished table, the three of them, with the candles lit and all the food in Royal Doulton tureens. They had hare paté, and duck with orange sauce, and chocolate mousse, and a bottle of Chablis. Nicholas was as silent and intent as his parents. He was allowed a sip of port at the end, and some camembert cheese.

'A bloody good meal,' Edward said.

'Must you use that word?' Jean sighed.

'Nicholas knows all about swearing,' Edward said, 'he knows when bloody is swearing and when it isn't.'

'It's always swearing,' Jean said. 'You mustn't use it when Mother is here.'

'We're off,' Edward said. 'Have you pinned the lists of do's and don'ts up yet?'

'There's no point in aggravating and upsetting her from the beginning, now is there?' Jean asked.

'No, there isn't,' Edward agreed, quicker than she had thought. 'It would be totally ridiculous to do that. So I shan't swear in any sense while she's here.'

'Thank God for that,' Jean said.

'Ha-ha, taking the Lord's name in vain,' Edward said gleefully. 'We don't thank the Lord unless we are really thanking him, and that brings me to grace. Do I have to endure grace?'

'I like grace,' Nicholas said. ' "For what we are about to receive may the Lord make us truly thankful, for what we have *just* received may the Lord make us truly thankful." '

'That,' Edward said, 'is not your grandmother's idea of grace. That's a mere burp to her. I meant all twenty-three verses of whatever John Knox prescribed.'

'It will be a relief,' Jean said, 'when Mother is actually here and Nicholas can see what nonsense you make up.'

They were all silent for a few minutes, then Nicholas went to watch television and they were left in the candlelight staring at each other.

'You must promise me,' Edward said, 'never to cry in front of her.'

'And you must promise me never to shout at me in front of her.'

Neither said anything.

'Shouting and crying,' Edward said. 'When did we last do either? We haven't shouted or cried for centuries, have we?'

'Yes,' Jean said slowly, 'I've cried.'

'When?' Edward said, genuinely shocked. 'When have you cried in the last—oh, the last five years?'

'Often,' Jean said.

'Oh rubbish. I'd have known.'

'You wouldn't. I cried when I was on my own, or when you were asleep.'

'How very silly. I don't believe you—you're seriously main-

49

taining you've been in the habit of long bouts of regular weeping?'

'I didn't say long bouts. I said I'd cried.'

'What about?'

'How can I remember, just like that?'

'Well, if the reasons were so dreadful you'd to secretly cry I would have thought you'd remember.'

'You wouldn't like me to mention the main reason,' Jean said, longingly. 'Would you?'

'Oh that,' Edward said, 'if that was all you were crying about then I certainly don't want reminding. That doesn't count—which is another thing. Should you ever be mad or weak enough to tell your mother——'

'Do you think I'd humiliate myself?' Jean asked.

'I don't think you'd choose to,' Edward said, 'but you've told her stranger things, and regretted it. She has a curious effect on you, I've seen you change before.' He paused. 'Anyway, I've never shouted, not even into my pillow at night.'

'Is that a good thing?' Jean asked.

'It must be. A minute ago you were warning me not to do it in front of your mother.'

'I meant generally.'

'Well, I never knew you ever enjoyed me storming round the place.'

'It was more natural than all your silences.'

'We're getting very personal,' Edward said, 'a real old heart to heart, eh.'

Jean got up and put the electric light on. Edward blinked.

'What did you do that for?' he asked, crossly.

'I'm clearing the table,' Jean said. 'I can't see everything properly with just the candles.'

'Don't clear it yet.'

'It's late.'

'Not all that late.'

'Why don't you want me to clear it?'

'I like sitting with you and chatting.'

50

Jean thumped side plates on to a metal tray. 'What a liar you are,' she said.

'Well, there won't be any more chances for three or four months,' Edward said. 'I was relishing the experience for the last time.'

'You've never relished it,' Jean stated.

'Now you're a liar. I have.'

'When you weren't busy elsewhere,' Jean said, with emphasis.

'Oh God,' Edward said, 'you're so bitter and so stupid and so bloody short sighted. Let me remind you——'

'I don't want to talk about it, especially tonight,' Jean said.

'You've wanted nothing else, any night,' Edward said. 'You're always harking back to it. You're a masochist, like your mother.'

Silently, Jean finished stacking the tray and carried it through to the kitchen. Edward went to join Nicholas. She thought she ought to indulge herself with one last good howl, but as usual, immediately afterwards, she was stimulated and felt elated, not depressed. She would miss the fencing. She got down to doing the dishes, extra carefully in preparation for Maudie's scrutiny.

CHAPTER TWO

They were ready half an hour before there was the vaguest need to go, which Jean achieved because they were now back to their original desire to do what was right and do it properly. Edward wore a dark suit and a very white, stiff-collared shirt. Nicholas suffered the indignity of literally having his hair brushed by his mother, and his grey flannel pants were straight back from the cleaners. Jean had limited herself to the most natural coloured of face powders, and the palest of lipsticks. Her hair was carefully combed back into a French pleat, and she had green gloves toning exactly with her coat. They were all as stiff and immaculate as they would have been for a funeral.

Edward whistled as he drove the short distance to the bus station. His mother-in-law hated whistling, particularly when driving. He felt grimly virtuous at the manifest effort he was making to extend the olive branch, and so forth. There were not many sons-in-law who would go to such trouble, and he hoped she would be fully aware of this. He parked the car, with exaggerated precision, as near to the station as he could. The first thing they saw when they arrived was a blackboard saying the Glasgow bus was behind schedule and would not stop on its way through to Victoria. They all turned and ran back to the car, their neatness easing at the edges.

'No need to rush,' Edward said, feeling light-headed, like a reprieved man. 'We've got a big start and we can get through the traffic quicker than any bus.'

'I think we ought to go on the North Circular,' Jean said.

'Don't be silly. That's miles from Victoria.'

'Well, we ought to take some roundabout way in case we get held up in town.'

'Nonsense. We'll sail through,' Edward said, firmly. 'We're bound to be ahead of the bus anyway.'

Jean sat tensely beside him all the way. Her ridiculous anxiety made him jam his gears and stall at traffic lights. Inevitably, he became irritable, and to show he wasn't irritable, that he was casual and amused and at ease, he put the radio on and sang tunelessly and loudly. Jean bent and turned it off. He snapped it back on, and as she furiously groped for the switch he turned to her and said, 'For chrissake what's the matter with you?' and drove through a red light as Nicholas yelled a warning.

No one was hurt, not even shaken. His left wheel grazed the side of a taxi, leaving a long, thin scrape down the door of the taxi and the slightest of dents, a mere indentation, in his own wing. But the horns hooted and the taxi driver got out and swore, and above it all the radio blared out and everyone started to say what could you expect. Trying hard not to scream, Edward produced his wallet and made money talk, and the taxi driver got back into his cab, still grumbling, and then, just as the traffic was about to move again, a policeman appeared. Edward instantly told him there was nothing the matter and not to be so officious and the policeman promptly settled down for an enjoyable ten minutes being just that.

They set off again, rigidly silent, after Edward said 'Don't bloody well say anything, I'm warning you.' He drove attentively, taking all the short cuts he could think of, trying not to think that the curse had begun. Even on the way to meet her, the jinx had settled. Very suddenly, the car started to make odd groaning noises.

'Bloody hell,' Edward said.

'Oh, what have you done now?' Jean wailed.

'I haven't done anything. My God, you're so keen to blame me.'

'Well, what's wrong with the car?'

'How do I know?'

'It's your car. The least you might have done is make sure it was in working order. First you drive like a maniac and smash it——'

'Smash it? What do you mean, *smash* it?'

'Dad,' Nicholas said, 'you've run out of petrol.'

Edward stared at the dial. It registered O. The car hiccupped. He barely had time to pull it into the side of Park Lane before it spluttered and stopped.

'I can't understand it——' he began.

'You're a stupid, incompetent idiot,' Jean said, 'that's all there is to understand. You're incapable of looking after a car. An accident is excusable——'

'I didn't notice you excusing it.'

'——but to run out of petrol! It's sheer thoughtless inefficiency.'

'I checked my petrol last night. The tank was half full.'

'Then why is it empty now?'

'I don't know. I'm not a mechanical genius.'

'You're not any kind of genius, don't worry about that. You're a selfish, arrogant man. You simply enjoy the thought of Mother arriving and being lost.'

'That would be too much luck to expect.'

'Exactly. That's precisely your attitude. I suppose you'll be glad if she's had a heart attack.'

'Wildly delighted, but she happens to have a heart like pressed steel.'

They wrangled furiously on. Nicholas had long since got out of the car. He re-appeared to tell them the petrol tank must have sprung a leak because there was a puddle under the car and a trail behind them. Edward demanded a fulsome apology. Jean said not at all—he ought to have his car maintained properly. By the time they had stopped shouting at each other, it was obvious they could never beat the bus. Jean then gave up and began to cry, moaning everything was spoiled, ruined, everything was bound to go wrong.

54

It took them well over half an hour to get going again. A hotel garage deigned to lend them a mechanic, at a price, who told them if they filled up with petrol again and he wedged something into the small hole where it seemed to be leaking, they might get home alright. This they did. The rest of the drive was spent by Jean trying to restore her former outward poise, and Edward trying to control the shake his hands had alarmingly developed. Nicholas alone was serene and undisturbed, not upset either by his parents' fighting or their lateness. Neither seemed to him of any importance beside the fact that his grandmother would still surely be there.

Jean shouted 'There she is!' and Edward braked hard. The car stopped completely. Before he had time to start and park it, Jean had jumped out and was running across the road. He watched and waited. Anyone would have expected an effusive kiss and hug. He saw her stop and fling her arms wide, and then bring them flapping to her sides like a bewildered penguin. Slowly, he heaved himself out of the car, measuring the number of footsteps between them with his eye, and told Nicholas to come with him to meet his grandmother.

'—and we were held up,' Jean was saying, lamely.

'I've been near dead of shock,' Maudie said, 'and not a soul I knew to help.'

'Sorry about the delay, Mother-in-law,' Edward said, 'it was the change in your bus schedule. We were at Golders Green in lovely time. How are you?' He held out his hand. Maudie ignored it and sniffed.

'Dear God,' she said, 'alone knows how I've survived.'

They tried, unsuccessfully, to get her moving towards the car as she told her adventures, but she would not move until she had finished her saga. They stood in a semi-circle in front of her, anxiously registering what they thought were the right expressions, their eyes not daring to stray from her face. Jean thought she had changed a lot—her face was thinner, tighter, her eyes seemed to water and she did not hold her head stiff and high, but let it sink now and again, like a bird burying its head in its feathers. Edward thought she had not changed at all. Her features were as sharp, her expressions as fierce, her voice rasping. Nicholas just stared and wondered.

'Are you going to keep me sitting on the pavement all night?' Maudie said at last, and they began to cross to the car. Maudie insisted that Jean and Nicholas should both get in the back with her. Edward sat isolated in front, the hairs on his neck prickling. She was so carefully ignoring him.

He drove slowly and safely home, eyes riveted on the petrol gauge. He hardly heard Maudie putting Nicholas through his paces, so intent was he on getting there without disaster. He sighed as he swung the car into their drive and managed to speak for the first time.

'The ancestral home,' he said. 'What do you think of it, Mother-in-law?'

Groaning slightly, Maudie was helped out of the back and stood on the gravel.

'A *yellow* door,' she said.

'We thought it would be cheerful,' Jean said. 'Welcoming. Don't you think it's welcoming?'

'It's yellow, that's all,' Maudie said. 'Are you spring cleaning, then?'

'No,' said Jean. 'Why?'

'Your curtains are down,' said Maudie, pointing at the large expanse of bare glass.'

'We like the view,' Edward said. They overlooked the park. 'We're not ashamed of anyone looking in. We've nothing to hide in there.'

Maudie turned, the gravel squealing under her heel. 'It's not a question of hiding, young man,' she snapped, 'it's a matter of decency. But if you want folks to know you're brazen, that's your affair. I haven't come to interfere.'

Trying to smile, Jean led her inside. The warmth from the radiator in the hall met them with a soothing rush.

'Dear God,' Maudie said, 'it's like Africa.'

'There's one thing I can't stand and that's cold houses,'

56

Edward said, loudly. 'You can go round our house any time of the year in your shirt sleeves and be comfortable.'

'No gentleman would want to remove his jacket,' Maudie said. 'Is no one going to help me off with my coat before I pass out with the dreadful heat?'

There was a tussle to get her tweed coat off. She gasped and pulled away the scarf underneath and undid the top press stud of her dress. Before she could ask if she was going to be kept standing in the hall all night, Jean led the way into the sitting-room.

'I thought you might like to relax before we had supper, Mother,' Jean said.

'I'm perfectly relaxed,' said Maudie firmly, 'and I won't be wanting any supper. I never eat after six in the evening as you know, Jean. A cup of tea and a biscuit at nine-thirty will be all I'll be wanting, thank you.'

'Treat yourself,' Edward said, 'have a supper and be a devil for once. Jean's made a delicious steak and kidney pie.'

'My digestion is no cause for frivolity,' Maudie said. 'I know what suits me, and I intend to stick to it.'

'Well, you won't mind if we have ours,' Edward said, 'I'm starving.'

'I'll stay with Mother,' Jean said, 'you two can help yourselves.'

'But you haven't eaten all day,' Edward said.

'I don't feel like anything,' Jean said, tensely.

'There's no call to stay with me,' Maudie said, 'if you want to go and eat a heavy thing like a steak and kidney pie at eight at night.'

Edward and Nicholas went. Jean sat down on the large, luxurious sofa beside her mother. She smoothed the creases in her dress and said 'It's nice to see you after all this time.'

'You knew where I was,' Maudie said.

Jean took a deep breath. 'Yes,' she said, 'I'm ashamed we never visited you. I'm sorry. I hope we can make up for it.'

'Is he always like that?' Maudie said.

'Who?' Jean asked, miserably aware that her hypocritical effusiveness had been swept aside.

'That Edward.'

'Like what, Mother?'

'So greedy and rude—leaving an older guest to go off and feed his face.'

'He's hungry, Mother. We waited specially for you. He works hard all day and he doesn't have time for a proper lunch.'

'No dentist knows what hard work is,' Maudie said. 'Fiddling about with people's teeth all day—where's the hard work in that?'

'He's on his feet all day,' Jean said, 'and operating a drill needs a lot of concentration. Just one slip and you could go through the roof of someone's mouth.'

'I expect he's done that often enough.' Maudie said.

'Oh Mother!'

'Not that these folk don't deserve it if they can't keep the teeth God gave them in good condition. There should be no need for dentists.'

'Or doctors?' Jean asked.

'Accidents will happen to the best of us,' said Maudie. 'There's a need for doctors. Our good Lord was a healer.'

Jean got up, and without thinking walked to the fireplace and took a cigarette from the gold box on the mantelpiece. With it in her mouth, she turned to get the lighter on the coffee table, and saw Maudie's face. She giggled, then coughed, and smiled apologetically. It was so ridiculous to feel ashamed of smoking a cigarette in her own house. Showing she was aware of Maudie's taste, but that she was choosing to override it, she went ahead and found the lighter, and lit the cigarette. Carefully, she inhaled, and blew what smoke there was away from Maudie's direction.

'I'm sorry, Mother,' she said, 'but I enjoy a cigarette.'

'There is no uglier sight,' Maudie said, and averted her eyes. 'The cancer will be all over your lungs.'

'I'll take the risk,' Jean said, cheerfully.

'It's depraved,' said Maudie.

'Oh now, Mother,' Jean protested, 'you can't argue it's a sin.'

She listened half-heartedly as Maudie expounded her theory on why smoking was one of the worst possible sins, and as she realised she was neither taking it all in, nor letting it upset her, she thought perhaps she had found the formula with which to beat her mother even before they had really started fighting. It gave her a tremendous sense of self-rightous superiority to let the old woman rattle on and not let a word of it penetrate. She longed for Maudie to finish just so that she could test her newly formed resolution to say 'I expect you're quite right, Mother,' and nothing more. The moment came, and she said it, with just the right amount of affectionate humility. Her spirits soared and she longed to go back thirty years to start doing it from then so that her whole life might have been different. There was no need for shaking hands and thudding heart and tremulous attempts at defiance. It was far, far better to say 'I expect you're quite right, Mother,' and go on doing exactly what she wanted.

'Of course I'm right,' Maudie said. 'Put it out and promise me never to touch another.'

'I expect you're right,' Jean said, still smoking.

'I'm waiting, Jean,' Maudie warned.

Slowly, Jean extinguished the cigarette. Let Maudie think she had won, then, later, she would simply light up another, and another, and the message would penetrate. No useful purpose would be served by making an issue of independence now. So preoccupied was she with her own cunning, that she barely noticed Maudie get up. One hundred cigarettes cascaded from their box into the fire before she had time to note her mother's action. It was a very small fire, there only because Jean liked a real fire even with the central heating. Automatically, Jean found herself on her knees trying to shovel the main heap of cigarettes away from the few flaming coals. With an expert shove, Maudie pushed her away, and they were both left red faced crouching in front of the merrily burning blaze.

They sat in silence until Edward and Nicholas finished their meal and came through. Maudie was flushed with triumphant exertion, Jean pale with the new, incredible tension inside her. She deliberately picked up a pile of old magazines and flicked through them, ignoring her mother's sermon on the wisdom of what she had just done. Even when the sanctimonious drone stopped and Maudie sank heavily on to the sofa, she kept silent in spite of the quickly begun barrage of pointed remarks about talking to one's own mother after twenty odd years.

Edward, restored by his excellent meal, stopped half way into the room, repelled by the quality of the women's silence. Realising they had quarrelled, and quarrelled badly, he was glad that it had not been because of him. With his sympathies lying on Jean's side, no matter what might have happened, he felt this would be recognised and that he must accordingly make overtures to Maudie first.

'I expect,' he said, in her direction, 'you're exhausted with that journey.'

'I'm never exhausted,' Maudie said.

'Still, you must be pretty tired,' Edward said.

'If you want me to go to my bed, then say so outright, young man,' said Maudie.

'I didn't mean that at all,' Edward said. 'I was merely making social conversation.'

'There's no need for that,' Maudie said. She swallowed hard, aware that she might have been too hasty. Never let it be said that she was rude. 'My back aches a little, that's all,' she admitted grudgingly, 'and I'll be glad to rest it soon.'

'Would you like your tea and sandwich now, Mother?' Jean asked. It was still an effort to speak and be sure her voice would not shake.

'I'll make it myself,' Maudie said, struggling to get up.

'You'll do no such thing,' Jean said quickly, already on her way out of the room. Once she had gone, the restraint deepened, even if it was of a different and less obvious kind. The going out and coming back of Jean would remove what remained of that antipathy, while it only emphasised the gap between the men and her.

'Do you mind, Grandma,' Nicholas asked, 'if I have the television on?'

'Nicholas!' rebuked Edward. 'That's a most impolite thing to ask. It's your grandmother's first evening here and you can do without tele for one night.' He felt virtuous forbidding Nicholas's pleasure for Maudie's sake.

'I don't want to spoil your fun,' Maudie said, surprisingly. 'There doesn't seem any harm in it to me.'

'How much have you seen?' Edward asked.

'I haven't seen the thing at all,' Maudie said, 'but the minister has one and everyone seems to set great store by it.'

When Jean came back, with the tray, the room was in semi-darkness and her mother was following a film of wild life with absorbed interest. Quietly, she laid the tea things on a table and pulled it up Maudie's side.

'Tea, Mother,' she said loudly.

Maudie shushed her into silence, pointing significantly at the screen. She poured her tea with breathless accuracy, wincing at the noise the sugar lump made as it hit the liquid, and lowering the spoon on to her saucer with anxious precision, lest its tinkle interrupt the commentary. The noise she made sipping her tea obviously upset her, and she seemed relieved that the soft sandwiches could alone cause no offence. Edward sank further and further back in his chair to hide his smirks at the ludicrous luck Nicholas had had. He knew his mother-in-law. First impressions were all. If it had been 'Z' Cars, or Ready! Steady! Go! television would have been outlawed forever. But now, even when the horrors of these hit her as they eventually must, the sacrosanct quality of that first experience would remain. For which, he thought, praise be.

The minute the programme ended, Edward leapt up and turned the set off and switched another lamp on, Maudie sat blinking, her hands folded in her lap.

'Very interesting,' she said, 'you'd never imagine dumb animals led such a life.'

'I watch it every week,' Nicholas said, virtuously.

'Then I will too,' said Maudie. 'God willing.'

They all smiled at each other, and Jean held her breath, prolonging the sudden burst of affection on all sides. Too soon, Maudie was gripping the arm of the sofa and rising to her feet.

'I'm sitting here,' she said, 'and I haven't unpacked a thing. I'd best go to my room and leave you all be.'

'I've taken your cases up,' Edward said, absolving himself from accompanying her.

'I'll show you your room then, Mother,' Jean said. She hesitated, wondering if she ought to start preparing Maudie on the way up, or simply let her work things out for herself. She waited, wondering and worrying, while Maudie and Edward and Nicholas exchanged most cordial and complete goodnights.

In the hall, Maudie lingered to examine the table and mirror. It was a semi-circular mahogany table with a design inlaid in the centre. Maudie's fingertips touched the wood briefly, and stole up to the ornate gold frame of the mirror for an even more fleeting caress. She sniffed, and moved towards the stairs. On the third stair, she stopped to feel the pile of the carpet and the thickness of the underlay, and when a mark on the white painted stair caught her attention she rubbed at it surreptitiously. The framed engravings of cathedrals set symmetrically up the right-hand wall held her gaze for some time before she moved on to the first landing, but she continued to say nothing.

Jean, not hurrying her, did not need the spoken commentary. She knew exactly what Maudie was thinking. Good wood, but needs a wax polish more often. Not gold, only painted metal. Expensive carpet, skimped on the underlay. Pointless painting stairs a showy colour like white if you aren't going to keep them clean. Funny place to have dark pictures like that, make people fall downstairs trying to look at them.

'This is our bedroom,' Jean said. She stood aside to let Maudie pass through, and saw her eyes drawn instantly to the twin beds with their blue satin counterpanes. Maudie grunted, and Jean turned and led her into Nicholas's room and lastly to the guest room, tidy, cold and quite empty. Before anything could be misunderstood, she said quickly, 'We haven't put you in the guest room, Mother. We've made a rather special room for you,' and then she led the way up the next flight of stairs and flung the attic door open.

'We thought it would be nice for you to get some peace when you wanted, somewhere to feel private when we got too much for you. See, there's a little stove if you want to make a snack during the night, and an electric kettle for tea, and a washbasin, so everything's handy. It's all centrally heated and you can control it yourself with these knobs. Edward had it decorated and newly furnished and if there's anything else you want, you've only to ask and it's yours.'

Her speech finished, Jean watched her mother take it all in, and then without saying a word, walk to her cases in the centre of the room where Edward had dumped them, and start untying the leather straps round them. She suddenly wanted to rush across and put her arms round her and tell her she hadn't meant it, of course she must move into the guest room next to them and she, Jean, would love to make her tea in the middle of the night, and she wasn't going to need privacy because they would all love and want her every waking minute.

'Would you,' she said, 'like a television set up here, Mother?'

'I would not,' Maudie said, grimly. 'I seem to have everything else.'

'Don't you like it?' Jean asked.

'Very nice,' Maudie said, 'you could let it for a lot of money. I expect you will after I'm gone.'

'We did it for you,' Jean said. 'We wanted you to be comfortable.'

'Oh, I'll be very comfortable,' Maudie said, proudly. 'I won't

63

have to trouble you for anything, will I?'

'Nothing will be any trouble,' Jean said.

'Well then, you can leave me to unpack and get to bed,' Maudie said, equably.

'Can't I help?'

'I don't need help.'

Jean sat on the grey bed and watched Maudie methodically take out her black and brown and grey dresses and put them away on hangers. The shoes came next and were put in rows, and her underclothes neatly piled in drawers. She handled bottles of things with loving care and stacked them on a shelf, the medical quack remedies next to the spirit cleaner and glue. The job was completed in utter silence. Every bend of her mother's back registered outraged disapproval, every click of a hanger and bang of a drawer told of her hurt and resentment. Still, Jean could not speak. She groped for something to say to show that she understood and was sorry and could find nothing. It was all exactly as she had known it would be, and she had let it go on all the same.

She couldn't go on sitting on the bed any longer. Maudie was waiting for her to go. I am dismissed, with ignominy, she thought, as she got up, and took the counterpane off for something to do.

'Goodnight,' she said, with it still in her hand, 'I hope you sleep well.'

'I never sleep well,' Maudie said, scornfully. She turned and began to unbutton her dress as Jean backed out of the room, bidding goodnight yet again.

CHAPTER THREE

Maudie woke in the divan bed, and reaching for her travelling alarm clock, she rapidly calculated how many hours she had definitely not slept. How she missed the striking grandmother clock at home! It was so easy to remember that she'd heard two strike, and three, but not four, and then the indeterminate half hour sound that meant she hadn't quite managed two hours' sleep and must be ready for five any second. She leant back on her pillow, and that instant the clock shrilled out that it was six. She let the alarm ring its full stretch. Best be truly awake.

Feeling for her morning spectacles, she put them on, and got into her dressing-gown, a cut down from an old overcoat. The day never began right if she put her afternoon spectacles on by mistake first thing, for they were a more recent prescription and never suited a dim light in her opinion. She had never been able to find an optician of the calibre of Mr MacIntyre of Sauchiehall Street who had made that original pair in 1927.

As she moved towards the door with her torch, not trusting the murkiness in a strange house, she felt the familiar constrictions in her stomach that meant the sennapod tea she'd drunk last thing at night was as usual taking its dependable effect. Hastily, she went down the stairs, taking care to creep past Edward and Jean's room, and into the lavatory. After a few brief seconds, she emerged satisfied and pulled the chain. She waited till the noise had died away, then she pulled it again, and to really clear the air she produced the fresh air spray she always carried in her dressing-gown pocket and sprayed it lavishly around. It had the most delicious smell for 1s. 2d.

Quietly, she crept back up the stairs and plugged the electric kettle in. The speed with which it boiled took her by surprise. When she had made her tea, she carefully examined the make of the kettle and wondered how much they were and if, should she invest in such a life-saver, you could plug them into a light because her room and kitchen had no power plugs. She admired, too, the pale pink tea cups and saucers that she'd found in the little cupboard beside the kettle. They were very nice. The kettle was very nice. Really, the whole idea of saving her the trek down to the kitchen was very nice. She warned herself not to be grudging, and began practising the words of proper thanks she would give Jean and Edward. Sitting in the quiet grey light sipping the hot tea, her inside comfortable, she was so sorry she had acted so ungrateful the night before.

It was impossible to bring herself to get back into bed. A rest was one thing, but bed after 6.30 a.m. carried things to extremes. Anyway, it wasn't as if she could get any extra sleep. That was out of the question. Her back would ache directly she got back in again on account of that dreadful soft mattress. So instead, she took out her prayer book and read the lesson for the day, a little too conscious that she was filling in her time virtuously, and listened intently for any signs below. She didn't want to disturb them. She didn't want to be a bother to anyone.

By seven-thirty, when the silence remained absolute, broken not even by a bus rattling by or a postman's knock, she could stand it no longer. Seven-thirty was a reasonable hour to stir, surely. Still trying to keep very quiet, she washed herself at the little sink and got dressed. Her bed couldn't be made because it had to be aired. She stripped it, examining the nasty mattress more closely, and flung open a window. She made everything tidy, and then went downstairs again, this time with a firm tread.

The kitchen, when she found it, seemed very large and bare. The floor was tiled with black and white tiles and felt as cold as a farmyard. There was a large wooden table in the middle and six chairs, and no other furniture except cupboards and pieces of equipment like the cooker and the fridge. She instinctively turned to open the curtains, and realised that the reason it was so light was because there were no curtains or covering of any sort over the big, four-paned window. You could see clearly into the garden, a large garden, full of trees and shrubs and no flowers at all. She shuddered and turned her back on such a brazen and hideous view.

She must make herself useful. Enjoying poking in all the drawers and cupboards, she managed to find their breakfast crockery and the butter and sugar and marmalade and so forth, but she was upset that she could find no tablecloth of any description. Puzzled, she went into the room next door, thinking it might be a dining-room, but it wasn't, it was some sort of laundry place and there were no tablecloths there either. She returned to the kitchen and looked about her for something to use and saw a pile of newspapers on a stool and selecting the newest, she spread them on the table. They would have to excuse her the first morning. Even with such a humble surface, the table looked neat and inviting and she was pleased with herself. There was nothing as nice as a nicely set breakfast table, she always said.

Her next shock was that there appeared to be neither porridge nor bread. In a way, she had guessed there might be no porridge and she was determined not to make an unseemly fuss about it. So she wasn't really shocked, only pretending to herself that she was as a sort of indulgence. But bread was a different matter. It was the staff of life. It was where every meal should begin and end. Prepared to do without the pan loaf, she had never expected to be entirely breadless. Panicking slightly, she moved rapidly from cupboard to cupboard, from box to box and tin to tin and shelf to shelf, and there was still no bread. Saying aloud 'Dear God, dear God', she gave up her search, and shakily reached for a chair. The kettle boiled its head off as she remained sunk in a bottomless gloom of an entire three months without bread. Even when she saw the clouds of steam, she hardly had the spirit or energy to go and turn it off. What was tea without bread to dry it?

At that moment, she heard the clink of milk bottles, and rushed to get them in. The milkman looked up, startled, as she snatched the third bottle from his hand before it had time to join the other two on the step. If there was one thing Maudie couldn't bear, it was the sight of milk bottles lolling lazily on a step for the street to see and know you still hadn't opened your door. It was, in any case, a sinful temptation to thieves.

With the milk in the jug, and the kettle twice boiled nearly dry, and the teapot warmed and cooled several times, Maudie did not quite know what to do. It seemed wrong to start her own breakfast, and in any case she could think of nothing that was palatable without bread. Jean might yet come down and reveal a baker's dozen of crusty loaves. But it was now gone eight o'clock and her stomach rumbled. God knew, she hardly ate a morsel, but that morsel was badly needed.

It began to occur to Maudie that they might all be dead in their beds, and her down there doing nothing. Or at the best, slept in. She would look silly if she let it be known that she'd been up since six and not thought to wake them. She started up the stairs, and as she did so, heard the bedroom door above open and Jean come out. She backed down the stairs again as Jean came hurrying down them, tying her dressing-gown cord round her as she went.

'Dear God,' Maudie exclaimed, 'I thought you might all be dead in your beds. It's past eight o'clock, Jean, and the milk's been and I can't find any bread.'

'Dear dear Mother,' Jean said, taking hold of Maudie and guiding her back into the kitchen affectionately. She was resolved to be firm but openly affectionate. 'You shouldn't have got up until you heard me making the breakfast. I don't want you to do anything. It's to be a complete rest for you. Didn't you sleep well or something?'

'No, I did not sleep well,' Maudie said, shortly.

'I expect you were overtired after the journey.'

'I was not overtired. I was as tired as I always am but I could not sleep on that bed.'

'What was wrong with the bed?'

'It's too soft and saggy.'

'Well then, we'll get a firmer one. I'm sorry you didn't sleep. Oh dear, you've laid the table.'

'I couldn't find a cloth,' said Maudie, aggrieved. 'Have you no cloths?'

'No,' Jean said, 'we use mats.' She drew the thick straw mats out of their drawer. Silently, Maudie watched her pull off the newspaper and put down the nasty, scratchy mats.

'Well, I won't say what I think,' Maudie said, longingly.

'You sit down, Mother, while I take Edward his tea.'

'Edward his tea? Dear God, Jean!' She watched her smiling, defiant-looking daughter make a pot of tea and pour a cup for her husband and actually march out lovingly with it. Maudie boiled with rage. Of all the ungrateful, slave-driving tyrants, that son-in-law of hers was the worst. Not even Joseph had expected himself to be brought tea at half past eight in the morning, and she would have thrown the teapot at him if he'd so much as suggested it. She heard Jean pull the newspaper out of the door, and go toiling up the stairs with that too.

'My poor lamb,' Maudie said as Jean reappeared. It was her most demonstrative endearment. 'My poor lamb.' She shook her head sympathetically and reached out to pat her daughter's hand. Jean snatched it away.

'Don't be silly, Mother,' she said. 'I like taking him tea.'

'It should be him taking you a cup.'

'I wouldn't thank him for it—I hate tea in bed. Edward really appreciates it. He finds it difficult to wake up and it helps him. With such a hard day ahead of him, he deserves it.'

'Shocking,' Maudie said, tight lipped, but she admired Jean all the more. It was good to stick by your husband, however bad he was. One had one's pride. It was best to pretend everything was quite all right and that you were as happy as the next person.

69

'Now, Mother,' Jean was saying, 'what can I get you?'

'I hardly eat anything,' Maudie said.

'Well, what can I tempt you with? Bacon and egg? Scrambled egg? Sausages?'

'No, no,' Maudie said, shuddering with distaste, 'a little porridge, though I don't suppose you have any, and a slice of toast, that's all I could manage.'

'You're wrong,' Jean said. 'I have some porridge. It's in this bottom cupboard. I got it specially.'

'And the bread?' sniffed Maudie, feeling that she had been caught out and it wasn't fair.

'By the time I've made and you've eaten the porridge, the bread will be here.'

'There *is* none in the house, then?' pressed Maudie, triumphantly.

'No, there isn't. I get it fresh and warm from a van that comes round so I never bother getting more than a day's supply.'

Maudie sat, as far away as possible from that naked window, contemplating this woman who happily confessed she went breadless overnight. No provision in that scheme for sudden visitors, sudden pangs of hunger in the small hours, sudden strikes or wars or famines. And what's more, she didn't even go for her own bread when she wanted it—she waited for a motor-car, the most fickle of inventions known to mankind. It was very hard to swallow and remember it took all sorts to make a world.

Silently, she sat and noted an abundance of strange things throughout the breakfast. She wasn't going to complain or comment, but no one could stop her noticing. There was no sugar spoon. Edward and Jean both put the wet spoon that had been in their tea into the communal sugar, and him a dentist. Nor was there a butter knife. Each person was expected to use their own side knife. The butter itself was rock hard from the refrigerator and not at all nice or easy to spread, besides which it was most wasteful.

70

The waste was awful. The butter each left on their plates! The bread that was thrown into the bin and not even given to the birds, and new bread at that! Neither of them ate their crusts, both left half full cups of tea at the end, and nearly a quarter of a pot was poured down the sink. It took all Maudie's self-control to remain amiable and chat as if nothing was happening.

Edward went into his surgery at nine-fifteen and soon she heard the newly arrived receptionist, whom she hadn't yet seen, letting in the first patient. She felt relieved that the monster was safely out of the way, and looked forward to the morning's work. Her next shock was to discover that the table was to be left, indefinitely, for Nicholas, who apparently was allowed to come down when he pleased for his breakfast. Maudie gathered this was a fairly substantial affair and that when it was required Jean dropped everything and made it.

She and Jean hardly talked as they went about the business of cleaning the house, yet Maudie felt closer to her daughter than at any time since her arrival. Thank God Jean was as much a stickler for cleanliness and order as she was, even if she had slipped up on smaller matters. It made Maudie feel good to see how thoroughly the stairs were Hoovered and the ornaments dusted. No laziness at all—each table and shelf was meticulously cleared and then dusted properly, and each individual article wiped carefully and re-arranged in a proper fashion. She was overjoyed the way Jean immediately washed her dusters—that was the mark of a Maudie Tipstaff trained housewife. Always take care of your tools, for a dirty duster cannot make a house clean.

They made the beds together and neither hesitated to see how the other would do it. With one accord, they pulled all the clothes straight off, shook them and replaced them deftly, stretching and tucking in as they went. They worked in perfect harmony, and at the end each had exactly six inches of sheet to turn down.

At eleven, Jean said she would make some coffee and then

they would go to the shops before lunch. This wasn't part of Maudie's training. She herself never stopped, but so pleased was she with how things had gone that she agreed as though it was perfectly normal. The kitchen was now filled with sunshine, and she felt moved to hum a little as she sat down and watched Jean make the coffee. She was just going to tell Jean her house was a credit to her and she was glad she hadn't forgotten herself to the extent of getting someone in to do it for her, when Nicholas shouted. He wanted ham and eggs on a tray in his room. Horrified, Maudie watched Jean, admittedly shamefaced, rush to comply, murmuring ridiculous excuses about only having him home half the year.

The glow had gone. Maudie wasn't at all sure that she now wanted to go shopping and had to be most energetically persuaded. It seemed to her a somehow personal insult that the men in this house did exactly what they liked with her Jean. She simply could not tolerate it, and she couldn't begin to understand the mentality of any woman who would allow it.

Deeply upset, but struggling to hold her tongue, she grudgingly allowed herself to be coaxed into getting ready to go out. She did it for poor Jean's sake. What she would really like to have done was throw Nicholas's egg in his face and order him up immediately. Her features were set rigidly in an expression of ferocious disapproval as she stepped out of the door with the downtrodden Jean, who was explaining that she walked to the shops for a few things just for the exercise and Edward got the rest so she wouldn't have to struggle back with heavy baskets.

Maudie put her arm through Jean's as they walked down the road. It wasn't that she needed the support, but to show the world that they were mother and daughter. She tried not to look to right or left in a nosy fashion, but it gradually began to dawn on her that no one was looking at them anyway. No one called out a greeting, or betrayed any knowledge of Jean.

'Is there no one going to say good morning to you?' Maudie whispered.

72

'I don't know anyone, really,' Jean said.

'What about your neighbours? You have neighbours, don't you?'

'Not really, Mother. I know the people in the street by sight, of course, but we aren't as close as speaking terms.'

'What about your friends? Don't you have any friends?'

'Of course I do.'

'Then don't any of them live round here?'

'Yes, but——' Jean stopped. She could feel Maudie waiting for, demanding, an explanation. 'Not many of them go out shopping in the morning,' she said, and quickened her step so that they reached the first shop before Maudie had a chance to meditate upon that.

All the shops were very busy and sometimes Maudie waited outside and studied the window because she did not believe in people who did not intend to buy anything taking up room. The contents of these windows fascinated her. They were all so full, so prosperous looking, and she positively drooled over the meat. She was sure she had never seen such ample, magnificent cuts. The chops were huge and nearly all lean, the steak so red it must surely have been treated in some way. Wherever she went, Maudie paid close attention to shop windows and it was a matter in which she had no false pride. In this respect, Motherwell undoubtedly did not lead the world. That was her home town and she hated to have it beaten. Nor did Glasgow, though it had one or two fine shops. From the minute she saw those London shop windows, she knew she had found the mecca.

Jean said no. She said these were just local shops and to be really thrilled Maudie must see some of the food shops in Soho and go with her to the famous markets. She drew her mother with her into a fishmonger's and asked her opinion on whether they should have salmon or halibut, or did she think the trout looked good? Maudie tried not to show her scandalised excitement. She had never in her life bought a salmon and Jean knew it. She bought kippers and cod and herring and mackerel, and on rare occasions, plaice fillets. She looked at the lovely salmon and tried to whisper the price to Jean in case she had not seen it, but Jean said she knew the price and it was quite cheap for the time of the year. Quite cheap! Maudie nearly fainted as her daughter handed over the unmentionable sum of money. She honestly felt sick with the strain of being involved in such expenditure.

A little dazed, she followed meekly as Jean went to the greengrocer's and bought some tomatoes at 5s. a pound and something queer-looking called asparagus at 8s. 6d. for a few thin-looking stick-like objects. Fearfully, she tried to squint into Jean's purse each time it was opened, sure it must be at last empty, but there always seemed to be pound notes in plenty. When Jean suggested some early strawberries at 6s. 6d. a punnet, she could stand it no longer and protested vehemently. Laughing and saying Edward liked good things, Jean allowed herself to be led away, and Maudie's palpitations eased as they left the shopping area and entered the residential part. All the same, she had to lean on a gate-post for a few brief seconds before she was quite sure she could walk home.

All through lunch, Maudie kept up a running commentary on how much everything had cost. She had watched the salmon cooking most anxiously, unable to bring herself to move from the kitchen lest some dreadful disaster should overtake it. There was no pleasure at all in the succulent smell of it—it was too worrying to know what it had cost. And when it was eaten, she could not help remarking that, all things considered, a really nice smoked kipper or pickled herring was every bit as good and tasty.

Sorrowfully, she helped Jean wash up. It was so sad to see the head and backbone of such a fine fish going in the waste bin.

'Forget it, Mother,' Jean said, 'it was only a fish.'

'At that price——' Maudie began, when Jean turned the hot water on with a rush, and then Edward came in and took a tea towel from a drawer and began to help her dry. Dumbfounded,

74

Maudie shot him accusing glances, to let him know that no one got in with her that way.

'Thank you, darling,' Jean said, as they finished, and kissed him. Maudie tutted and turned away.

'You going for your rest?' Edward asked. She nodded. 'Then I'll be off.'

He went, with an affable nod in Maudie's direction, and she heard the car start. The house, centred in the tidy kitchen, was suddenly very still. Nicholas had unaccountably disappeared.

'Well, Mother,' Jean said, 'I have forty winks on my bed now.' She hesitated. 'Will you have a rest too?'

'Whatever for?' Maudie asked. 'Dear God, I haven't done a stroke all morning. Now's the time to get all the odd jobs done with the men out of the way and the lunch over.'

'There aren't any,' Jean protested.

'I'll find some. You be off for your rest.'

Unhappily, Jean went. Maudie heard the bedroom door open and close. Eagerly, she looked about her. The front step needed whitening. It was near grey with dirt. She had noticed nobody seemed to whiten their steps, but anyone could see they would look the better for it. She looked about her again, trying to work out where Jean might keep a pumice stone and some whitener, and after a long search she found what she wanted. They were wrapped together at the back of a cupboard in a newspaper ten years old. Flushed with her good luck, Maudie got together all the other materials she needed and hurried to the front door. Oh what glory was soon to break there!

Aching and tired, but completely satisfied, Maudie came in from her labours an hour later just as Jean was coming down the stairs. She stood waiting, the front door still open, one hand on her hip where her arthritis suddenly stabbed.

'Whatever have you been doing?' Jean asked, anxiously.

'You only need to look,' Maudie said, triumphantly, and gestured towards the step. Jean looked. Maudie waited, child-like, for her ecstatic praise, but none came. Her daughter frowned.

'That's ridiculous,' she said, quite sharply.

'It is not,' snapped Maudie, glaring. Waiting no longer, she thumped off towards the kitchen. Jean banged the front door.

The matter was not referred to again. When Edward came back from his golf and asked what they had been doing, Jean simply said she had rested and then pottered in the garden, and Mother had been busy. Maudie was too hurt to say exactly what she had been doing. They ate their tea, still with no Nicholas, and immediately Edward looked at his watch.

'Nearly seven,' he said, and paused. It seemed to Maudie that Jean lowered her eyes. 'Time to be going,' Edward said, and when Jean was silent, 'we go up to the Club on Saturday evenings,' he explained to Maudie. 'Jean and I, that is.'

'Edward!' said Jean reproachfully.

'We look forward to it,' Edward said. 'It's Jean's one night out.'

'I don't want to go,' Jean said, firmly.

'You do,' Edward said, 'you're just imagining that your mother will want you to stay in with her.'

'Nothing of the sort,' Maudie almost shouted, 'you both go. I've plenty to do.'

'I'd rather stay,' Jean said.

'I don't want you to,' Maudie said. 'I'm going to bed, anyway. I've my magazine to read and my letters to write. I wouldn't talk to you if you stayed. I'm off to my own room right now. Goodnight.'

Gathering her things up, she started towards the stairs, expecting at every step to hear Jean say she wouldn't hear of it and telling her to sit down again at once. But all she heard was a cheerful Edward exhorting Jean to hurry and get dressed so they could get out of her mother's way. Miserably, Maudie mounted the last flight as Jean began rushing around. She didn't put on the light, but walked over to her bed and sat on it in the dark. Minutes later she heard Jean calling that

Nicholas had his own key and would let himself in, and they wouldn't be late, and why didn't she watch television, and would she really be all right and not mind? Maudie went to the door and shouted down 'I'm busy'. Then she stood at the window and watched them drive off.

For a while, she went on standing in the dark, listening to the quiet of the house. No one was going to drop in, it wasn't that sort of place. She would have peace. Unfortunately, it was the one commodity she did not want. She knew all about peace. Peace was an enemy she was a little tired of fighting with self-created activity. And then, scolding herself roundly, she switched on all the lights and began organising herself. It was just like being at home, but that was something she must not think of.

CHAPTER FOUR

'It has been,' Jean said, 'the longest day of my life.' She put her head back against the car seat in exaggerated parody of total exhaustion. Guilt weakened her still further. She should not have left her mother like that. It was not as if she was for one second convincing herself that Maudie would be happy. 'I know exactly how she feels,' Jean said, 'that's the worst part. If only I wasn't so good at appreciating her feelings.'

'Maybe you aren't,' Edward said. He was so pleased to have got Jean away that he had forgotten that they never enjoyed their Saturday evenings out. He was just beginning to remember.

'Oh, of course I am,' Jean said impatiently. 'Putting myself in other people's shoes is about the one talent I have.'

'Then use it on me,' Edward said.

'Don't try to sidetrack me,' Jean said, sharply.

Edward stayed silent for the rest of the evening. He piloted her politely into the club and politely left her to go and play cards after politely buying her a drink. She sat with her three 'friends' and he knew she would be happy telling them all about Maudie. She was. She was able to put the case with such admirable clarity.

'You see, it's not as if I ever got on with my mother, we just never agreed on anything. She ruled us with a rod of iron and I never disobeyed her till I met Edward and he put me up to it. We haven't a thing in common. I admire her, in a way, because she's had such a hard life—oh yes, a very hard time of it. You can't help but admire her for the way she brought up we three children. But she's so overbearing, and she's such a moan—I mean, I don't blame her, I can see why she's a moan, but all the same she hardly ever smiles. I knew it would be like this. We don't dare have anyone to the house while she's there. But I had to welcome her, she is my mother after all, it was the least I could do—no, no it was. The absolute least.'

All the time, listening to herself, listening and enjoying it, Jean thought miserably what a bitch she was. She was bidding so obviously for a sympathy she didn't deserve, even if it was only to comparative strangers. She saw herself so clearly as wanting to be patted on the back and told how marvellous she was to put up with it all. Oh, she was so tired of her endless hypocrisy in this affair. Why couldn't she simply say she couldn't stand her mother, but that though she resented the fact, she did feel responsible for her? No, she felt tied to her. Say it, face it, and have done with it, instead of this endless inward whining. She felt she couldn't get through another single day if this turmoil persisted.

She did get through the days, without even, for such an acutely introverted woman, realising that the turmoil was flattening out into a merely stormy sea. It was Maudie's doing. She imposed a routine so rigid that it was impossible for the hours and days not just to glide by. It was a routine of conversation and thought, not only of behaviour. She opened each day with the same pattern of remarks, and continued it with the same rhythm of silences and outbursts of varying degrees of calm discontent. She really made it all very easy.

Every evening, at exactly 7.30 p.m., Maudie said she would bid them goodnight and go to her room, for she had things to do before she went to bed. Her retirement was no discreet departure. It was a flagrant slap in the face to their hospitality.

'There's no need to go off like that every evening, Mother,' Jean said, after a couple of weeks, 'Edward isn't even here tonight. You're not interrupting anything.'

'I have things to do,' Maudie said, relentlessly. She might just as well have said she knew when she was not wanted, Jean thought.

'It seems silly you sitting up there on your own and me

79

sitting down here on my own,' Jean said, with persistent masochism. 'Why don't we keep each other company?'

'I have my own room,' Maudie said. 'We see each other the rest of the day. I'll say goodnight.' And off she went, gleefully.

Jean, alone, could not read or sew or watch television. Night after night, when Nicholas had taken himself off to school and Edward had gone out, she sat literally staring up at the ceiling, trying to see through it what Maudie was doing. Off she went up the stairs each evening, proud to be going of her own accord, glad that she was the one to voluntarily leave. She seemed so pleased about it, so triumphant. Restlessly, Jean flitted from one inadequate pasttime to another, thinking her mother might just as well have stayed for all the peace her absence gave. I wonder all the time, she thought, what she is doing, I even ask her next day what she did, yet she never asks me. She has no curiosity about my isolation, as I have about hers. She never asks why Edward goes, where Edward goes, whether I mind that Edward goes. She never seems to think it is any business of hers. She doesn't want to discuss anything personal. She doesn't want to be involved. She watches and notices and weighs everything up, and she won't tell me.

Increasingly, Jean found herself wandering out into the hall after her mother. She would stand and fiddle with something at the hall table until Maudie was about to turn the first landing, and then, about to be seen, she would walk briskly back into the sitting-room. She began to want to follow her mother. At first, she was content to pretend to go to the bathroom, and stand inside with the door slightly ajar, listening breathlessly to the pointless and predictable sounds of an old lady going upstairs. Then she would go downstairs and ask herself what she wanted to hear. Eventually, not even that was shame enough. She had to go the whole way up, sweating at each creaking stair, and sit at the top, right outside her mother's door, eagerly waiting for familiar sounds. It was so ridiculous it made her alternately giggle and sob, when once she was back in her own room.

She knew she would have to go into Maudie's room, one night. It could not be resisted. Listlessly, she found herself waiting for an excuse, though when she had reached the door, with the request for Robert's address dying with age on her lips, she did not bother to use it. She walked in, without knocking, and knew Maudie had been expecting her from the satisfaction with which she turned and looked at her. Jean went and lay down on the bed.

'You don't mind, do you, if I come up?' Jean asked, for something to get it all going.

'I can't stop you,' Maudie said, sniffing. Her enjoyment was offensively obvious.

'Yes you can. You only need to say this is your room and it's private.'

'Nowhere's private in someone else's house,' Maudie said.

Jean raised herself on one arm and looked at her mother. Was she being bad tempered, or cunning?

'This can be if you want it to be,' she said. 'Do you want it to be?'

'Don't talk silly,' Maudie said. 'Dear God, do I want to be private from my own daughter?'

Jean lay back again. She heard Maudie put the kettle on and get the cups out.

'Do you like it here with us?' she asked. It was an inexcusable thing to ask.

'Well enough,' Maudie said.

'But do you really like it?' Jean pressed.

'I wouldn't want to stay forever, if that's what you mean,' Maudie said, fiercely. She clashed the cups on to the saucers, and flung the teaspoons together.

'Why?' asked Jean, praying that Maudie would violently criticise her life with Edward, then it would be so easy to get up and go.

'Folk like their own homes,' Maudie said. 'East west, home's best.'

Disappointed, Jean closed her eyes. She could feel the words

81

coming, and pursed her lips hopefully together.

'Sugar?' Maudie asked. She always asked, as though Jean was so fickle she might have changed her mind since last time.

'Please.'

Maudie put the sugar in, and the milk, without asking. Milk was good for you. You ought to have it in tea. Therefore she always put it in unless she was expressly forbidden. Jean sipped the tea, and then left it to go cold at the bedside. Maudie drank hers with concentration. The minute she had finished, she got up and washed the cup and saucer, and dried them, and put them away. Then she sighed, as though the tea drinking had been part of some dreadful ordeal. Jean watched her, and pondered the effect of suddenly asking, 'Tell me what happened to Dad? Tell me all about it from the beginning.'

'I get quite lonely when Edward's out,' she said, instead. 'Especially with Nicholas away. There isn't a great deal to do.'

'There's always plenty to do,' Maudie said, firmly.

'There isn't,' Jean said, feeling excited. 'What is there to do? Just tell me?'

But Maudie didn't reply. She ignored the plea to start an outspoken, personal discussion. One kept one's life to oneself.

'Oh well,' she said, 'I don't know.' But she said it as though she certainly did know. 'I must see about my bunion. Look——' and she began to roll down her stocking to show Jean the bunion on her big toe. 'It needs cut out,' she said, 'that's what it really needs, no getting away from it.'

Jean sat up, abruptly.

'I don't want to look at your bunion,' she said, 'put your stocking back on.'

Strangely, Maudie did not seem offended. She began to roll the stocking back up.

'I'm going to bed,' she said, 'you'd better go back down. Edward might come in.'

'Well,' Jean said, 'it wouldn't matter if he did, would it? It wouldn't matter at all. He would hardly notice I wasn't there. He often comes in and goes to bed and he doesn't even look to see if I'm in the other bed. Don't you think that's dreadful? Not needing me? Not even wanting to see if I'm there?'

Maudie's face went tight with disapproval. Jean's whole attitude, the way she was wandering around the room, all excited like that, it was all wrong. It made her go cold with the horror of it. The intimacy was unbearable.

'I'm going to bed,' she said, 'you'd better go down. He's your husband, when all's said and done. There's many a worse.'

'Like yours?' Jean said, quickly.

'No one knows what I had to put up with,' said Maudie, pointedly.

'Of course they do,' Jean said, 'everyone knows everything. You dragged Sally and I into every detail of it. We know exactly what you had to put up with—but at least you weren't ignored.'

'More's the pity,' Maudie said, and immediately regretted replying at all. 'Well,' she said, 'least said soonest mended. Your Edward is good to you in his fashion. He's given you a lot.'

'He doesn't love me,' Jean said.

She had gone too far. Maudie turned back the coverlet of her bed, decisively. Below, the sound of Edward's car could clearly be heard.

'There he is,' she said, relieved.

Jean was forced to acknowledge that that must be that. She couldn't just blurt out 'He had an affair, you know, with his receptionist.' She couldn't force Maudie to hear it all in five seconds while Edward mounted the stairs. She couldn't be done out of what she hoped would follow such a devastating announcement, without knowing what that would be. She had started her speech too late.

She said goodnight. Maudie almost rushed her through the door. She went down the stairs feeling cheap and miserable and confused, and above all, ridiculous. Slowly, she went into the bedroom where Edward was undressing with the light off, and began to undress too. The words she had been longing to say were still all there in her head, and she wanted to say them, to talk.

'It's really very funny,' she said, very loudly.

Edward grunted, and got into bed, not attempting to ask what was funny. as though he thought she wasn't capable of knowing anything funny.

'It is funny,' she said, not moving from the side of his bed. 'It's funny that you should imagine my mother as the sort of person who would want to find out everything about us and then cause trouble.'

'I never said she would cause trouble,' Edward said. He groaned as she switched the bedside lamp on.

'That isn't the important bit,' Jean said, 'it's the finding out part. She doesn't want to find out anything. In fact, she goes to great trouble to make it plain that she doesn't think I ought to tell her anything about you, or us.'

'What have you been telling her?'

'Nothing.'

'Then I don't understand what you're talking about. Can't you go to bed?'

'You're the same,' Jean said, 'you're exactly the same as her. You don't want to get involved in other people's troubles. You think "being personal" is indecent. You've a lot in common, considering you hate her.'

'I don't hate her,' Edward said.

'You always pick on the least important parts of what I've said to reply to,' Jean said.

'I would have thought the subject of hating your mother was quite important enough.'

'You know what I mean,' Jean said, insistently, 'you just like to pretend you don't.'

'I don't hate your mother. She annoys me to death but I don't hate her. In some ways, I'll be sorry when she goes. There, you never expected me to say that, did you?'

Jean turned round and stared at him.

'What ways?' she asked, sharply.

'Oh, you know, just little things.'

'I want to know precisely what things? List them.'

'For God's sake, it was just a compliment, that's all.'

'I don't care what it was. What did you have in mind that made you able to say you would be sorry she went?'

'I told you—little things. She's company for you. The days don't drag so much for you when she's here, and then she's there in the evening when I'm out.'

'You must be mad.'

'O.K.—forget it. Let's get some sleep.'

'You honestly think she's company for me? You think the days don't drag because she's here? You must be blind.'

'Right, I'm blind. I don't want to discuss your mother any more. Goodnight.'

'We're not discussing my mother, we're discussing me.'

'Well, whatever it is we're discussing, I'm not discussing it any more. I'm tired. I want to go to sleep.'

'I just can't believe you can live in the same house and not see how much worse it makes everything having her here. It shows up the whole emptiness of my life. I keep thinking she isn't making any difference, I'm doing what I would do anyway, and then I think that's exactly it—there's nothing she could make a difference to. I don't have to cancel or change one iota of my daily routine. All I do is live in an empty, luxurious haze.'

'Oh God,' Edward said, 'what have I started? I meant on a simple level. You have someone to talk to, for example.'

'She doesn't talk to me.'

'Oh Christ, Jean, stop being so bloody silly. Of course she talks to you—she can hardly help talking to you.'

'She makes remarks.'

'Well what do you want? Some kind of philosophical treatise?'

'She doesn't talk to me,' Jean repeated, stubbornly. 'I talk to her, I try to get close to her, but she just brushes me off. She only wants to talk about the weather, and the price of things, and what we're going to have for tea.'

'I suppose you want to talk about life and love and poverty and——'

'Stop sneering. I just don't want to go on chatting about trivialities to my own mother, as though we had no connection with each other. It's wrong.'

'There's nothing wrong about it. It's entirely natural. It's because she's your mother that nothing else should be necessary. You understand each other too deeply to need that sort of talk.'

'But we don't, we don't understand each other at all—and anyway, it isn't a matter of understanding. It's a question of caring about each other and that means wanting to know what affects each other's lives.'

'Your poor mother,' Edward said.

'Why?'

'Having to put up with you thrusting your nauseating confidences on her all day.'

'God, I hate you when——'

As Jean shouted out the words, Edward put his hand to his lips and she automatically found herself stopping to listen. Clearly, she heard Maudie's door opening and the quick patter of her feet down the stairs and the scurry into the bathroom.

'One, two, three, a quick pee for the night and away we go,' Edward said, and as the chain was pulled he laughed and Jean in turn made silencing noises at him.

'We'd better put the light off and go to sleep or she'll wonder what vile and dreadful things I'm doing to you,' he said, and quickly snuggled down into his bed, determined not to be tricked into replying to any of her absurdities again.

Defeated, Jean at last got into her bed and put the light out. He muttered a goodnight but she couldn't bring herself to say even that. She lay wondering who was the more distant from her, Edward or her mother. She tried so hard to come close to them, and both pushed her away. She was the odd one out, wanting what neither believed in giving.

86

She knew what troubled and disturbed her most about this when she saw Maudie's face as she lifted Robert's airmail letter off the hall table the next morning. The letters nearly always arrived on a Wednesday, and if they didn't Maudie immediately began to worry. Jean watched her lift the letter and put it inside the pocket of her dress, and then come through for her breakfast. Her mother's face was contented and yet eager.

'Robert's letter come?' Jean asked, slowly.

'Yes,' Maudie said. 'It was cold last night—nearly the end of March and yet you can still get nights like that. It was cold enough for snow. Is the temperature in the papers?'

'What does he say?' Jean asked.

'Oh, I haven't opened it yet,' Maudie said. 'I'll take it to my room after. I haven't time to read it now with my breakfast on the table.' She tried to say it crossly, as though his letter was a nuisance.

'Open it,' Jean said, 'I'll read it to you while you have your porridge,' and she stretched out her hand for the letter.

'You wouldn't be able to read his writing,' Maudie said, quickly burying the letter deeper in her pocket. 'He just scrawls when he writes to me, doesn't care at all about my poor old eyesight. Sometimes I can hardly be bothered to read his letters at all.'

You liar, Jean thought, watching her take her porridge extra-slowly, though her rush to be away shone from every pore. You are dying to get up those stairs to open his letter, and you'll disappear every half hour the rest of the day to have another quick read. Tonight, it will be by your bedside and you'll read it last thing at night, and again when you wake in the night, and first thing in the morning when you wake up. You'll cling to it like a leech till the next one arrives.

Maudie finished her breakfast and was heavily casual about washing up, acting as though there was nothing more delightful than prolonging the task. The minute it was finally done, she went off, 'to give her room a turn-out' and Jean was left to scrub the sink with Vim and wonder what magic those letters had in them. It wasn't, she knew, that she was jealous of Robert. Robert had been no closer to Maudie than she had been. He had suffered the same puritanical lack of affection, and could never have had one emotional exchange with his mother in his life, except in sudden anger. It was the letters she was jealous of, the power of the written word over the face to face contact. She suddenly realised, those Wednesday mornings, that what her mother ran away from in the flesh, she drank up on paper. Jean remembered how affectionate her own letters had always been, how she enjoyed settling down for the evening and beginning 'My Dear Mother'. The thoughts and endearments flowed, and they were never cast off. Maudie had never written back and said let us write only about the weather. She had even been as revealing as it was possible for her to be about Joseph and his goings on. It was as though their letters were between deep and mutual friends.

Jean dried her hands. In a moment, Maudie would come down, guiltily, and start doling out snippets of Robert's news. It was never any good asking her what he had said. His communications were too important to be passed on in one consuming rush. It all had to be given in dribs and drabs, until the end was reached.

Patiently, Jean went through the day receiving the news and commenting accordingly. Everything was Robert this and Robert that until she longed to shout that Robert was far away and she, Jean, was right here and that ought to be of more value than a letter. But her irritation began to pass as she realised Robert had this yet to come. He had the strangeness and coldness of actually being with his mother still to endure and puzzle over. She felt she ought to write to him and warn him that all this warm demonstrativeness would have to stop. It wouldn't do. Keep that for the letters, brother.

It was the same, basically, with Edward, but with him it wasn't letters. He had even maintained, when he confessed it all to her those years ago, that he hadn't really fancied Phillippa at all, not really. Oh, yes, he had slept with her, of course he had, that was what an affair meant, wasn't it, but that wasn't what had been important. It was being able to really talk to her, even though they hardly knew each other. You didn't have to know Phillippa to be able to talk to her, about anything under the sun. Apparently, it was marvellous how you could talk to her and really enjoy the talking, and yet leave her just like that, no ties or anything, no being pinned down at all.

I want, Jean thought, as Edward went out of the front door and Maudie hurried upstairs, to pin them down. I want them to cry and laugh and break down and rejoice in front of me because I am part of them and they are part of me. I don't want to have to be ashamed because they are seeing me being emotional. Surely it wasn't too much to ask of one's husband and mother? Who else but them could she ask it of? Yet they thought she was being so unreasonable, so demanding. It was all so strange and peculiar to think that they were part of her in the two closest ways possible, and yet they spent all their time repudiating the closeness.

She was glad she hadn't told Maudie about Edward and Phillippa, and what it had meant to her and still meant to her, however foolish. It was good that Edward had interrupted her attack, for that was what it had been—a deliberate, shock attack to force her mother to become implicated in her life. She wouldn't try again. She would spend the remaining month keeping their relationship on the cool and distant plane that was required. Feeling happier, she settled down to write a long and newsy letter to Nicholas. 'My darling Nicholas,' she began, as she went to find her pen, 'My darling son ...'

CHAPTER FIVE

Maudie began packing exactly four calendar weeks before she left Jean's. As soon as the date was fixed for going to Sally's, and her ticket bought, she washed her heavy cardigan and folded it, duly dried and aired, and put it at the bottom of her case. She knew it was in a way tempting fate, that this action might immediately bring on an unseasonable cold spell, but it was a risk worth taking with only four weeks to go and so much to be done. Besides, it wasn't really a risk. She could always wear two thin cardigans.

There was going to be nothing left behind to collect next time, because there wasn't going to be a next time. She wasn't going to come again, ever, unless, of course, the call of duty should be heard. At no time did she actually say to herself that she wasn't going to come again—she just knew it. There had been no arguments, no fights, no unpleasantness. They had all got on remarkably well. But she wasn't needed, that was the point. Jean didn't need her. She didn't really need anything done for her, any help was superfluous. And she was cold. Maudie hesitated to say or think this about one of her own flesh and blood, but it was an undeniable fact.

Maudie, to herself, put it like this: you couldn't feel comfortable with Jean. You couldn't get housework done and the meals over and the menfolk out and settled down with a sigh of relief for a cosy evening by the fire. Jean was *there*, and so was the fire, but she wasn't a companion and the fire didn't make the atmosphere cosy. It was no good sitting there with her, content to jog the evening away with a nice, desultory conversation and later, some supper and scalding tea. As sure as anything, she would start staring at you and everything would become strained and awkward. You would look up from your knitting, about to say this was a very complicated pattern, and there she would be, staring hard at you as though she didn't know who you were. It was enough to give anyone a proper turn.

Then she had no friends or neighbours that could be discussed and compared. Maudie could not understand this. She had waited and waited for someone to drop in, but nobody ever did. Jean either didn't encourage it, or there was no one to encourage, but whichever way you looked at it, it was a bleak state of affairs. It was eerie sitting there in the utter silence, knowing that the knock on the door or tap on the window could only be a cause of alarm and not anticipation. It created, too, a dearth of gossip, though Maudie did not put it quite so frankly to herself. No one's hairstyle to discuss, nobody's health to ponder over, nobody's family to get involved in. Nothing that was real and mattered to talk about.

So awful was this lack that Maudie found herself saying her prayers aloud at night just to reassure herself that she still had a tongue in her head. Either she had been alone in her room since seven o'clock when Edward went out, or she had sat with Jean and felt her vocal chords slowly freezing. She had to hear her own voice before she went to bed saying something spontaneous. She even began to read Robert's letters aloud just to have a bright, newsy voice breaking the hush.

Maudie was not so blind that she thought only *she* felt this cruel ban on human warmth. Edward felt it too. Far be it from her to take any man's side against her own daughter—or any man's side at all, ever—but she felt there was definitely a bond between them. No wonder the poor man went out each night. He had to find some jollity and company somewhere. She had seen him come up from his surgery and make some agreeable remark, only to have Jean spoil his promising opening with an aggrieved stare. So he went out, and who was to blame him? He didn't drink, of that Maudie was sure. He just went somewhere for a bit of company.

Why Jean didn't provide it was the key mystery to Maudie. The girl certainly had a high regard for him. That hardly seemed to have diminished from their early days. You could tell just by the way she did things for him, and the way she could never hide her unhappiness at his absence, that all was still well there. But she had some grudge against him, something that made her how she was. Maudie could only surmise, without being at all convinced, that there was, or had been, another woman. It seemed the only possible explanation, and if that was the case, it only confirmed her opinion that Jean was a fool.

There were women, Maudie reflected in the evening solitude of her soulless room, who did not know when they were lucky. She was prepared to criticise Edward on all the grounds that mattered, and never give him the benefit of any undeserved doubt, but carrying on in a discreet fashion with other women, so long as the carrying on did not infringe any of the wife's rights, was not one of these grounds. Men, much more than women, were mortal and had mortal needs. In Maudie's opinion, no woman could get past forty and still have those needs. She put it in just such veiled and coy terms to herself, never referring to anything crude in her thoughts just as she would never refer to it in speech. But she knew exactly what she meant, and she knew that any honest woman would agree with her. It seemed only logical to go on from that and say let the men get those needs from the sort of woman who was willing and save yourself the whole sordid trouble.

It was on lines like these that Maudie thought about Edward's nightly departures. Tackled on the subject, she would have expressed, out loud, the most utter disgust with the man and condemned him roundly. But privately, she thought it inevitable and could not see why Jean acted as she did. She ought to be thankful her husband wasn't like her father, instead of looking for a god-like self-sacrifice that didn't exist in men. Edward was a good worker and a good provider. He was clean, neat and sober. He didn't, so far as Maudie knew, gamble. He was pleasant to talk to. All these were the things that were important and that Jean ought to be judging him by, and not any other standards.

Whatever the ins and outs of it, Maudie knew that she could never live with Jean and Edward. It was like being a stranger. She might as well be living in a hotel, up there in her room, coming down only for meals and to help with the housework, never seeing a living soul from one day's end to the next. If it wasn't for Robert's regular letters she would hardly know that one week was slipping into another.

There was nothing that she would miss. The rich food didn't agree with her—she had used up her whole stock of anti-acid powders. She didn't like the peace and quiet, nor the endless resting. The way she looked at it, there was nothing to rest from. And she most certainly would not miss London. From what she had seen of it, it was a nasty big place, none of the homeliness of Glasgow at all. The sights were sights and she had enjoyed seeing them, but they made her head ache. They were always rushing to get there or get back before the crowds began to pour in or out of the city. And then, of course, the saddest miss of all was the lack of children.

Maudie personally regarded children as her weakness. Give her a child to spend her day with and she became shamefully soft and indulgent. When people said how good she was with them and how she must have enjoyed her own, she knew that it must have been something that had come with age. She couldn't remember having experienced what one would call pleasure in the bringing up of her children. They had been her life, but she had worried and fretted over them rather than enjoyed them. She thought her family the only reason in the world for struggling on, whereas her husband beside them had rated as nothing. But it was other people's children, when her own had grown up and gone away, who had been her great delight.

It had begun, this half-secret passion, with the little girl in the room and kitchen below. Her name was Fiona, and

Maudie had actually brought her into the world. She had watched Fiona's mother moving in, very pregnant indeed, and she had said to Annie McAllister that that woman's time was going to be brought a lot nearer by all the heaving about. She had hoped, as she said it, that she might be part of the drama but had never expected to be the sole witness. Sitting in her room, late at night, she had heard the urgent banging from above and had gone up and found the poor body panting to hold the baby in and half mad with fright because her husband was on night shift and she didn't trust herself to even go outside the door, never mind to the phone blocks away. Maudie had only time to get her on the bed before the wee baby burst its way out, howling even before she was held up and slapped. There had never, surely, been such an easy birth and Maudie could hardly credit it. She had wrapped the baby in a shawl, and wiped its nose and mouth clear, and then knocked the nearest neighbour up to run for the midwife.

All this had given her a proprietary air where Fiona was concerned. She had helped to look after her right from the beginning, and events had played right into her hands to give her an even greater share of the girl's time than she already deserved. Fiona's mother, to Maudie's utter disgust, had gone out to work six months later, informing everyone that she was going to pay Mrs McIntyre down the road ten shillings a week to look after her. That Mrs McIntyre was famous. She already looked after four other babies and it was the scandal of the neighbourhood. So Maudie had had no alternative. Calling down fire and brimstone on the respective heads of Fiona's mother and that Mrs McIntyre, she had said she would look after Fiona. It was a duty. Not even her scalding contempt for such heartless treatment could prevent her recognising this duty.

There had followed four of the pleasantest years of Maudie's life. Wee Fiona was a constant joy. From her first appearance at eight in the morning, to her departure at six, she never gave Maudie any trouble. As soon as she could sit up, they spent hours trekking off to the far distant park. As soon as she could walk, they took buses to watch the boats. And when she began to talk they had long and serious conversations about Jesus and the stars and Australia and the little princesses. Fiona's gems were gleefully treasured by Maudie and passed on as a staple diet in Robert's letters. Then Fiona went away. Her mother simply said one day that they were going to Aberdeen the next week. The next week, they went, and Maudie cursed and raved and finally wept her anguish away.

She got over it. She never took in and mothered another like Fiona—in fact, she vowed she would never be 'caught' again. But her resistance was gradually worn away by a cheeky little monkey called Hamish who came to live opposite on the same landing. Hamish was seven and he confided his all to the world at large. Persistently, he sat on the stairs after school and attempted to engage Maudie in chat. She snapped at him at first, but soon his amazing line in friendly banter wore her down and from sitting on the stairs he was promoted to sitting in the kitchen.

Hamish led to Angus, his little brother of five, and Angus led to Mary, his girlfriend, and so to Mary's brother, and Mary's brother's friend, until half the building gathered at four o'clock in Maudie's kitchen for jam pieces. She kidded herself she was very strict with them. No dirty shoes, no wiping noses on sleeves, no impudence, no fighting, no leaving crusts. She also protested to all her neighbours that she didn't want anything to do with them and didn't know how they got into her kitchen, but that, as Annie McAllister observed, was all my eye. Everyone knew by that time that Maudie Tipstaff wasn't right in the head about children.

Only Maudie thought she was very right in the head. With Hamish and his crew she knew just where she stood. She was the dispenser of jam pieces and the judge of all problems, moral and otherwise. They accepted the food and the judgements as gospel, and took Maudie's breath away with their simplicity. They plagued her with questions, but they never queried any final pronouncement. They told her anything and everything and caused her endless heavily concealed mirth.

At Jean's there were no children. Nicholas, the short time he had been around, was no child. He was a young adult. He watched and weighed Maudie in a manner she fancied was his mother's in embryo. He was polite and quiet and careful. She had given him up as hopeless from the beginning. Like his parents, he seemed to have no friends, or only friends who lived some distance away who had to be visited but didn't visit him.

Watching from her window, Maudie had noticed the almost sinister lack of children in the area. If there were any, none of them played in the street like they did at home. At six o'clock, there were never any mothers shouting at the gates for their offspring to come in this minute. Occasionally, she saw a child coming out of one of the houses, but only to get into a chauffeur-driven car and be whisked away. There weren't even any babies in prams. Once or twice, when they had been to the park, Maudie had been amazed by the numbers of babies being wheeled there in prams. She was sure they must all have been dropped from the sky.

The thing she was looking forward to most about Sally's was her grandchildren. There were five, the eldest only seven and the latest fifteen months. Maudie thought that was going too far, really, but at least it erred on the right side and the prospect of all the chatter and noise and bustle to come made her sigh with anticipation. There, she was going to be sorely needed. From the beginning she would be surrounded, and she privately thought she wouldn't be a bit surprised if she never had a minute to herself and her feet ached at the end of every long and full day.

Thinking ahead all the time, and with Jean suddenly much less nervy, the last few weeks went quite quickly. Maudie could never be surprised by a date, but she was at least able to put on a convincing pretence of being astounded when she realised there were only two days to go before she left.

96

'Fancy,' she said at lunch-time, 'only two days left and then I'll be off.'

'Time flies,' Jean said. She knew her mother would like her to say a few platitudes on those lines. 'It only seems like yesterday that you came,' she added for good measure, and then wondered if she had overdone it.

'Why don't you stay a bit longer?' Edward asked. Jean felt her heart constrict as she rushed to add, 'Yes, yes, stay another week.'

'Oh no,' Maudie said.

'Why not?' Edward asked.

'Because I said I would go on the sixteenth,' said Maudie, simply but firmly.

'Promises are made to be broken,' Edward said.

'Not mine,' Maudie said, and that was the end of the matter. The next day was taken up with packing proper. Jean helped. At least, she came up with newspapers to wrap shoes in and sat silently on the bed watching Maudie put in the last things. Maudie hoped there wasn't going to be any last minute awkwardness, especially when she saw Jean looking at her in that unnerving way again.

'Did you ever go to stay with your mother?' Jean asked suddenly.

'No,' Maudie said, relieved. She could handle simple information requests. 'My mother died the year after I was married. You've often asked about your grandmother and I've told you before.'

'I forgot,' Jean said, 'tell me again.'

'Tell you what?'

'About my grandmother and you and your family.'

'There's nothing to tell,' said Maudie, rather sharply, for she suspected the drift of this.

'Tell me what she looked like, and what she was *like*, and what she did.'

'She was a big woman, dark haired,' Maudie said, briskly.

97

'Always very cheerful. She liked company, and she was easy going.'

'Did you like her?' Jean asked.

Maudie tutted with annoyance. 'She was my mother,' she said, 'of course I liked her.'

'Did you get on with her?' Jean asked.

'She was my mother,' Maudie repeated, exasperated, and shut her case with a click.

Jean got up and walked to the window and turned and faced her.

'Tell me about me,' she said, and added, before Maudie could express her impatience, 'about me as a little girl, from the beginning, from when I was born.'

'You were born in Johnstone Hospital at six in the morning,' Maudie said, 'and I'd been in labour for forty-eight hours and I thought I was dying. That's all I can remember about you being born.'

'Tell me about me as a baby,' Jean pressed.

'You were a puny wee thing,' Maudie went on, in the same matter-of-fact tone, while she wrote the label for her case, 'never slept at night till you were two years old. I never got a night's sleep with any of you. How do you spell Yorkshire?'

'Tell me about me as a girl,' Jean said, 'about what I was like, how I behaved, the things I liked to do.'

'You were a good little girl,' Maudie said, 'very quiet and properly behaved and you liked your dolls. You used to hum to them.'

'Did you talk to me?' Jean asked.

'Oh, this is silliness,' Maudie snapped. 'Of course I talked to you, for goodness sake. What do you think I did?'

There were no more questions. With everything packed, they went to have tea, and it was only when she was half way through her second scone that Maudie thought about talking to Fiona and to Hamish and then a very long way back to talking to Jean, and she stopped eating. She couldn't trust her memory absolutely, of course, she knew better than to do that, but she couldn't honestly remember treating Jean and Robert and Sally as she did her neighbours' children these days. For one thing, she had always been in a rush. Always hurrying and always worried. Her children had never seemed such objects of enchantment and amusement.

Carefully, she pushed the crumbs together on her plate and put them into her mouth. She looked furtively at Jean. Perhaps she ought to tell her what had just occurred to her, but as she tried to form the sentence in her head, it suddenly seemed quite clear that she had nothing to tell and no way of telling it without sounding foolish. She did not want to start anything so she kept quiet.

On the last evening, they went out. Edward and Jean took Maudie to see the 'Black and White Minstrel Show' at the Victoria Palace. They had the most expensive seats in the front row of the circle, and chocolates to eat and coffee brought to them in the interval. Then they went home and had a very nice supper and Edward opened a bottle of cherry brandy. They talked about the show, and compared it with the television show, and then Maudie said she had better be going to bed.

Upstairs, she checked her cases again, set her alarm with even more attention than usual, and got into the hateful soft bed for the last time. She lay awake for a good while, thinking that it was typical that they should wait to the very last evening before they took her out. They hadn't asked her what she might like to see—they had just chosen for her. It was a celebration, Edward said. They hadn't, Maudie thought, celebrated at the beginning or the middle, only at the end. Oh, it had been quite nice, quite pleasant, but not what one would have expected. Not what one would have wanted. Determinedly, Maudie shut her eyes. There was no need to think back. It had really all gone quite well and she was a silly old fool to have expected anything else from such a source. She fell asleep, and had a lovely dream all about Sally and her children.

'Well,' Edward said, 'freedom, eh?'

Jean stood watching the bus move out. She stared stonily after it, waving listlessly. Her mother waved back, vigorously.

'What shall we do?' Edward said.

'Oh, really,' Jean said, crossly, and began to walk towards the car.

Edward was humming as he started it and they drove home. He felt immensely cheerful. It hadn't been too bad having her, but now that she had gone he felt repressed in retrospect. Perhaps now Jean would get back to her old self and stop moping about. She was always quiet, but there was a difference between being quiet and moping.

He knew better than to remark on this. They arrived home and went inside in complete silence. Edward sniffed in the hall.

'God,' he said, 'that vile spray she used in the lavatory still stinks the house out. Another week and I would have gone mad.'

Jean ignored him and went into the sitting-room. She sat down, her hands clasped on her knees, and examined her shoes. Edward came and sat beside her with an exaggerated sigh.

'How about,' he said, 'going on holiday?'

'Why?' Jean asked, dully.

'You need a rest.'

'You mean after Mother?' Jean asked.

'Well, after all the tensions of the last three months. We both need a change, a break.'

'You do mean after Mother,' Jean stated.

'Alright then, I don't see what's so terrible about saying it—after Mother.'

'Oh God,' Jean said, 'we're worse than I thought.'

'Now don't be silly—and don't let's argue over it. It was a simple suggestion. If you don't want to go, that's absolutely that.'

He was relieved when Jean did not go on worrying the subject like an agitated dog, He thought it would be a nice gesture, comforting, if he made some tea, so he went into the kitchen and made some and set it all out on a tray and carried it through to her. She didn't thank him, but she took the tea. Encouraged, he tried to begin a conversation again.

'What shall we do with her room?' he asked. 'I mean, not that there's any hurry but we might as well start thinking about it.'

'Leave it,' Jean said.

'Leave it? But that would be a waste. It's ridiculous to have gone to all that trouble——'

'I thought we went to all that trouble for Mother.'

'Yes, we did, but it was always intended to use it afterwards.'

'What if she'd stayed?' Jean said.

'We knew she wouldn't.'

'Yes, we did, didn't we,' Jean said, viciously, 'we made absolutely certain.'

'Now look,' Edward shouted, 'I don't want all that to start again. We've had your mother for four months, we've given her a nice time, we've more than done our duty by her. I will not have all this stupid moaning about failing her and all that silly nonsense. Just shut up about her, do you hear? Let's just drop the whole subject of your mother once and for all. Everything that's worrying you is in your head, that's all. You're imagining the whole situation.' He stopped for breath, and wished he hadn't shouted. 'No, but really,' he said, quietly, 'forget your mother for a while. Agreed?'

Jean began tidying up the tea cups, her head bowed, to hide her own disappointment, not only her mother's.

PART TWO

SALLY

CHAPTER ONE

There was, at the last minute, only time to send Sammy on his bike. They had intended to all dress in their Sunday best and go in the car, if they could get it started. And they had alternatively intended to send the menfolk and bring Maudie back in style in a taxi. Finally, Sally and William had intended to go just on their own and get Grace to look after the kids. But, in the end, Sammy, seven-year-old Sammy, was sent helter-skelter to get his bike and meet Grandma and tell her to leave her case and walk her home and say sorry mam and dad can't come and tell her what had happened.

Happy to rush off like that, an ambassador on such an important mission, Sammy was clear about everything except the last bit. What had happened? It didn't seem to him that anything had happened. Dad couldn't be found—he was off doing something for Mr Grant, as he always was, and might be anywhere on the farm. Grace hadn't turned up at all, having had a row with Sally the day before. So Mam was on her own, as she usually was, and the dinner wasn't properly ready and all the kids were screaming round her. But nothing had happened, nothing that he could tell a Grandma.

His mother, too, knew that nothing had actually happened, just the day had gone too fast as usual and caught up on her and left her standing. Maudie's bed hadn't been aired—in fact, it hadn't been finally settled where Maudie was going to sleep at all. The dinner wasn't the special roast she had wanted, but a shepherd's pie that hadn't gone into the oven till after twelve. Nothing was tidy, none of the children were clean, and God only knew where William was. It was all a muddle.

Sally leant on the draining board and suddenly, out of her

kitchen window, saw the lilac at the bottom of the lane. Quickly, she dashed out, swooping Angie into her arms, for it was never safe to leave her for a second, and ran with her to pick some lilac. Singing and laughing, she broke some low branches, and ran back, and plunged them into a milk can and set them in the middle of the cluttered kitchen table. Then she turned back to leaning on the draining board and wondered what she had been trying to remember. Nothing would come. She bit her lip with vexation, and slowly began to wash some of the dishes, letting them slip and slide into the bowl as they liked, and often selecting one particular piece to wash and dry, only to put it back again.

Sammy could be trusted. He would meet his grandmother and talk to her nicely all the way back. She would really take to him. It was a lovely walk from the green where the bus stopped, up through the woods and over the hill past the church and along the lane parallel with Mr Grant's house. She should have told Sammy to take his grandmother round by the back, so she could see the blossom thick on the trees of the Grants' orchard—she would enjoy that. He might even do it of his own accord and that would really please her.

The memory of first coming to Cokeham was still with Sally. It was in the winter and it was the most beautiful place she had ever seen. She had come straight from Manchester, where she had been in service and met William at a dance, and she had almost swooned at the pure whiteness of it all. Manchester and Glasgow were the only places she had ever known and the dales were a revelation to her, for she had never had the imagination to imagine them. Nothing put her off. She did not mind the draughty, cold-water-only cottage that William brought her to, nor the long pull up the hill back from the nearest shop. She thought it was all lovely and she had gone on thinking that the whole eight years. She could hardly wait for her mother to see it and be entranced, as she had been. It was so perfect that she was coming in the early summer with the blossom still out and everything looking at its best.

Sally went on sloshing about, free from any worries, except one little one that wasn't worrying her too much yet—she had not given much thought to her mother's visit because she didn't give much thought to anything. There was, to her, nothing to think about. Her mother was coming and that was nice. All visitors were nice. She didn't try to work out whether Maudie would be happy because she never worked out anything. She didn't worry about what Maudie would think of them because she didn't care. She was pleased to accept life as it came, and did not even value the enviable simplicity that this permanent state of mind showed.

Neither, as Sally messed about, breaking off to rearrange the lilac or kiss one of her children, did she go back in her mind over her previous relationship with her mother. If anyone had suggested to her that her whole childhood had been one long scold and bullying, she would have thought them raving mad. She couldn't remember being shouted at for being a slut. She couldn't remember the constant prodding and poking to dress herself neatly and hold herself straight like Jean. She couldn't remember the various puritan punishments for absent-mindedness and daydreaming. If the truth were known, she couldn't remember much at all before she was sixteen. And then she remembered not the day-to-day things but the big dramatic things like the day her red-faced, cheery father had thrown his dinner on the floor and her mother had hit him with the hot teapot and she had had to run for Mrs McAllister. So it wasn't a question of forgiving and forgetting and trying to be nice to her mother. Sally was nice to everyone, and it was as though her mother was a new person in her life. There were no shadows at all to spoil the sunny day.

Up the hill Maudie plodded, gripping a case in each hand, doggedly keeping abreast with Sammy's battered red bike. Her heart was doing incredible dances and somersaults and it only made it worse to stop and rest, as Sammy kept anxiously suggesting. But the mere idea of leaving her already once-snatched cases on that village green, to be picked up by a man she had never met at some far off, unlikely, unmentioned time, was more than she could bear. It was the most outrageous suggestion she had heard this side of Glasgow, and only the rapidly rising affection for her little grandson had kept her from exploding.

They had proceeded, at first, with one case resting on the seat and handlebars of the bike, but Sammy's struggles to keep the bike balanced and moving had put an end to that. He had then insisted on carrying one case, and trundling the bike, but he had steered himself into a ditch twice, and Maudie was afraid he would do himself a mortal injury. She was also afraid he would scratch her case.

They reached the top of the hill and Maudie collapsed on the grass verge.

'There's our house, Grandma,' Sammy said, and pointed down the lane.

Maudie's eyes were closed. Diffidently, Sammy touched her lightly on the hand. 'Our house, Grandma,' he whispered, 'you can see our house.'

'Oh dear God,' Maudie said, and wet her lips slightly. She opened her eyes and looked past the massed blossom to where the land opened out into a shallow valley and saw a red-tiled cottage a very long way down it. She moaned, and passed her hand over her forehead.

'We turn off the road here,' Sammy was saying, 'and go down this lane past Mr Grant's and along the stream and across the bridge and then we're there. It's a short cut, Grandma.'

'In heaven's name,' Maudie said, 'what is the long way round like?'

'Down this road to the crossroads and——'

'Don't tell me,' Maudie said, crossly.

Puzzled, Sammy scratched the ground with his foot, making patterns in the loose gravel at the edge of the road where the tar had been too thin to set it.

'And don't do that, you'll waste your shoes,' Maudie added.

'What would your mother do to you if you wasted your shoes?'

Gravely, Sammy stared at her. He didn't know what she was talking about. His mother had never mentioned wasting his shoes, and she never did anything to him. He dropped his eyes and fixed them instead on the wheel of his bike, waiting for his grandmother to show she was willing to go on.

'Why we couldn't get a bus, I don't know,' Maudie complained. 'If I find out we could have got another bus, young man, I'll skelp your backside.'

'There isn't a bus,' Sammy persisted. 'The buses only go to the green, Grandma.'

'And has that father of yours no car to meet an old woman?'

'It's broken,' Sammy explained. 'Dad's waiting for a new part.'

'Could he not have hired one?' Maudie asked, still querulously pursuing a subject they had already been over. Sammy didn't reply because he couldn't think what to say. He wasn't too sure what hiring meant. Unconsciously, his toecap began scratching the ground again.

'Dear God!' Maudie shouted, 'haven't I told you about that foot? You're old enough to know better.' Suddenly, a thought struck her. 'How old are you?' she demanded sternly.

'Seven and threequarters next Wednesday,' Sammy replied, promptly.

'Aren't you at school?' Maudie said.

'Yes.'

'Then what are you doing off it today?' Maudie said, quickly.

'Mam said it was too nice to go to school,' Sammy said, 'and anyway you were coming. Mam said some days were meant to be natural holidays. Mam said there are enough rainy, miserable old days to go to school on.'

Horrified, Maudie stared at him, taking stock for the first time under the awful weight of what he had just said. He was undoubtedly very like his mother to look at—solid and sturdy, with the same wide, freckled face that she had had as a child. Not at all a handsome little boy. His hair was thick and untidy, a dull, neglected brown colour, and he hadn't one noteworthy feature. The expression in his eyes was anxious, and he hunched himself defensively over the handlebars of his bike. Noticing this, Maudie chided herself. The child could not help having a mother so wayward and wicked as to encourage truancy. Nor was it anything to do with him that she had not been met properly off the bus. The poor wee soul would think her a very cross, unfair old lady from the beginning if she went on at him like that, and already she loved him and wanted him to like her. She must be careful. Children were strange ones for first impressions.

'Well, I don't know,' she said, a little less fiercely, 'we'd better get on, I suppose, away from this nasty damp grass.'

Sammy looked at the grass closely. He bent down and felt it. 'It isn't damp,' he announced, 'it's dry.'

'Grass is always damp,' Maudie snapped, 'and don't contradict your elders.'

Stiffly, she got up off the large boulder she had perched herself on, like some withered Puck. She put a hand on her back and stretched and groaned with the agony of the ache. Sammy watched with interest. He didn't make the mistake of asking what was the matter. He didn't need to, for Maudie's pantomime was brilliantly clear. Instead, he watched her carefully to see when she was ready. When she made to pick up her cases, he set slowly off down the lane and she began to lurch behind him.

All the way down Grant's lane, the cherry blossom hung over the railings, already dropping and scattering pink flowers on the overgrown verges. There were bluebells, still stiffly in bud, standing behind the trees in the long grasses that stretched in a tangled mess from the big farm house to the lane. The path was not tarmacked, but deeply rutted in two big ruts where the tractor had forced its way umpteen times. Between the ruts, the grass had grown quite high, whereas on either side it was short and stubbly with people walking on it.

Maudie chose the central grass to walk on. She did not fancy descending into one of the ruts, and did not consider there was enough room at the sides for herself and her load. She concentrated on keeping her balance and keeping Sammy in view, and ignored the blossom and the flowers, except to wonder why no one had cleared the mess up. The cottage looked to her such a long way off, all those fields to pass yet and that dangerously rickety bridge to cross.

At the bridge, they rested.

'Nearly there,' Sammy said. 'Mam could hear us if we shouted now.'

'Shouted!' Maudie whispered, and had to sit down. Sammy squatted beside her and began to throw pebbles in the stream. 'Don't splash my coat, it's my best one,' Maudie warned him. The minute she got in, it would be put in its polythene bag and never taken out again as long as she remained in this God-forsaken place. She was very hot, but did not want to undo it. An undone coat was one of the untidiest sights in the world. She would have taken it off altogether, for she was perfectly decent underneath, but that would only be cluttering herself up more.

She sat and sniffed in the sun. She looked sharply about her, while she waited for her breath to come back. Not a shop in sight. Everywhere was grass and trees. Thank God she would be gone before the winter. She looked at her shoes, dusty and dirty with the walk, her ankles were swelling with the heat.

'Well, young man,' she said, 'if it's really not far off I can maybe just manage it before I drop.'

Sammy got up, and rushed eagerly ahead, wanting to be relieved of his responsibility as soon as possible. Then half down the slope to the house, he thought his mother might not like him leaving his grandmother alone like that, and so he waited impatiently for her to catch up so they could do the last lap together. But as she caught up with him, Maudie stopped, and looking ahead, said 'Dear God!' and seemed incapable of moving.

At the bottom of the incline, where the cottage lay, she could

111

see a rabble of children with a wild-looking tramp in the middle. They were all decked with blossom and they were singing 'For she's a jolly good fellow' over and over again. Seeing Sammy and his charge, they began to surge forward, until they reached the pair and surrounded them, and Maudie did not dare move, though she knew quite well that the tramp was Sally and the rabble her grandchildren.

'Welcome home, Mother,' Sally said, and to her mother's horror, swept her into an embrace that included the runny-nosed, bawling Angie.

'That child needs a handkerchief,' Maudie said, glad to have something to do to cover her horror. She searched out a handkerchief and wiped Angie's nose.

'Isn't it a lovely day?' Sally said, gaily.

'Not when you've to walk fifty miles in the blazing heat,' Maudie said.

'And isn't it a lovely walk?' Sally said. 'I could walk there and back from the green all day long when the blossom's out.'

'You're welcome,' Maudie said, grimly. They were all moving towards the house, Sammy leading on his bike. 'Dear God, Sally, how many children have you, in heaven's name?'

'Six,' Sally said, cheerfully, 'the other three are all friends.'

'Haven't you enough to do without looking after other people's bairns?'

'I don't look after them,' Sally said, simply. She smiled, showing the missing two teeth on her denture plate, and linked her arm through Maudie's for the last few yards.

They all crammed into the kitchen and Sally began shouting at them all to sit themselves down and be ready to eat. Maudie was pushed on to a rickety bench between Sammy and Richard, the next in age, who plucked immediately at her sleeve to show her how far he could get his index finger up his nostril. Feeling faint, Maudie wrenched the finger out, only to see it plunged into the mound of shepherd's pie which had suddenly appeared before him. As she opened her mouth to protest, a scalding helping appeared on her own plate, grazing her right ear as it passed from Sally's hands over her shoulder. To the left and right and all around children were devouring the mixture without forks or knives, shovelling it in with spoons, or like Richard, with their fingers. She felt she might faint.

The feeling persisted through the next hour. After the shepherd's pie came apple crumble and custard, and soon the table was running with yellow puddles and the room full of shouted songs about green snotter pie. Water, so urgently demanded, cascaded from the plastic tablecloth, and empty plates were sent spinning on to the flagged floor. With her head splitting, Maudie could not eat a thing. She waited for Sally to scream at them and clout their ears and restore order, but all she did was stand at the head of the table supervising the frenzied scraping of the dishes the meal had been cooked in. Now and again, she nodded and raised her eyes to heaven when Maudie gestured but she did nothing to stop the pandemonium. Then, dramatically, they all began to run outside, screeching, and the latch clashed again and again as the door was flung open and another well-fed Indian whooped his way out. Angie alone remained, crawling among the remains under the table with a rapt mongrel dog.

'Oh, the peace!' Sally said, cheerfully. She sat down on a chair and put her feet on the table and ran her hands through her already wildly disordered hair. She yawned again and again, before finally settling her features into a broad, sleepy smile.

'I don't know why you put up with it,' Maudie said. She felt she had been personally insulted. 'They haven't any notion of manners, not one of them.'

Sally wrinkled her nose. 'This isn't a great place for manners,' she said, 'and anyway, they're all too young.'

'They are not,' Maudie said, 'a child that is old enough to eat is old enough to learn manners. From the age of two I taught you all to chew your food with your mouth closed and to handle a fork and spoon cleanly and properly.'

'Ah well,' Sally said, 'they'll learn some day.'

'Not if you don't teach them.'

'I will, then,' Sally said, and finished the argument before it had properly become one with her usual smile.

Tutting with annoyance, remembering that Sally never kept her word because she was too lazy or she forgot, Maudie bent to retrieve Angie from under the table. The little girl was filthy. She had on a shrunken pullover with a large hole under each arm, and a pair of stained and creased denim rompers. Her auburn hair was thickly matted with what Maudie divined as marmalade, and her nose was running again, forming a thick, sore crust between her nostrils and lip.

'This child is a disgrace,' Maudie said. 'I cannot hold my peace, Sally. It's the wonder you haven't had the N.S.P.C.C. man around.'

'There isn't one,' Sally said, amiably. 'She's happy, aren't you Angie love?'

'And what has that to do with it?' Maudie asked. 'It's a matter of cleanliness, not happiness. Where's the bathroom, or the sink so I can give her a bath?'

'She doesn't like baths,' Sally said. 'She'll cry.'

'And since when did crying harm anyone?'

Good humoured, Sally stirred herself and ferreted out the large tin tub they used for baths and put the biggest of the kettles on for hot water. She then sat and watched Maudie clear a space among the dishes on the table to put the tub on it. Angie, unsuspecting, was stripped to her very dirty vest, then Maudie filled the bath and tested it and removed the vest and plonked Angie in. Grimly, she held the screaming, struggling child with one hand and soaped her with the other, while Sally made sympathetic noises. When both body and hair were clean, Maudie opened her own case to get a towel fit to receive the newly bathed angel, and smothered her in it, and crooned her into a gulping silence.

'Now where's her clean clothes?' she asked Sally.

'There aren't any,' Sally said.

'Surely to God the child has something other than those rags?'

'Yes, she has, but they're all to be washed. I got behind, with Grace not coming——' and Sally gestured towards a big basket in the corner full to overflowing with clothes. 'She has a clean nightdress, though,' she said, helpfully.

'She cannot put a nightdress on in broad daylight,' Maudie exclaimed.

'Then she'll have to stay in her altogether,' Sally said. 'It's warm enough—she won't come to any harm.'

'Don't be ridiculous,' Maudie said, angrily. She pulled back on Angie's horrible clothes, and set her down on the floor. The child immediately raced for the door and was gone.

Breathing heavily with indignation, Maudie stood up.

'What are we doing first,' she demanded, 'the dishes or the clothes?'

'Oh, sit and rest awhile,' Sally implored.

'Rest? In this muck heap?' Maudie shouted. 'I couldn't rest for a minute.'

'Oh well,' Sally sighed, 'whichever you please, then. But there's really no need. There's nothing at all to do now till William comes in for his dinner.'

Maudie laboured the whole long afternoon to put at least the kitchen to rights. She kept sending Sally for clean rags and brushes and disinfectant, and Sally willingly disappeared on these errands for half hours at a time, only to eventually return with something quite different and useless. She admired the results of Maudie's work, while repeating often that she shouldn't, and none of it was necessary, and when her mother sat down, as though the jobs were finished, she rushed around upsetting everything in her efforts to make a cup of tea.

'I'd better sort my things out before I stop for tea,' Maudie said, rising again with an effort. 'You just show me where my room is and I'll manage.'

'Well,' Sally said slowly, 'I'm not quite sure where it would be best to put you. Where do you fancy?' she asked, engagingly, with all the easy confidence of the manager of the Hilton.

'Where is there?' Maudie asked, wearily.

'Sammy and Richard have the little room at the top,' Sally said, her fingers spread out to tick the members of the family off. 'Rosie and Betty and Alan have the big room at the back, and Angie is in her cot with us. But then there's the parlour, we could put something up there, or a bed would fit nicely in this kitchen and it would be very handy....'

While she was still listing the possibilities, Maudie went off on her own to discover the full horrors of the other regions. The parlour stank. It was also damp. She wouldn't have dreamt of sitting there, never mind sleeping there. Poking among the unmade beds, it seemed best to her to move Alan up with the other two boys, put one of the girls on the camp bed delegated to her and sleep in one of their beds. Without consulting Sally, she set about heaving and carrying and re-arranging, and with what was left of her strength, got her cases up the stairs. With Sally shouting, 'Anything you want, you just ask for,' she lay down and took what was only her second tablet since she had left Glasgow.

CHAPTER TWO

William finished work late that evening. The milking machine broke down, and with over thirty cows waiting to be milked, he had to set to and help everyone else, even though it was years since he had milked a cow. Then, when the job was done, Mr Grant would have him drive down to Coledale and personally contact the supplier of the machine so that he would be sure of coming as soon as possible. It was after eight when he parked Mr Grant's estate van and set off down the lane to his home.

If Sally could not get any work done for admiring the blossom and the lush beauty of that perfect early summer's day, William too had not been able to set his mind to his jobs. This was partly a permanent condition and had a lot to do with the fact that he had no easily defined job at all. He was a general man-about-the-farm. Mainly, he looked after the sheep, but he also took a hand with the small herd of cattle and the pigs, and ploughed, and helped harvest and drove Mr Grant about. His position was precarious, though anyone might have thought him indispensable to hear his name so constantly on the lips of the Grants. But he was not indispensable, and the knowledge of this was a constant source of worry to him.

Unlike Sally, William worried, even on fine summer days. The sun and the blossom and everything happening all over again set off in him a train of reactions. It reminded him that he'd said last summer that the next summer he would definitely have gone. It made him think of holidays and the fact that, if there was a slack time at all, this was it and he ought to have one and he'd never had one in his life. It brought to mind the one and only time he'd made a break for it and gone to

Manchester to find work, and married Sally and come hurtling back to what he had just left.

William trudged down the lane, his jacket over one shoulder, his torn sleeves rolled up. There was something very wrong with the world, that much was certain. He worked hard, and he got next to nothing. He was out at six every morning and often not home till eight and he'd just seen that morning in the *Daily Express* that his wage was five pounds under the national average. Five whole, enormous pounds under, and him thirty-four and with six children and no hours left in the day to work harder.

None of this would have been so bad, he told himself, if he had had a few home comforts. If Sally had been a hard worker like himself and a good manager, he could still have looked forward to something—a square meal, a clean house, a bit of spoiling. But Sally was useless. He was lucky to get a meal at all. Some days, it was a feast, some days a sandwich, and the feasts always came when he was least hungry and the sandwiches when he was ravenous. He could never count on getting a decent bait, either. Sometimes, he opened his box and there was the most delicious leg of cold chicken and sausages and pickles. Today, there had been a stale roll, unbuttered, with a grated carrot inside.

It was no good shouting and raving. Nothing upset Sally. She would either laugh at him, or simply go for a walk, and then he would be left with the kids. He had seriously thought about beating the living daylights out of her, but he had not the energy. Actually, she was bigger than he was and that made the thought of beating her not half so attractive as if she'd been a skittery thing he could have bent in two.

There was one satisfaction Sally gave him, and that was in their brass-posted marital bed. The laughing, big, warm, easy-going Sally, the ever affectionate, never-say-no Sally was a pleasure in bed. That William acknowledged, and of late bemoaned. For these pleasures, he paid the price of one child a year with what was becoming monotonous regularity. He felt that with a little self-discipline on Sally's part, this number could have been kept down. But she had no self-discipline, and always obliged, and almost always conceived. She never complained about this. Indeed, she seemed always pleased. It was William who was sick of her productivity.

They were by now, after seven years of marriage, heavily in debt. Mostly, the creditor was Mr Grant, so in one way that was a good thing, but in another way it was a very bad thing. Although it gave Mr Grant an interest in keeping William on, it also meant that William couldn't leave Mr Grant. Furthermore, he had worked it out that Mr Grant could at any time tell him that for the next two months he wasn't going to get any wages until the debts were paid off. There were also other debts. They owed fairly large sums to every shopkeeper in the village, and to quite a few in Coledale, the nearest town. They owed Grace, their so-called daily, almost as much wages as William owed Mr Grant. And all the time they were needing more, not less money as their family increased.

Near the house, William stood on the bridge a few minutes, not because he was lost in wonder at the scenic beauty, but because he very often wanted to put off going in at all. It was at least quiet out here. The trees made orderly patterns to his experienced eye, the sky met the fields cleanly, the stream kept within its banks. In there, there would be waiting children—couldn't he surely hear one from here?—and a cluttered kitchen and everything messy and comfortless, and Sally in front of the television she adored, hardly heeding his greeting as he came in. And tonight, in addition, there would be her mother.

To William, it was inconceivable that Sally's mother could be anything except an overgrown version of Sally. There would be two of them cackling all over the place, letting everything go to rack and ruin. He based this assumption on the belief that the forces of heredity could not be escaped. People were like their parents. He was like his father, Sammy was like him. Girls especially were like their mothers. Sally could only have picked up her habits from a mother likewise inclined.

William hoped that some night he might get drunk enough to tell Sally's mother what he thought of a woman who brought her daughter up like that.

Sally had only told him the day before that Maudie was coming for four months. She said she had told him before, but he couldn't remember her doing any such thing. Now that he was being told again, he couldn't think why he was being told at all. It had nothing to do with him—he hoped. It was just something else that must be put up with. So he had gone on eating his dinner and silently turning over the information to see which way he should react. When he'd gone out in the morning, Sally was shouting all the ideas she had for meeting her mother. He had simply closed the door very quietly and gone off up the lane.

He turned away from the bridge and went towards his house. It wasn't such a bad house, for a rented place. Mr Grant liked all his property to be kept in good order, and the work William liked best was when he was set to put something right in his own house. The roof was watertight, the walls freshly re-pointed, the windows and doors were regularly painted. It was undeniably better than a council house, even if it wasn't his own. His mother-in-law wouldn't be able to find fault with his house, though if, as he reckoned, she was like Sally, she would be past finding fault with anything.

It wasn't until he actually reached the door that he realised the yard was empty. Usually, there were at least two kids still up, no matter how late the hour, and they would scutter away, like field mice, in case he was in a bad mood and was going to give them a clout over the ear. Tonight, there were no children. He lifted the stiff latch of the old wooden door, and the silence seeped out almost eerily. He peered into the now dim kitchen. The television was blank, the room empty.

Thoughtfully, William switched the light on and instantly noticed the tidiness. He'd always, before he'd married, been used to a tidy place. He recognised the look of a newly cleaned kitchen with an astonishment and pleasure all the more acute for not having had the experience in the last seven years. He sat down on a chair and took off his boots and placed them on the fender. Then he removed his pullover, worn and filthy with farm work, and turned his collar in and went to the sink to wash. Usually, he had to fight his way through the dishes, which always made him roar with rage, and he often smashed a few of the offending articles. Tonight, he could have had a bath in the vast, empty space before him. He was quite sure, as he turned the tap on, that never before had the sink been completely empty.

He ducked his head under the tap and swilled the soap and water round his neck and ears, and then rinsed it all with his hands. Gasping and spluttering, he groped for a towel, knowing there wouldn't be one, but tonight there was. He dried himself tenderly and squinted at himself in the cracked, plastic-edged mirror propped precariously on top of the tap. He was just examining his teeth and wondering if, on this magic night, he might even find a toothbrush, when Sally came in.

'Hello,' she said, and yawned, and then immediately gave him her big, feckless grin.

'Hello,' William said. He watched her lower herself into a chair, yawning and scratching her head. 'Well,' he said, smiling in anticipation of his own joke, 'have the fairies been, then?'

'No,' Sally said, 'it was my mother. You mustn't mind her—she always has to have a clean out whenever she arrives anywhere.'

'I should have arrived here years ago by the look of the place,' Maudie said crossly from the doorway. 'How a man could put up with it, I do not know,' she said accusingly to William, who had turned awkwardly to look at her, not knowing what to say or do. Sally did not bother to make any introductions.

'Sit down, Mother,' Sally said.

'I can hardly bring myself to stand still never mind sit still, the state this place is in,' Maudie said. 'And what are you doing sitting down, madam? Where's your man's dinner?'

'Oh, I'll rustle something up in a minute,' Sally said.

'Dear God!' Maudie said. 'Your father never walked in the door without the smell of his dinner greeting him and the sight of it on the table cheering him. A man's entitled to his dinner after a hard day's work.'

Sighing, Sally heaved herself up. She winked at the dumb-founded William as she went past him to the larder. Breaking into song, she made a tomato sandwich and set a delicious pickle beside it, and brought it to the table.

'I'll make you another if you've room for it,' she said generously, and sat down, exhausted.

'What in heaven's name is that?' exclaimed Maudie. 'A tomato sandwich? A cold tomato sandwich and a cold pickle— one cold tomato sandwich and one cold pickle?'

'He wouldn't fancy them hot,' Sally said, and was immediately convulsed by her own wit. Maudie's lips were twitching with the heat of the words stored within, but all she said, above the giggles of the near-paralytic Sally, was 'Sit down' to William.

William sat, grinning foolishly. He watched while Maudie whisked the sandwich away and placed it contemptuously on the floor near its maker. Anxiously, he saw her go to the larder. He wanted to warn her that there probably wouldn't be anything else there and he would settle for the sandwich. But she seemed to know what she was looking for and was sure of finding it. There was a great deal of clattering of pans and rustle of paper and muffled, mild curses, and then, in what seemed seconds, things were bubbling and steaming on the stove. His mouth went dry and he had to rub the palms of his hands on his knees to conceal the agitation such culinary preparations aroused in him. When Maudie set the dish before him and took off the cover, he wasn't quite sure what she had after all conjured up, but he plunged into it and found it to be a sort of magnificent pancake, with cheese and potatoes and bacon in it. Hardly had he finished, blowing with the goodness of it, than she was hovering at his elbow with another.

As William loosened his belt, Sally sidled across to the table, and sitting down, leaned over and opened her large mouth very wide, revealing acres of fillings. When William ignored her, she picked up a piece of pancake with her fingers and popped it in the waiting cavern. She munched it appreciatively.

'It's good,' she said, 'make me one, Mother.'

But Maudie was already putting away the frying pan and did not bother replying. Her last act, before she at last sat down, was to set a pot of tea at William's elbow.

Sally managed to snatch another morsel before regretfully withdrawing to the other easy chair, which was not very easy at all. The springs hung out at the bottom and it had only one arm. This left William at the table, where he drank his tea noisily, very aware of the noise but unable to swallow quietly for some reason. His noisy tea-drinking had always embarrassed him. When he had finished, he pushed his chair back and thought how full and warm he felt. He had not yet spoken to Maudie. Slowly, he rehearsed several sentences, but none of them came out. He realised Maudie was staring steadily at him, and he began to blush. He could feel the blush spreading down his face to his neck, and in desperation he got up and went over to the window. In agony, he blurted out 'Chickens' and dashed from the room.

He needed to go outside to the lavatory, but if he went straight out, she would think he was ungrateful. Yet he could not bring himself to say he was going to the lavatory.

'What did he say?' Maudie asked Sally.

'He was making the chickens the excuse to go to the lav.,' Sally said, 'he didn't like to say that was where he was going. He's very shy.'

'Is that how you got him?' Maudie snapped.

'Yes,' Sally said, beaming. 'He isn't shy with me.'

'He must be wrong in the head to put up with all this,' Maudie said, 'and never complain.'

'Oh, he complains,' Sally said, 'you should hear him sometimes.'

'Then why don't you heed him?' Maudie asked.

William came back into the room at that point. He had come to a resolution in the lavatory. With a determined air, he strode over to Maudie and held his hand out and said 'Pleased to meet you'. Sally laughed.

'Be quiet, Sally,' Maudie said sharply. She stood up and shook hands firmly with William.

'And I'm pleased to meet you, young man,' she said, loudly. Awkwardly, William inclined his head in a sort of bow. Maudie sat down. 'Sally, let your husband take the weight off his feet,' she said, seeing William was left with nothing but the hard kitchen chair to sit on.

William did not like to say he walked into the village to the pub every evening. He was so surprised when Sally did vacate the doubtful chair that he sat down heavily on it. Maudie had her hands folded on her lap and was continuing her pre-lavatory visit stare, but now she was also smiling at him, a tight but approving smile. He smiled back and then Sally guffawed again, and unable to resist the temptation, he turned on her and swore at her and told her to belt up. Uneasily, he waited to see what reaction this would bring from Maudie. He was relieved to see that he did not seem to have sacrificed her implied approval.

They sat there, the three of them, for an hour, without stirring to put the television on. William thought his mother-in-law might not like him to put it on, Maudie did not think it her place to suggest putting it on and Sally was dying to have it on but alone knew that it was broken. She had tried to get some life out of it earlier and there had been a sharp flash and crackle and then silence. She wanted it kept from William for as long as possible that it would need at least a visit from the repair man. The repair man meant contact with the shop in Coledale, and contact with the shop meant a demand for payment of their arrears and their last repair bill. Eventually, he would have to know, but Sally believed in letting things slide for the longest time possible. She secretly hoped he could be persuaded into thinking that it had broken itself, or that in a couple of days, having had a good rest, it would right itself.

No one bothered to put the light on, either, though the kitchen soon became quite dark and they could barely make each other out. Sally soon began dozing, even though her chair was so hard and straight. She had once been pleased to read that Sir Winston Churchill was in the habit of taking ten-minute cat naps all over the place. She knew just how he felt. Cat naps, of much longer duration than ten minutes, were the staff of life to Sally.

William heard her very soft, light snoring and felt relieved. Maudie heard it and was disgusted.

'Fancy falling asleep at the table,' she said, quietly, for William to hear.

'She often does,' William whispered back. They were both leaning forward to catch each other's words, like conspirators. William racked his brains for something to say to show he enjoyed the intimacy. After deep thought and a lot of deep breathing all round, he said, 'Had a good journey?'

'Except for the walk at this end,' Maudie said, and sat back. William sorrowfully realised he had somehow asked the wrong question.

'Lovely day, though,' he said, still whispering, but he had broken contact with Maudie. She had given up whispering.

'You don't think it's a lovely day when you're an old woman and you've two heavy cases to carry,' she said loudly, and Sally woke up. Thereafter the atmosphere was destroyed. They went on sitting there, gazing at each other through the dark, until Sally got up and put the light on and they all blinked foolishly and Sally said she would make some more tea and William said he would take a turn outside to see everything was alright.

Maudie went to bed before William came back. She had managed to find some clean sheets and spare blankets, with some difficulty, and had made her bed reasonably comfortable, or so she hoped. It wasn't a full length bed, but then she was small so that wasn't too serious. She had her own hot water bottle with her, of course, for even on warm May nights her feet were cold. As she filled it from the kettle, thinking her exhaustion might at least give her a good night's sleep, Sally was telling her to have a nice lie in in the morning and not to let the children disturb her. Maudie merely snorted, and took herself off.

She let herself into the bedroom very quietly, not putting any light on. Both little girls seemed to be heavily asleep. She bent over Rosie and pulled the covers up to her little shoulders, and then had a look at Betty who was splayed across the bed in a most extraordinary position. Carefully, Maudie turned her on her side and rearranged the bedclothes, and as she did so she felt that both the child and the bed were sodden with urine. Tutting with consternation, she gently pulled the bottom sheet off, thinking Betty could sleep on a blanket for the rest of the night. But there was no rubber sheet under the cotton one and the blanket and mattress below were wringing wet. 'No rubber sheet' Maudie found herself saying aloud. The very idea of putting a child of three in a bed without a rubber sheet! She did not know what to do. Appealing to Sally would be no use whatsoever. Groping around, she found Betty's pants and managed to slip her pyjamas off and get the pants on without waking her. Then she lifted her into her own bed, which was short but quite wide enough for a thin woman and a three-year-old child.

A little more satisfied, Maudie undressed and got in beside her granddaughter. Tenderly, she crooked her body round the baby's, and drew the clothes over both of them. Instantly, she remembered doing the same with both Jean and Sally, when Joseph had driven her out of their bed, or rather when she had had her own reasons for wanting to vacate it. She had always loved sleeping with her children. They were so cuddly and soft, so reassuring in the effortless way they breathed, so beautiful to simply lie and look at when you couldn't sleep yourself. She took one of Betty's hands in hers. It lay there, podgy and dimpled, until some dream sent it sprawling above her head, as though in surrender.

Cautiously, Maudie got out of the bed. She was going to have to draw the curtains. The moon was shining full into their room, right on Betty's face, and would surely waken her. She looked out of the window, with a hand on each of the curtains, and saw the figure of a man leaning on the gate. A little startled, she drew back, and then realised it was William, and pressed closer to the window to see what he was doing. As far as she could see, he was just leaning on the gate staring at his own back door. She thought he might see her, and for some reason did not want to attract his attention, so she did not after all pull the curtains in case, in this acute stillness, the slight rattle would draw his attention.

She stood watching him for ten minutes or so. Once, he turned and put his back against the gate and looked towards the bridge, but soon turned back to his original position. He seemed to be enjoying himself. There was something languid and leisurely in his stance. One would not have thought here was a man killing time at his own gate, but here is a man watching some enthralling spectacle, or listening to a riveting conversation. It made Maudie impatient. She wanted to ask him what he was doing, to tell him to come in and stop being so silly, standing there gaping. Finally, his absorption irritated her so much that she had to get back into bed and be damned to the moon.

Once in bed, she could not forget William. She retained the image of him standing there, and willed him to come in. She was relieved when, soon after, she heard his slow, heavy footsteps crossing the cobbled yard and the rasp of the latch as he opened the kitchen door. Then she heard Sally's laughter, and irritation of a quite different sort took hold of her. It was dreadful to see such a silly girl had become such a silly woman. More than all the mess and muddle, Sally's fecklessness had upset her deeply that day. It was something she hadn't really reckoned with and now it was discovered, she did not quite know what she was going to do.

While she was still worrying, the two of them came up the stairs and went into their bedroom which was next door. Sally made no effort to be quiet. She was singing 'Rule Britannia' all along the passage, and even when she was in her own room continued humming and tra-la'ing, even when she must have been in bed. Maudie could tell she had not been to see all her children were safely tucked in. They might be smothered in their beds for all the carousing Sally cared. The bed springs creaked as the pair of them got in. They were making enough noise for twenty-year-olds and Maudie waited for Angie to wake and scream in protest, but it must have been her regular lullaby, for she slept on.

Thinking how altogether scandalous Sally was, and thinking how nice it was to share her room and her bed with her granddaughters, and thinking it was a good job she'd brought her working clothes, and lastly thinking what a change it all was from Jean's and not sure whether it was a change for better or worse, Maudie at last fell asleep.

CHAPTER THREE

It did not take Maudie very long to discover that Sally was the talk of the neighbourhood. She was known over hill and dale as a good-natured slut who sent her children to school, if she sent them at all, in clothes that everyone else would have sent to the church jumble sale. In fact, looking at Sally's mob, it might have appeared that Coledale and district didn't bother with sales but sent its jumble straight to her. Everyone knew the state she kept her house in. Everyone knew she was in debt all over the place. Everyone knew that she was quite likely to be found at midnight padding along the lane in her bare feet like some mad Meg Merrilies. Everyone knew everything, and everyone pitied William.

Maudie found all this out within the first week because people made it their business to tell her. She found out first of all from Grace, who was the woman who was supposed to come and clean for Sally. The very minute Maudie saw Grace, she knew that here was no cleaning woman. Grace was a trollop if ever she had set eyes on one. She had dyed red hair hanging in thick, uncombed clusters round her head, like a golliwog's. Her freckled, flat face was smeared with all the cheapest brands of make-up, badly applied. She was full-bosomed and displayed her cleavage in even the coldest weather with a selection of V-necked pullovers or blouses that were everywhere too tight and too short. She always wore high heels, with sling backs. She looked like a camp follower, or an actress in a wartime musical comedy.

Maudie did not believe Grace knew what a scrubbing brush was for. She came into the house, sat down, blasphemed and lit a cigarette, and all this when the dishes were stacked high, the beds unmade and the place crying out for good, hard work.

'Oh, what a life,' she said to Maudie, and blew smoke over the bread still on the table. 'Oh, I don't know,' she added, and sighed.

'Did you want Mrs Harrison?' Maudie asked.

Grace hooted. 'Mrs Who? You mean old Sal? Here, are you her mam?'

'I am,' said Maudie, stiffly.

'Oh, well, I'm Grace. I'm Sal's cleaner.'

A thousand retorts went through Maudie's head. She selected one with care. 'You've got yourself a full time job,' she said, distinctly.

'Part time,' Grace said, 'mornings, three times a week. I do Mrs Williams on Tuesdays and Fridays and in the afternoons I serve at the Co-op butter counter in Coledale. I like the variety.'

'I won't keep you back, then,' Maudie said, 'I expect you'll want to start with the dishes first.'

'Hang on,' Grace said, blowing away, 'I haven't said good morning to Sal yet. Is she still in bed? Isn't she awful? Them kids of hers'll murder themselves one of these days. Sal! Sal!'

Grace disappeared, cigarette in hand, to Sal's bedroom. Soon, their gay, girlish laughter rang merrily through the house. No one could accuse Sal of being stand-offish with her staff. Stiff with rage, Maudie washed the dishes and cleaned the kitchen, and then began sorting through the laundry basket for the children's clothes, all the while keeping her eye on the three little ones playing in the yard. She was hanging the newly scrubbed clothes on the line when Sally and Grace came down. Sally said immediately that she shouldn't have. Grace said she was soft in the head. Grimly, Maudie got on with it and said nothing.

By the end of the morning, it was clear that Grace brought more mess with her than she took away. She and Sally slopped round the house, doing things in a half-hearted sort of way, never once stopping their chatter, except to drink tea. Their standards were appallingly low. Maudie did not know how anyone could start cooking with pans that were not clean, or make up a bed with sheets that were soiled. But Sally and Grace did not seem to notice these things. They were 'all done' at eleven, and pleased as punch with themselves.

Down in the village, where Maudie took herself to buy some Vim and Domestos and other essentials which Sally seemed to regard as exotic mysteries, it was obvious that everyone knew who Maudie was and that they were dying to find out if she was like her daughter. One look at her, and her shopping list, and they knew that she wasn't. From the beginning, they were therefore all sympathy, and this Maudie found very hard to endure. She hated it when they looked at Betty and Rosie and said 'poor little things'. She could not stand it when they asked her if she wanted credit, and watched her slyly when she said no to see if they could get her to pay Sally's bills.

All the way home, pushing the two little girls in a beaten up push chair she would have been ashamed to go for coal with, Maudie was trying to hold back her tears. The shame was killing her. She did not know how she was going to bring herself to go back to those shops, ever. To think that her daughter was looked down on throughout the entire area! Maudie pushed and with every yard she pushed she tried to work out what had happened. She had brought Jean and Sally up in exactly the same way. Why was one a credit to her and the other the very opposite? Anyone looking at Sally's home and children would think she had been brought up in a slum. Grieving silently, Maudie was driven to one inescapable conclusion: the bad in her father was coming out in Sally. She was shiftless because he had been. She was feckless because that was his nature. The strong hand she needed was lacking and this was the result. There was nothing of her mother in her at all, not a scrap, and the fact that she had borne her was a mere accident of breeding.

Towards the entry to the Grants' lane, Maudie began to see that the good Lord had sent her to Sally's to try and put her on the straight and narrow path. All that lounging around at Jean's had had its point. She was fit and strong and rested, and she must set her shoulder to the wheel, and leave no stone unturned, and not cease from the fight until she had made that Sally see the error of her ways. Those poor wee bairns had found their champion in her, and that unlucky William might be made something of yet.

Humming 'Onward Christian Soldiers', Maudie turned into the lane, and saw a lady coming out of the gate half way down. She was a very neat-dressed person wearing gloves, and Maudie took an instant liking to her. Not many people wore gloves these days, especially in the mornings. They were rather a crowd, strung out across the lane, as they approached the gloved lady, so Maudie pushed the pram into the hedge, and pulled Rosie, who had been walking since the top of the hill, into her side. The lady came on, and stopped when she was abreast with them. As well as gloves, Maudie saw that she was also carrying a very carefully rolled and buttoned umbrella.

'Good morning Rosie, good morning Betty,' the lady said, and nodded and smiled at Maudie, who had a sudden and quite uncharacteristic feeling that she ought to curtsy.

'Say good morning,' Maudie instructed her granddaughters sharply, and shook them when all they could manage was a mumble.

'You must be Mrs Tipstaff,' the lady said, and held out her hand. 'How do you do? I'm Mrs Grant.'

Maudie took her hand and they exchanged fingertip pressures most politely. She saw that Mrs Grant was staring at her rather hard for one so obviously genteel.

'I do hope you enjoy your stay,' Mrs Grant said, still smiling.

'I doubt it,' Maudie said, confidentially. 'What I've seen already is enough to break any mother's heart. All I can hope to do is try to put some things right for the sake of these dear children.'

That was the end of their conversation then, but it was, of course, only the beginning. Mrs Grant asked Mrs Tipstaff to come and have tea with her that afternoon, if she felt she could be spared. Maudie, highly gratified, and glad she had not overstepped the bounds of decency with her confession, accepted. She went and stayed two hours and knew she had found a woman after her own heart. It seemed, for a start, that Mrs Eliza Grant had seen which way things were going a very long time ago and had tried to give advice to Sally when and where it was needed. But she had been rebuffed. It was not that her advice had been rejected—it was much worse. Anyone could understand advice being rejected, especially such a humane woman as Mrs Eliza Grant, but to have it simply not listened to was quite a different matter. Sally had laughed at her. She had ridiculed her. Mrs Eliza Grant had never forgotten her attitude.

Maudie spent most of the first hour, sitting in Mrs Grant's dark and plush parlour, making fulsome apologies for Sally's behaviour. She did not normally tolerate any attacks on her family from outsiders—family solidarity was a law of nature—but she felt Mrs Grant to be so sympathetic that she had to make an exception. She spent the second hour getting a most horrifying message. This message, though horrifying, was really quite starkly straightforward, but such was Mrs Grant's delicacy and such was Maudie's naïveté, it took a whole hour of undertones and overtones and meaningful facial expressions and background noises.

Home truths were things Maudie hoped she had never been too proud to face and own up to, but even so this one shook her. It was not a question of not being able to believe what Mrs Grant had at last made clear. It was more that she could not understand such behaviour. When a woman was thirty-six and had six children, it was not normal to enjoy the pleasures of any man's bed. In Maudie's opinion, it was not normal at any age, but that was something one did not talk about. For Sally to be a woman of loose morals was not only utterly despicable and shocking, it was also, Maudie felt, mental.

Mrs Grant was quite specific in her accusations. Everyone,

133

she said, including William himself, she was quite sure, knew about Sally's jaunts with Grace Wilson on Saturday evenings to Coledale. Everyone knew they went to dances—at *thirty-six*—and got drunk and went with anyone. They did not try to conceal their activities, but went about them quite openly as though there was nothing to be ashamed of. And no one had been able to make Sally at least see that there was.

In the exhausted silence that followed Mrs Grant's diatribe, Maudie felt near to tears. The room seemed to get even darker than it was, and the stiff, shiny furniture crowded in on her. Her heart thudded dangerously. She fixed her eyes on Mrs Grant's cameo brooch and concentrated on remaining calm and in control. Not since her cases had disappeared at Victoria Coach Station had she felt in such spiritual turmoil. Sally's vile and awful wickedness made her feel tainted. It was one thing to see her slovenly habits and sigh over them and wonder how it could have come to pass and where one had gone wrong, but to be told one's daughter, one's married daughter, was a whore, was something to make one cringe.

At first, Maudie felt she could in no circumstances return to Sally's house. Then she realised she must in fact return, both out of practical necessity and moral obligation, but she did not know how she was going to carry on as though everything was normal. It would be impossible to act as though she knew nothing, but equally impossible to admit all. She had always been prepared to have scenes over untidiness, but never over emotions. She could go into the sins of all her family in minute detail, except sexual sins. These could not bear being talked about. She would not know what terms to use, how to start, how to say what she was getting at. Maudie hated all intimacy and all crudeness. To confront Sally on this matter, or to let on that she knew about it, was something she physically shied away from.

She would just go back to Sally's and have nothing to do with her. She would get on with doing everything she had outlined in her head that morning. There was no other alternative. She immediately told Mrs Grant this, adding that she would carry the burden of her recently acquired knowledge to the grave, and that she would never be able to hold up her head again, and that it had been a mortal blow, and little did she think when she left Scotland—and so on. Mrs Grant at once produced some medicinal brandy to have with the remainder of the tea.

That over, Maudie was ready to learn quite a lot of other things about Sally and William from Mrs Grant, who it appeared had always kept a maternal eye on William. She explained to Maudie that Mr Grant had always looked after his workmen. He was a gentleman farmer in the true sense of the term—that is, he really did farm and he really was a gentleman. He wasn't interested in branching out or going into a big combine. All he wanted to do was keep going the land that had always been in the family, and with this Mrs Grant was in full agreement. She assured Maudie that she liked the life. If you knew how to treat the villagers, they would respond accordingly. There were some nice people in the district, to whom she was going to introduce Maudie, and she would personally see that she did not suffer from being Sally's mother.

They then proceeded to skate round the subject of Mrs Grant having no children. It had not all been left to God's will. Mrs Grant had had Tests and she had had Examinations and she had even taken Temperatures, but all to no avail. It was a great sorrow, but it had its compensations. She could interest herself more in the church and the village community and they were naturally all very grateful for this. It was nice to do good and be appreciated. It also, as she had said, gave her time to help the young workmen and their families. Mr Grant employed six men altogether, and two boys, as well as a farm manager, and Mrs Grant knew them all very well and all their families and what their backgrounds were and what could be expected of them.

She remembered very well the day William had first come to the farm. His father was killed in the war and his mother was a very respectable widow who lived in Coledale and was a most valued charlady of a type not to be confused with Grace Wilson. She had come to see Mr Grant and asked if William could be taken on in any capacity as she wanted him to have a good boss, not having a father. They had immediately taken him on as a farm hand and Mrs Grant had been pleased to regard him as her special charge.

William had always been a credit. He wasn't over-bright, but he was hard working and trustworthy and good with animals. All had gone very well until he had got in with a very bad sort of youth who had persuaded him to go to Manchester and make his fortune. Nothing the Grants could have said about fresh air being his fortune would have made any difference, for he simply upped and offed. It had been a great shock. Not all his mother's apologies could get over that. Only the week before, Mrs Grant had given him Mr Grant's old sports jacket and several worn shirts, and one would have thought he would have found it impossible to leave after that.

Mrs Grant did not know what happened in Manchester. All she knew was that William turned up late in the evening six months later saying he had just got married and could he have his job back. They had given it to him. Others wouldn't have, but they had. It was no good being a Christian if one bore grudges against people. They had let him have the house at the bottom of the lane, and had prepared to welcome his wife. But could anyone have welcomed a woman clearly much older than William who arrived, a bride of two weeks, about to have a baby in three months' time?

William's mother had felt not, and Mrs Grant could quite understand this. The poor woman had forbidden William to set foot in her house again. She wanted nothing to do with his wife, who did not even have the decency to look ashamed but beamed around her as though she was proud. But the Grants had allowed them to stay and trusted they would make amends.

Maudie felt very weak and ill by the time she left the Grants' house and set off down the lane. She ought never to have let Sally leave home, but then it would have been extremely difficult to restrain a fully grown woman from going off to what sounded a respectable domestic post in a good family in England. She tried hard to remember the exact circumstances of Sally going, but could not. She had stirred her lazy, idle self one day, when, as ever, she was between situations, and had replied to an advertisement in the paper and that had been that. What could a mother have done?

The baby must have been Sammy. Maudie decided she was simple minded—she had never doubted that it was only Sally's usual lethargy that had prevented her writing to say she had got married last year and had a little boy this year. She had been so delighted about her grandson that it never entered her head to think there was anything funny about it. Oh, it was all so deceitful and shabby.

At the end of a very wearying day, Maudie had yet to face another disclosure on the same subject. She felt there was now nothing about her daughter she did not know, to her eternal sorrow, but she had reckoned without Sammy. He was waiting for her on the bridge, his face self-consciously serious, his arms folded in a determined but somehow comical fashion. Maudie was cheered by the very sight of him, so she said, extra-crossly, 'Well, young man, haven't you a tongue in your head?'

'Yes,' Sammy said.

'Yes Grandma,' Maudie snapped.

'Yes Grandma,' Sammy muttered.

'Can't you be more civil than that?' Maudie complained. 'Dear God, you've none of you any manners at all.' The minute she had said it, she was sorry. 'What are you looking so sulky for?'

'I'm not looking sulky,' Sammy said.

'Yes you are.'

'No I'm not. I can't help what my face does.'

'Then you can start learning how to help it now,' Maudie said. 'I don't like sulky little boys, and I don't like cheeky ones either.'

'I wasn't cheeky,' Sammy protested.

'Yes you were. It's cheeky to answer your elders back and I'm your elder and that's what you're doing.' Sammy sighed. 'Don't sigh at me,' Maudie said immediately, 'or I'll smack your bottom.' Sammy smiled. 'And you needn't laugh—I've smacked many a bigger bottom than yours in my time.'

'Did you smack Mam's?' Sammy asked.

'Hundreds of times,' Maudie said. 'I smacked it till she couldn't sit down.'

'Good,' Sammy said, defiantly. He waited to see what his fierce little grandmother would say to that.

'Don't speak like that about your mother,' Maudie said, firmly.

'I didn't say anything,' Sammy said indignantly, 'I just said good. There's no law against saying good is there? It's a free country, isn't it? I can say good if I like. I never mentioned my rotten old mother.'

Maudie was used to small boys' indignation. She realised now was the time to forget the tellings off and find out what was troubling him before he either ran away or said something that was going too far or burst into tears.

'I've got my good shoes all muddy,' she said. 'Find me a stick to scrape the worst off.'

Sammy reluctantly unfolded his arms and scrapped around till he had found what Maudie considered a suitable stick. She then perched herself on a big stone and commanded him to clean her shoes, which he did very well.

'Now we'll go home,' she said.

'I'm not going home,' Sammy said, instantly.

'Why not?'

'Don't want to.'

'Why don't you want to?'

'Don't want to see Mam.'

'Why don't you want to see her?'

'Don't know.'

'Then you're stupid.'

'No I'm not.'

'Yes you are.'

'No I am not.'

'Why don't you know why you don't want to see your mother then? If you don't know you're stupid, and that's that.'

'I do know.'

'You don't.'

'I do so,' Sammy shouted. 'I do so know why I don't want to see her. I don't want to see her because she'll make me go down to Carters and I don't like going to Carters and I'm not going to go.'

Carefully, Maudie regarded her shoes.

'You've left a bit of mud on that one,' she said.

'I'm not going to Carters,' Sammy said.

'Nobody said anything about Carters,' Maudie said, mildly. 'Now finish that shoe off properly.'

Sammy finished it and when he had put the stick down, Maudie took hold of his hand and said she would guarantee he wasn't going anywhere except home with her and nowhere else. She led him along, and out came the garbled account of Mr Carter and the meat and delivering it and not liking wrapping bloody meat up and the money he took home to Sally, about which he was to tell nobody but everybody knew. He didn't like Mr Carter either. He made queer jokes about Sammy's mother that Sammy didn't understand but could tell were queer jokes. He had a nasty face as well, and he always stood very close to you.

Maudie seethed. She wanted to rush off and bring the cruelty officer. Getting a seven-year-old boy to go and do a butcher's delivery round after his schooling and taking the money for your own—it was the limit. Both the butcher and Sally ought to be horsewhipped. Why had nobody objected? Who were these people who took meat from a little boy and never thought how young he was for the job? Never, never, in all her hard-up days had Maudie descended to the depths of child exploitation. Child exploitation. She rolled the phrase grandly round her tongue. That's exactly what it was.

Already shouting 'Child exploiter, Adulterer, Harlot!' in her head, she marched towards Sally and the house with all the fervour of a slave abolitionist.

CHAPTER FOUR

'She can't help herself,' Sally said, 'she just has to be on the go. It was always the same, sweeping and cleaning till it drove my poor dad nuts. She can't lay off.'

'Lucky for you,' Grace said.

'Oh, I don't mind her ways. I wouldn't interfere with her. If she gets pleasure out of it, why not let her do it? She could have a holiday here if she wanted, go for nice country walks and that, but if she'd rather work herself into the grave that's her affair.'

'You'd never recognise this place,' Grace said.

'I don't mind her bossing me, as long as she doesn't go too far. She's going a bit far with our Sammy. Made a real song and dance about him helping out old Carter, as if the kid didn't enjoy it. He's got cheekier than ever since she came.'

'What can I smell?' Grace said.

'Shoulder of best English lamb.'

'Going up in the world, aren't we?'

'Mam bought it. She's mad about good hot meals, drives you crazy.'

'You mean she paid for it?' Grace said.

'Yes. Well, naturally she wants to help towards her keep, doesn't she? I mean, if she buys the odd bit of meat or two that's more or less right.'

'Have you touched her for anything?' Grace asked, shrewdly.

'Not really. It wouldn't be fair. I've got a loan off her to tide me over, but I wouldn't just take her money. It's not right.'

'What's the loan?' Grace asked.

'Not much. Paid off one or two things, not that I was worried.'

'Does William know?' Grace asked.

'No, and don't you tell him. He's soppy about my mam. Keeps going on about why aren't I like her. He can't see further than the end of his nose.'

'Reminds him of his own mam,' Grace said, 'she's the same—all bustle and drive.'

'Oh well, it takes all sorts. That's what I keep telling my mam.'

'She's thick with Ma Grant,' Grace said.

'Makes a friend for her.'

'Don't it worry you?' Grace asked.

'No. Why should it? I don't grudge the two old dears a chinwag.'

'She might tell her things,' Grace said.

'She can tell away.'

'You wouldn't want your mam to know—things,' Grace said.

'I don't care what she knows. Doesn't make any difference to me. I've got to baste that lamb.'

Slowly, Sally heaved herself out of her chair and made her leisurely way to the oven where a very large and handsome piece of meat sat on the middle shelf. She spooned the fat over it lovingly, and over the potatoes around it, then, exhausted, returned to her chair and Grace and the tea they had both been drinking for the past hour.

'This tea's cold,' Sally said.

'Then make some more,' Grace encouraged.

'Make it yourself.'

'You're a lazy faggot,' Grace said, amiably. 'You get worse and worse.'

'Here, who's paid to work here?'

'Who?' challenged Grace. 'I never got none of that loan, remember.'

Sniffing, Sally got up again, and put the kettle on. She gazed vacantly out of the newly cleaned window. It was another glorious day. The heat haze hung over the Grants' house in the distance. She suddenly wanted to get away from the house and its fierce fresh cleanliness.

'Wouldn't it be lovely,' she said, 'to go off.'

'Where?' Grace asked.

'Oh, anywhere. For a ride.'

'In a Rolls, I supose,' Grace said.

'No, a bus. Or any old car. Or a train.'

'An excursion,' Grace said, brightening.

'A day trip to the sea,' Sally said.

'Blackpool,' Grace shouted.

'Too far. Scarborough.'

The kettle boiled its head off. Sally pounded up the stairs, using several weeks' ration of her usual energy quota, and began ratching through her drawers looking for a dress to wear. Grace applied new lipstick and eye shadow in the kitchen, to the tune of 'Five Minutes More'. Without any more preamble, the pair of them rushed out of the house, leaving the door wide open, and ran giggling up the lane until Sally got a stitch with laughing and they slowed down. They linked each other's arms so that their bodies stuck together in one fat bundle.

'Your mam'll be mad,' Grace gasped.

'So what? We're not kids. I'm entitled to a day out when I feel like it,' Sally said.

'You haven't told her.'

'Do you think I'd tell her?'

'She'll wonder where you are. You haven't left a note or anything.'

'I can't write,' Sally said. Grace was convulsed anew. They stood and howled against the hedge.

'Oh!' Grace moaned. 'Oh, you're wicked.'

'Come on,' Sally said, pulling at her arm. 'We'll never get anywhere.'

They set off again, this time at a smart trot, Grace struggling to keep up in her outmoded stiletto heels. Mrs Grant saw them passing and wondered if they could be drunk so early in the morning. They looked a disgrace. A grown woman with a family leaving her house in that sort of dress with no hat or gloves or coat, laughing and shouting like a two-year-old, and in the company of a common little chit like Grace Wilson. You would think they thought they were gay schoolgirls. If only they could *see* themselves. What would poor Mrs Tipstaff say?

There wasn't much point in Maudie saying anything. There was no one to say it to, except Angie, Rosie and Betty. She came back from the village with them and the smell of scorching meat took precedence over everything else. Flinging open the oven door, she saw the rapidly shrinking, juiceless joint and she knew there was no hope for Sally. To neglect such an occupation as meat basting was a crime too heinous ever to overlook.

Tears with children around are no good at all, as Maudie knew well. So she controlled hers, and laid the table and washed everyone's hands and got everything ready for William coming in at twelve as he had said he would that day. She tried not to give a thought to Sally. When she reappeared, Maudie planned to tell her straight out that she was going on to Robert's without more ado. Enough was enough. She didn't mind being a dogsbody, but when it came to being expected to buy the best meat and watch it be ruined, then the time had come to admit defeat and go.

As she moved about, Maudie rehearsed several conversations with the likes of Mrs Grant in her head. They all began, 'I tried to show her the error of her ways. I didn't preach at her or scold, I just did things as they ought to be done and hoped she would take the hint.' Then she went through all the things she had done in detail. The most difficult bit was when her hearer might suggest she should not walk out. 'I have thought of those poor, dear children, believe me. I've tried to work out how I could take them with me, but I can't and that's that. All I can do is commend them to the good Lord's care, and hope their father will be watchful.'

William did come in at twelve. In deference to Maudie, he had rolled his shirt sleeves down and put a jacket on. His three daughters were neatly arranged around the ladened table, and he was moved to smile with pleasure at the sight of them.

'Grand smell,' he said, and sat down, then remembered Maudie liked him to wash his hands before all meals, so he got up again and did so.

'It's ruined,' Maudie said.

'Smells a good ruin,' William joked, shyly.

'It's a dreadful mess,' Maudie said, putting the still near perfect lamb on the table. 'Your wife forgot to baste it regularly. She went off and left it.'

'Oh,' William said, and lifted his knife and fork in readiness.

'The Lord only knows where she's gone,' Maudie said, carving the meat tenderly. William said nothing, his eyes watching the long, lean slices. 'It's a disgrace the way you let her carry on, William.'

'What can I do?' William said.

'Bring her to her senses,' Maude said. 'Tell her that's not the way a wife and mother should carry on. Get rid of that Grace for a start.'

'I've told her to go,' William said. 'She takes no notice. Neither of them takes any notice of anything I say.'

'Then you ought to make them,' Maudie said.

'How?'

'Do I need to tell you that?' Maudie asked. 'Do you have no idea how to exert your authority?'

William's plate was by now full. He began filling his mouth, hoping Maudie's well known opinion on eating food while it was hot would save him the trouble of replying, because he had no reply. He did not know what anybody could do about Sally. What did Maudie mean? Did she want her daughter beaten? Sally would only beat him back, and he did not like fights. He couldn't keep her in the house when he had his job to go to. It was no good reasoning with her. What could he do?

Vaguely, he wondered if Maudie intended him to tell her to go away forever, but how could he do that with six children? He couldn't manage on his own and no woman, even if there had been another woman, would have him with that lot.

Treacle tart followed the lamb. William stuffed himself, thankful that Maudie was now so preoccupied with the children's table manners that she had no time to turn on him. He wondered if he could get up the minute he had finished the pudding and bolt for the door before she saw him, but the children finished first and to his horror, she sent them out to play, leaving them alone.

'Now William,' she began.

William dropped his eyes and concentrated on the custard streaks round his plate.

'Now William,' she said again. 'What are you going to do about Sally?'

William gave an embarrassed smile. 'She'll be back soon,' he manged to mutter.

'That's not the point,' Maudie said, pouncing on the start he had given her. 'She has no right to wander off like that.'

'You tell her,' William suggested.

'The idea!' Maudie exploded. 'Whose wife is she, indeed?'

To her fury, William simply shrugged and began to amble towards the door. As he stood in the open doorway, hesitant, unsure, indecisive, Maudie consciously longed for a man such as her own awful husband. At least Joseph knew how to deal with a woman. He was master in his own house. Sally would not have lasted five minutes married to him. He would have gone out and dragged her back by the scruff of her neck and knocked the living daylights out of her. She had hated him for his violence and crudeness, and had prayed that her daughters would marry good and reasonable men, but in that moment she wished heartily that William would take off in a roaring, towering rage, instead of trailing sheepishly back to work.

The afternoon was a long one. Maudie had her bags packed, her speech ready, but still Sally did not come. The boys, when

146

they came in from school, wished aloud that their mam might never come back and grandma stay for always to go on making girdle scones. When they were tucked up in their clean beds, prayers all said including God bless mother, and William's tea ready, and all the evening tidying done, Maudie's impatience began to be uncontrollable. She could not stop herself talking aloud. Backwards and forwards she went, between window and table, cursing very mildly, though she knew it was wrong and she shouldn't. Not even William came so that she could have another go at him and get rid of some of the anger choking her.

Slowly, in place of the anger, or rather mixed with it to a sickening degree, she began to feel worried. Suppose Sally was lying dead somewhere? Suppose she and Grace had got in with a bad crowd and been left dead by the roadside? Suppose she never came back? Maudie put her hand to her mouth and kept it there. She would have to stay. It would be her plain duty. She would have to look after the children and see they were brought up properly. She would have to live in this house and this village and this godforsaken place till she died. She would have to worry all the time about being ill or dying and wouldn't feel she could do either when she felt like it.

William's mother would have to look after them temporarily. After the funeral—would Robert come?—she would go back to Glasgow and sell most of her furniture and clear things up and then come back here, never more to leave. She must have a room to herself so she could get a decent night's rest, for she found the little girls increasingly restless rather than comforting companions. They would have to convert the parlour into her room, and buy a proper bed, or maybe the boys could move in with William and she could have their room.

Maudie felt very ill. She stopped patrolling up and down, and went and sat in the easy chair. Her fate, so quickly and sensibly conjured up, appalled her. She did not want to stay here, for all her love for her grandchildren. What she wanted was for them to somehow live near enough for her to see them often and yet not all the time. Say, twenty minutes away in a bus. Guiltily, she realised she was already looking forward to the childless peace of Robert's house, away from the endless whining and exhausting demands that had to be met. She was too old to cope with six young children from morning to night.

Sitting there, moaning to herself, her resentment towards Sally for getting herself killed built up. One expected in one's old age to be looked after and cared for, to have paid back in kind the attention lavished on one's children. It was too cruel to find instead that one had to become a substitute for one's daughter, to have to start all over again a job that had already been done once. Sally had never given her anything. She had always been a liability. It was typical of her that she could not die in a grateful way.

The thought of flight before William came back and before any bad news was brought, did enter Maudie's head, but only fleetingly. She could leave a message saying she had been called away urgently to Robert's or Jean's. But that would mean leaving the children alone, which did not bear thinking about. No, she would have to stay and make all the arrangements. People would pity her from the bottom of their hearts, and admire her decision to take on the family. She would become a kind of heroine, a local saint, someone whose history would always be related to newcomers. To everyone, she would simply say, 'It was my duty' and go quietly on with whatever she was doing.

William's hand on the latch interrupted Maudie's tearful outburst.

'Oh, dear God!' she said, standing up.

'It's only me,' said William, half in and half out of the door. Gloomily, he saw that Sally was not yet back and his delaying tactics had been wasted. Never had he tried so hard to get himself sent on some long job in another valley, but Mr Grant had seemed determined he should be finished on time. He had hung around the village for hours, had several drinks and yet still it had seemed early and he could not bring himself to go home. Only his awful hunger had driven him in.

'Have they found her?' Maudie asked.

'Who?'

'Oh for heaven's sake! Sally, who else?'

'Oh. I don't know. Who was looking for her?' William asked, genuinely puzzled.

'She must be lying in a ditch,' Maudie said, beginning to weep again. 'Oh, what an awful thing to happen.'

William watched her rocking dramatically back and forwards. He scratched his ear and cleared his throat. Embarrassment stifled him.

'Now, now,' he said, gruffly.

'What are we going to do?' Maudie wailed.

'Nothing to be done,' William said, uneasily. 'She'll turn up soon enough, don't you worry.'

'She won't,' Maudie said decisively. 'I've had a premonition of disaster ever since I arrived. Twice I've dreamt of a crying baby and I've seen crosses in the tea-leaves nearly every day. I knew something dreadful was going to happen, I knew it, I knew it.'

William frowned, horrified by all this hysteria. He mustn't let her upset herself so. Doubtfully, he went over to her, but it was impossible to think of any way in which he could reassure her with some physical act. He could not put his arms round her. The thought made him go cold all over. Nor could he stroke her hair or do any of the other things he felt vaguely might be called for. All he could manage was a pat on her hand, and just as he reached out to pat it, she moved it and he patted the arm of the chair instead.

'We must be brave for the children's sake,' Maudie said, leaning back so that the tears got caught in the wrinkles of her cheeks and fascinated William. 'It's no use getting upset.'

'It is not,' William said emphatically.

'I suppose you want your tea.'

'Yes,' he said promptly.

149

Sighing, Maudie heaved herself out of the chair. She would have been disappointed if William had said he did not want his tea, for in spite of all the inner turmoil she had found time to bake.

William ate his very delicious meal in silence, with Maudie watching and calculating every mouthful, and accompanying his champing jaws with short, breathy exclamations of concern about Sally and the children and what was to be done. It was as he pushed his chair away from the table that they both heard voices singing. William stood quite still, and so did Maudie. The singing stopped. Quite far up the lane, they heard laughing, and then that stopped too, and there was no sound until the yard gate clanged shut and footsteps pattered surely over the cobbles. The latch was lifted quickly, almost noiselessly, and the door very quietly opened just wide enough to let Sally in.

She had no shoes on. That was the first thing Maudie noticed and it became her abiding memory of the scene. She had no shoes on, and her large, knobbly-toe'd feet were covered with dust and grit and small pieces of grass. They looked as though they did not know what shoes or stockings were, as though all their lives they had been used to freedom and had forgotten to wince at a tarmac road or prickly path. The legs above them were red and mottled with the sun, right up to the big, fat, scarred-looking knees. A varicose vein stood out prominently on one. The skirt which dipped and twisted its way around these limbs had a long tear from where the side-zip ended to where the hem began. It looked like a barbed wire tear, the edges frayed and jagged. Tucked into this sad garment was a once white blouse, with only two out of six buttons still intact. There was a large hole under one arm. Hanging down from the breast pockets were two chains of buttercups, quite fresh still, and thrust through the empty buttonholes a series of drooping wild roses.

All this Maudie took in instantly, but William saw only the languor of Sally's stance, and the dreamy, I-have-been-away look on her face. It was exactly like she always came back, a cat who had lapped the cream and did not care how many beatings there were to be for it knew the cream was fully digested. Her hair, usually coiled in an untidy knot, hung down her back and around her face in a magnificently intricate tangle. The skin on her prominent, wide nose was already peeling, and her cheeks were like the rising sun, with the white creases around the mouth showing that she had sunbathed with a smile. Her eyes were half-closed, each blink taking its own long slow time. William knew there was no point at all in talking to her. All she wanted was to be taken to bed, to have a response to her sunbaked sensuality. He felt himself weakening all over.

But all this was lost on Maudie, she sensed no spell. Moving swiftly forward, she thrust her face into Sally's and began sniffing. 'Drink,' she said, viciously, and prodded her daughter in the stomach. 'If I had thought I would live to see this day...' As she searched for words dreadful enough, Sally walked past her and put her arms round William's neck and kissed him.

'Oh, dear God!' Maudie said, feeling sick. 'Oh, she's out of her mind! Oh the wickedness of the woman.'

With difficulty, William got himself out of Sally's heavy embrace.

'Where've you been?' he asked, his voice thick with the attempt to conceal his desire from Maudie. Sally just looked at him and smiled and he knew she had gone off somewhere with Grace and they had acted daft and now she was back and glad to be back and wanting him. She was going to kiss him again. 'Your mam's been worried,' he said, 'she thought you were murdered.'

Sally laughed. William gazed from her loose, untidy, full figure to the ramrod back straightness of his mother-in-law. He had to shut his eyes to ease the tension, and missed Maudie's rush up to Sally and only heard the smart slap of her stiff hand on his wife's face.

Sally made no move to slap back. Maudie was crying. She sat down and sobbed and William could not bear to look. But all Sally did was yawn, and shake her head to clear it, and put her little finger in her ear to clean it, and yawn again so that her tonsils danced. Then she went off towards the stairs, and stood waiting for William. He did not know what to do. He hated to leave Maudie so upset, just as he well remembered leaving his mother upset, and yet he wanted to go. There wasn't going to be a scene. He knew Maudie longed for a scene, but that Sally would never rouse the energy to become part of one, and he could not bear them. So there was nothing he could do but clear his throat and try to say something about forgetting it, and follow Sally, knowing that she ought to be horsewhipped and the only reason he was going to lay a finger on her was to take her, and tomorrow it would all go on as before, and there was nothing Maudie could do about it, because that was how they were.

CHAPTER FIVE

Embarrassment was luckily an emotion Sally knew nothing about. She eventually stirred herself the next morning to get up and go into the kitchen and face her mother. To her it was not a question of 'facing' anyone. She just behaved as she always did not out of any deliberate intent, but because yesterday was only a hazy memory.

Maudie, of course, knew this. She might have reared Sally in vain, but she did at least remember her capacity for treating every day as a shining new one. Not that this was anything to be proud of. If it had been a case of Sally being the wronged one, then this could have been called turning the other cheek and would have been very noble. There was nothing very noble about forgiving and forgetting when you were the one who had done all the wrong. Somehow, Sally had to be made aware of the enormity of the gulf which now existed between herself and her mother.

After a long, uncomfortable night planning yet more campaigns, Maudie had reached one resolution: she was not speaking to Sally again. Anything she might have to say could be communicated through William or the children. For the remaining three weeks of her stay she would not talk to Sally unless some suitable act of penitence was proposed. Reason and arguments and good example had all failed: the pariah must now be shunned.

Maudie realised some people might have called this childish behaviour. They might say it was a sign she was entering her dottage. But as she saw it, she had no desire to have any more to do with Sally if she would not mend her ways, therefore even if ineffective, sending her to Coventry meant Maudie lost nothing. And there was always the faint hope that garrulous, easy going, sociable Sally would crack under the strain of such a spartan attack.

It is always difficult to make people like Sally appreciate that you are not speaking to them. Maudie could not say, 'I am not speaking to you,' for that would ruin the whole point of the thing. She clattered around the kitchen waiting for Sally to put in an appearance and make a remark which could be pointedly ignored, but when Sally did slop down the stairs it was only to say 'What a lovely morning' and that was an opening gambit Maudie never replied to on principle.

Half the morning went by in a spate of vague pleasantries and still Sally had not seen the light. The only question she asked of Maudie was 'How can anyone resist going out on a day like this?' and she could never in her wildest dreams have expected an answer to that one. She sat on the doorstep shelling far too many peas and sniffing at the sun till Maudie was driven to going upstairs lest an irate shout spoiled her ruse. It was so difficult to resist letting forth a good harangue. Consequently, Maudie used up her whole range of facial expressions, all made at nothing and nobody. If only Sally had been listening, the sighs and grunts, the clash of pan lids, the very sweeping of a brush, would have told her a lot.

Sally was not listening, but she was not totally unmoved by Maudie's performance. She watched her mother and wondered lazily what made people do unnecessary jobs all day long with far too much energy. She pitied her, without being stirred by her own pity. The neat, stiff little figure rushing about was to her as pointless as an ant. She thought of her sister Jean and imagined what a successful combination she and her mother must have made. It was surprising Maudie had ever left Jean's house, in Sally's opinion.

Dreamily, Sally fed peas to Angie and the cat. Her mother's banging around grew more violent and began to disturb her serenity. She balanced a pea on the tip of her finger. Old folk were a liability. Maudie was good with the children and useful about the house, and as she had said many times, she did not mind who stayed with them or for how long. She loved company. But it was annoying when they tried to interfere with your life and with things they were too old to understand. It was, Sally thought, like having a vicar permanently billeted in the house, forever trying to make you feel you had done wrong.

She had done no wrong. She had simply gone out for a nice day in the sun, harming nobody and not being harmed herself. She had come back at the end of her day overflowing with love for everyone, yet you would have thought from that crabby crow's face that she had been out robbing and stealing and doing all manner of wicked things. Well, let her and that moany minny Mrs Eliza Grant think what they liked, if it gave them any pleasure, as long as they kept their findings to themselves. If you lived as your mother wanted you to live, there was no fun in anything.

Sally, for her part, thought she was doing very well to patiently put up with a mother who tried to turn a woman's husband against her. That, in her opinion, was what Maudie was trying with poor William. Hardly had he been rescued from the clutches of his vinegary mother and bitchy Mrs Grant, hardly had he been turned into a nice, easy, unworried sort of man, before Maudie was coming along and trying to undo all Sally's good work. Sally found herself laughing aloud. Maudie did not realise what she was up against with William. He would give every appearance of agreeing with his mother-in-law and her like, so that they would imagine they had an accomplice in him, but underneath there was the same lazy self-indulgence which made him a suitable mate for Sally. He was willing to swing along with anyone willing to provide the ideas and the initiative.

Sally had finished shelling the peas. She chewed a pea pod and thought how her head ached with all the thinking she had been doing. She got up and went inside, fancying a cup of tea. It was not one of Grace's mornings or she would already have had several. Idly, she glanced around the kitchen. She wouldn't have to clean for months after her mother had gone. Filling the kettle, she gazed, as usual, at the apple trees outside and let the water go gushing everywhere in her admiration. Maudie came in as she was rubbing the water aimlessly into the flagged floor with her toe. It was as her mother tightened her lips and got down to mop it up properly that she wondered if the lack of any accompanying biting comment meant Maudie was 'not speaking'.

'I can't take my eyes off those trees,' she said, brightly. 'Watching them makes me do daft things.'

Maudie said nothing.

'What did you fancy for lunch?' Sally asked, looking at her slyly. Maudie went and sat down. Amused, Sally put her to the test again. 'Maybe we'll just have a sandwich?' she suggested, knowing Maudie's views on sandwiches. Her mother's face twitched alarmingly. Now certain of the situation, Sally began to enjoy herself. 'I'm glad you think it's a very good idea,' she said.

All day, the one-sided warfare continued, with William and the children only half understanding what was going on. Sally took shameless advantage of her mother's self-imposed vow of silence, attributing to her the most nonsensical and violently contradictory ideas. Maudie just went on determined not to be worn down or caught out, so that the whole affair took on the ridiculous tension of a radio quiz programme where the first to be tricked into saying some word lost the game. The only way Maudie could hit back was by answering through the children, particularly Sammy, when they turned to her for corroboration that she agreed with what their mother said she agreed with.

But by evening, it was Sally who was tired of the farce.

'Well now, Mother,' she said, after the children were in bed. 'Can't we call it a day?' Maudie inwardly brightened, but maintained her stony expression. 'You tell me what the matter is and I'll see what I can do to put it right.' She knew if

Maudie could be prevailed upon to even say 'Nothing's the matter' or 'You know fine well what is the matter' then all would be well. But Maudie was not budging. 'Oh,' said Sally, clicking her tongue with exasperation. 'It's so silly to act like we were children.' Maudie permitted herself a satirical smile. 'You've only three weeks left and I want you to enjoy yourself,' Sally said, 'not sit there like an old misery.'

With that, Maudie got up. 'Where are you going?' Sally asked, quite sharply for her. 'To bed? In the sulks?' Maudie continued towards the stairs. 'Oh well, go to bed. I just hope you wake up feeling less sour-faced in the morning,' and she added, much lower 'You silly old faggot.' She felt uneasy with the insult still on her lips.

'She's making me all cross,' she said to William. 'Now she'll go to bed and cry and try to make me feel bad about it,' she complained. 'She was always trying to make people feel bad.' William rustled his newspaper. He was genuinely trying to read a report of a houndtrail. 'Oh, you,' Sally said, in disgust. She sat down heavily and bit her fingernails for a few minutes. 'Let's go for a drink,' she said, suddenly. She got up, and got her cardigan, and opened the door, knowing William would follow. She stood outside in the yard and shouted 'Come and have a drink, Mother,' under Maudie's window, and even pretended, as she linked arms with William, to be waiting for a reply. As they moved off down the lane, she deliberately started singing, and fondled the reluctant William for any window watcher to see. She tried turning very quickly once or twice to catch her mother's eye so she could wave, but all she saw was the curtain twitch and even Sally got no kick out of waving to a twitching curtain.

On the second day, Sally decided not to give her mother the satisfaction of being wheedled and coaxed out of her ill-humour, as though she was somebody special. 'Mother's lost her tongue,' she said when Grace slopped in. 'Can't find it anywhere. She's swept it out with all the dust.' Grace giggled, but eyed Maudie nervously. 'Don't ask Grandma anything,'

Sally said to her children, 'the fairies stole her tongue in the night.'

'Did they, Grandma?' Sammy asked.

'No they did not,' Maudie said.

'Then why did Mam say they had?'

'I have no idea,' Maudie said. 'Just you get on with your dinner.' Undermining a parent's authority, whoever the parent, was something she hoped she would never lower herself to do.

'Why did you say the fairies had stolen Grandma's tongue?' Sammy duly asked his mother.

'Because she won't talk to me,' Sally said, adult solidarity not being a thing she worried about.

'Won't you talk to Mam?' Sammy asked.

'I've told you to get on with your dinner,' Maudie said, furiously, and as he opened his mouth again: 'Now not another word.'

Sammy reluctantly got on with it, eyeing first his smiling mother and then his glowering grandmother and longing to know what was going on. He tried all day to find out, but not even his mother seemed prepared to explain any further if Maudie would not.

Regularly, Sally began every day that week forgetting the situation, and regularly, by about midday, Maudie had made sure she remembered and all the annoyance of it began all over again. There was no way out. She wasn't going to have a row with her mother, and she wasn't going to start apologising when she had done nothing wrong. Since she had no principles, this latter wouldn't have been too difficult for Sally to do, but she knew that 'I'm sorry I went off like that' would not be the end of the affair but the beginning of the inquisition. Every detail would have to be gone over, every sin catalogued and final absolution would be dependent on an abject penance Sally would never be able to even feign. So she didn't attempt it.

Maudie's last weeks were therefore spent in an atmosphere

quite unlike anything Sally had ever dreamed possible. It was soon no secret that she wanted her mother to go, that she was counting the days to her departure. She repeatedly asked Maudie the times of her buses and trains and in this case, aeroplanes, and worried almost as much as the traveller herself about the tickets coming through safely. Her conversation with everybody was full of references to after mother has gone, as though it was a case of her dying.

Maudie felt it was in a way like dying. She was pleased she had made some effect on her daughter, but she genuinely cried in the night at the outcome of her stay. She might not have seen Sally for years and years, she might never have approved of her anyway and said so many times, but she had still been a daughter, there, as it were, for the having. Now she wasn't. Oh, if asked, she must still say she had two daughters and one son, but she would always feel Sally was no longer a part of her. She felt she wanted to go and tell someone this, someone like Mrs Eliza Grant, someone who would appreciate the dreadfulness of such an affliction. But she resisted the temptation, and said instead long, pious prayers for Sally, in which was included a laborious amount of background detail, covering the parting of the ways.

But to make Maudie happier, there was the prospect of her four months with Robert, the thought of which made her cross herself frequently as such happiness seemed to be tempting fate. It was not just the thought of Robert himself, but the thought that there would be no one else at all. No in-laws, no grandchildren, no other people to interfere with their content-ment. She would have him completely and utterly to herself, and he would be able to devote himself to her. This lack of complications in their relationship was what gave Maudie her greatest anticipatory joy.

She worried a little about leaving her grandchildren, glad though she might be to have peace again. She had made something of all of them, especially of Sammy, but all they had learnt would be lost in a matter of days with no one to watch

159

that their new standards were kept up. It would be back to dirty necks and soiled clothes and revolting table manners and no sense of right and wrong whatsoever. Were she to return in a week, the same rabble would doubtless greet her—and God only knew what worse evils lay ahead for them.

The heartbreak of it moved Maudie to have a long but careful talk with Sammy. She walked with him half way to school one morning in order to have the necessary solitude to underline the importance of what she was going to say.

'Sammy,' she said, 'I'll be leaving in a week.'

'Why?' Sammy asked, though he knew.

'You know fine well,' Maudie said crossly. 'To see your Uncle Robert, that's why.'

'Why do you have to go and see him?'

'Because I want to. I've a right to see him, as much as I have a right to see you, so don't be impudent.'

Sammy no longer asked what impudent meant, nor, understanding, did he say he wasn't. He had learnt a lot in four months. He kept silence and waited.

'I want you to promise me,' Maudie said, and Sammy inwardly groaned, 'I want you to promise me that you'll always wash your face and clean your teeth every morning. Now promise that for a start.'

'What if there's no toothpaste?' Sammy said.

'I'll send you toothpaste regularly,' Maudie replied.

'What if Mam says don't wash I want you to do a message and you'll be late?' he prodded, slyly.

Maudie took a deep breath. 'If you get up early you'll have time always to wash. Now promise.'

'O.K.,' Sammy sighed, 'promise.'

'Don't say those letters,' Maudie snapped. 'You should talk in proper words.'

'Everyone says O.K. It means——'

'Never mind what it means. You don't say it. Now listen, I haven't finished. I want you to promise as well that you'll say your prayers every night——'

'Kneeling?'

'Kneeling, of course. And that you'll always tell the truth and do your best to be a good boy and try to see that the others follow your example.'

'I promise,' Sammy said, quickly. 'On my honour to God and the King.'

'There's no need to make a meal of it,' Maudie said. '"I promise" is quite enough. The word of a gentleman is quite enough without any fancy additions.'

'I promise, then,' Sammy said, huffily. 'I was just trying to make it a better promise.'

'Well, then,' Maudie said, 'I'm pleased you're taking it seriously. Put your tie straight.'

'No one else in my class wears a tie.'

'You're not no one else,' Maudie snapped, and that was the end of the conversation.

To have a go at William, she considered worse than useless. He had already shown himself lacking in all the qualities needed in a husband for Sally. She was therefore gratified and even touched when William himself opened up a discussion on the very topic that had been troubling her.

'You'll be leaving soon,' he said, 'more's the pity,' and immediately blushed.

Maudie looked at him sharply, and noted his more than usually red face.

'What do you mean by that, young man?' she asked, upbraiding rather than inviting him.

'I mean it's a pity you're going, what with all you've done,' William said, bringing out each word with great distinction, giving his sentence a ludicrously heavy emphasis.

'I've done no more than you could do if you wanted,' Maudie said. 'You've a fine family of children. They only want shown the way.'

'I know,' William said, and paused. He could think of nothing better to say than 'I know' again.

'You just keep an eye on them,' Maudie instructed, 'and you won't have any trouble.'

'It's not just the children,' William said, and stopped.

'Anything else is up to you,' Maudie said, 'as I've told you over and over again. The remedy is in your own hands and I've no sympathy at all for a man too idle to set his own wife and home in order. There now.' She pursed her lips to show that was her final word.

William shifted uncomfortably in his chair. She had missed the point. He wasn't too clear himself on what the point was exactly, but he knew it was very important and had nothing to do with clean, well-behaved children or a tidy house or hot, satisfying meals. He had meant to compliment her and she had thought he had just meant he'd liked the law and order of her stay. That was a compliment too, but not of the kind he had meant. It was Maudie as a person he had valued, with her inflexible standards and uncompromising ideals. It had been so good to have certainty in the house. Each night, coming in, he had imagined this as something tangible—you knew, as you opened the door, that here resided someone who knew black was black and white white. The responsibility of being the father and husband and in charge didn't exist when Maudie was there. She took it all on herself, a magnificent family matriarch, relegating him to an insignificant subordinate.

All this was still framing itself into words in William's head when the day came for Maudie to leave. She was going by bus to Coledale, and from there by train to Manchester, where she would catch a plane. To everyone's amazement, including his own, William insisted on going to Manchester with her and actually seeing her on to the plane. Once he'd thought of the idea, he was adamant. The Grants gave him a day off willingly, there was nothing to stop him accompanying his mother-in-law, though she protested she neither needed nor wanted chaperoning. William, quite excited by his own chivalry, was not to be put off.

There were no farewell celebrations of any kind, as Maudie

162

and Sally were still not speaking. The only slight crack in the hostilities came two days before Maudie was due to leave, when Sally was sick into the kitchen sink and again in the yard later on. The mopping up done, Maudie made her daughter a cup of tea, and watched her narrowly as she sat down to drink it.

'You don't have to look like that,' Sally said, 'I haven't been drinking. I'm always like that the third month.'

Maudie tutted, and turned away.

'What you tutting at?' Sally asked. 'I can't help having another. There's no law against having babies is there? I don't have to apologise for that as well do I? Anyway, I don't mind. I like babies, the more the merrier.'

'God help it,' Maudie said, and thereby broke her long silence, but as a general exhortation it did not really count.

William and she were up at five in the morning. The Grants' car had after all been borrowed so there was no need for the early morning bus, but getting away still took time. Everyone else slept, Sally soundest of all, having said no goodbyes whatsoever. Sammy had vowed he would be up, but when Maudie went to take a peek at him he was, thankfully, giving very gentle snores. She was glad all the children had remained asleep. For one thing, it would be nice to remember them looking so beautiful and angelic, for another it meant no tears on her part. It was a clean, unfussy, unwearing break, and with a long journey ahead of her she needed such a calm start.

The two of them hardly talked at all, but Maudie had to admit that she enjoyed William's presence. He made all the little things easy for her, and she did not have to worry about her cases or where she was going. She arrived at the airport entirely unflurried thanks to him, and it was a relief, when she heard the roar and saw the aircraft taking off and landing, to have an arm to clutch at and someone to hear her 'Dear God!'

He sat stoically with her till her flight was called, not knowing any more than she did about how things were organised, but determined to see her through to the end. When they heard her number and moved towards the correct exit, he forced himself to go up to the young lady in uniform and ask her to look after his mother-in-law. As Maudie passed through the door, he gripped her hand hard and she said, 'Do you want me to go with a bad hand?' and he said 'No' and she said 'You're a good boy, William' and they both smiled, truly, at each other, and that was that.

'There now,' William found himself saying as he walked away. 'There now.'

PART THREE

ROBERT

CHAPTER ONE

Peace was so perfect on Comino that Robert was never wakened by noise, not even by the noise of the sea or the birds. It was always the light which woke him. He had grown so used to the varying degrees of the sun's brilliance, according to the hour, that he could open his eyes, realise it was only six o'clock, and go back to sleep again. He never got up before nine, and even then his getting up was an affair so leisurely it was hardly worthy of the name. He remained half in and half out of his bed for so long that he often forgot in which direction he was going.

Robert lived in a two-roomed stone hut on a rocky promontory overlooking a small bay at the uninhabited end of the island. Not much of the island was inhabited at all. In the centre was an almost derelict village containing the remnants of the four families who had not moved lock, stock and barrel to Malta, six miles away across the Mediterranean, or to Gozo, four miles in the other direction. There was also a new, luxury hotel, out to catch the holiday maker who wanted something different, to the south of the island on the largest and deepest bay. Then there were a dozen holiday bungalows still in construction. And there was Robert.

His house was not his in any legal sense whatever. He had slept in his tent till he found this derelict burrow, and then he had simply moved in and waited to see if anyone would object. Nobody did. This was perhaps because it was not exactly a prize possession. It was built completely of stone boulders, sandwiched together with a cement that was more hardened mud than the proper stuff. Its doorway was so small you almost had to go down on all fours to get in, and the only window was a gap in the wall overlooking the sea. The floor was flattened earth and there were no facilities whatsoever.

It had taken the resourceful Robert some six months to get his shelter comfortable. This was always the part of his entirely nomadic existence which he liked best. Everything he wanted which he had not brought with him in his rucksack had to be brought from Malta, which meant cadging a trip in the hotel boat, and the hotel was not, as a body, overfond of Robert the Tramp. He made, altogether, only four trips to Malta, and then he was satisfied and never went there again.

In those six months, the two-roomed hut had blossomed forth into a three-roomed home. Robert had built another wall, using the same materials as the original architects. One room was a storeroom, for Robert was truly Maudie's son in that he could not bear mess. In this space he had all his food neatly arranged on shelves, all his canvasses carefully stacked away, his spare bedding rolled up in one corner and all his possessions placed in piles around the walls, with labels attached to anything not immediately recognisable. The second room, which was surprisingly large once you were inside, was his kitchen. He had made another window, and a shutter for it. Here he had a Calor gas stove and a table he had made himself from wood stolen from the builders of the holiday bungalows. The last and largest room was his bed sitting-room and into this had gone the most care.

The room was oblong. The original window had been a one-boulder gap. Robert enlarged this to a four-boulder gap. He would have liked to have made it six but was worried that the whole wall might collapse. Even so, the resulting view of the bay made it seem that the room sat on the sea itself. The emerald green line of the horizon swam up and down the window all day long, and the rivulets of sand curved in and out of the corners according to the shallow tides. Stuck in the middle of the window like an ornamental support was the jetty where fishing boats, mostly smuggling, occasionally tied up.

On the floor was a carpet of rush matting which had taken

168

Robert two months to weave. There were no real rushes on the island, but there was a type of thick, tough grass which dried to the consistency of hemp. He had plaited this together into squares, and then sewn the squares together, rather loosely, so that the most worn parts would be easily replaceable. The walls—merely the insides of the boulders which Robert did not wish to spoil by covering up—were whitewashed. Now and again Robert had painted a motif to relieve the starkness. He had his easel set up in one corner, where the most light slanted in from the window, and his bed, covered with a Mexican blanket, in the other. It was a folding canvas bed he had always had, but double the normal width and with its own very comfortable inflatable mattress, for in some matters Robert was very civilised. For light when it was dark, there were three storm lanterns suspended on metal hooks from a strip of wood hammered on to two pillars at either end of the room.

That completed the inside. Outside, Robert had built a lean-to and made a primitive lavatory, for hygiene was another of his strong points. He washed mainly in the sea, keeping his fresh water in a cask near the kitchen. This he got from a well in the village, about two miles away, and it was therefore very precious. Robert was always very careful to boil it before he drank any. He had a crate of bottled water he'd bought from the hotel for emergencies.

When Maudie came, Robert had been living on Comino for nearly a year, and he was almost ready to move on. He felt that he was almost ready without actually fixing in his mind any date for going. He was not discontented with the island: rather the reverse. Every day, he appreciated it just a little more. But he was beginning to feel that restlessness which made him want to do the whole thing again. The satisfaction in wandering around, as he had done the last eight years, lay in the discovery of a new place, the making of a new home, the establishing of a new routine and the drawing from it of new pleasures.

His homes had not always been nearly deserted islands—it

was only as his tastes had become more sophisticated that he had developed a taste for those. He had started off, like many before him, in St Tropez and led there the brightly coloured beatnik life in keeping with the newly acquired tradition of the place. He had shared a house with six others. Then he had moved to Israel with two of the original six, and then to America with one of them, and he had moved around America for nearly four years, going from New York to California, from city to country and back again. Finally, he had come back to Europe on his own and spent a few months in Italy before finding Comino.

All these meanderings had been financed not just by the odd jobs any man can find in most places, but by Robert's savings as a schoolteacher in the years before he left England, and by his fairly regular sale of articles to travel magazines. As a schoolteacher, he had been well off in a generally impoverished profession, since he had a physics degree from Glasgow university. He had saved carefully and methodically till he had one thousand pounds, and that remained his capital, of which, at the end of eight years, he still had four hundred pounds left. When his capital had gone, he would be quite ready to go and earn some more. He would even enjoy doing so.

Robert saw nothing remarkable in his life. It seemed to him ideal, something everyone should do. He could not understand those who valued material possessions and got themselves bogged down in the struggle to get them. Nor could he understand those who drifted without resources, so that their freedom was a continual lesson in the degradation that comes from being dependent on circumstances. Robert considered himself truly independent, in that he was master of his own fortunes. He was not happy-go-lucky. He was not a bum. He was not an escapist. He was a very shrewd, cautious Scotsman who had worked out exactly what he wanted and then set about getting it.

To look at, Robert might have been exactly what he had been: a schoolteacher. He was small, thin, pale, holding himself very erect and walking with precise little steps as though he was picking his way over sharp points. He wore glasses and had a neat black beard more because of the obvious reasons of convenience than anything else. His hair was always combed, parted down the left side and kept very short, almost crewcut. He cut it himself once a week with nail scissors and had some years ago invested in clippers to do the sides and back. Although in the open air so much, his skin remained untanned. He was naturally sallow, but the sallowness had remained that unhealthy post-jaundice colour and had never somehow deepened to brown.

Robert nearly always wore the same clothes: khaki knee-length shorts and a drill shirt. He had three sets and wore them for two days each, washing them immediately he took them off. The rest of his wardrobe consisted of a polo-necked grey sweater, a tweed jacket, a pair of long drill trousers, a pair of flannels, a white shirt and two short-sleeved checked shirts. He had four pairs of shoes—canvas espadrilles, tough brogues, wellingtons and soft leather slip-ons. All were regularly renewed, except the wellingtons which he had had since Glasgow. The last item was a plastic pack-a-mac.

Robert's expression was a habitual serious look, not so much stern or worried as calm and contemplative. His face, although he was nearly forty, was virtually unlined because he taxed the skin and muscles so little. He hardly ever smiled or frowned and thus his brow was unfurrowed. He got plenty of rest and sleep and therefore had no shadows under his eyes. He remained always at the same weight, and was never ill. He never lost his temper or got particularly excited. He had no nervous mannerisms or twitches.

Yet for all this, Robert was, to most people, an alarming individual. He was, for example, very rude. He would walk away in the middle of a conversation, he would deliberately ignore your greeting in the street, he would tell you to your face that you bored him or nauseated him or that he couldn't stand the sight of you. He was very mean, too, never standing anyone a drink or a meal. It was impossible to pressgang him into hospitality, and he was known as the sort of man who earned Scotsmen their reputation. But the most alarming thing about him was, people thought, his selfishness, which was of a kind so complete and engrossing that it made you forget everything else.

On Comino there had been until recently—until Eleanor in fact—no one to be bowled over by this selfishness. Robert did not belong to any community, he had no contacts. Being selfish on one's own is an unrewarding business. Having been told often enough how selfish he was Robert often tried to work out whether, in his present circumstances, it was not a contradiction in terms, or at least a logical impossibility. It was, in any case, not at the moment true, for by having his mother to stay he was, he felt, earning himself future redemption.

Robert's relationship with Maudie was a very strange one. His letters to her were designed to be famous, but they were not, as anyone with any knowledge of Robert ought to have realised, letters to her at all. They were essays, weekly essays most painstakingly executed, beautifully written. They were stylistically perfect—and quite unreal. They were, in fact, letters from Robert to Robert. True, they showed a most touching concern for the person they were ostensibly sent to, but on examination this concern consisted mainly of a string of endearments, quite foreign to Robert's nature, and certainly to Maudie's. But he enjoyed putting them in. He thought they read well, and he liked to begin and end with something informal. When he read the copy over, as he regularly did, he thought them rather a master touch. They would look well in book form when the collected edition was published.

The last letter Robert had sent to Maudie had been full of the joys of the life he led which she was soon to share. He had dwelt on the peace, on the beauty, on the freedom—two paragraphs to each. He had told her how she would take the simple island to her heart. Being a realist, he knew of course that this was a load of absolute rubbish. His mother would go raving

172

mad on Comino. She would leave within twenty-four hours. And that was in part why he was letting her come.

At first, when she had suggested the idea, he had thought how ridiculous it was and had prepared a draft letter saying, in the most regretful terms, that the roughness of his present existence precluded such a visit. But then he had begun to toy with the notion of Maudie coming and it had quickly taken on a sort of fascination for him. The whole perversity of the encounter was irresistible. There he was, separated from his mother for eight years and during that time choosing her, for the want of anyone else, as the recipient of his polished, intimate letters that were going to be of such importance. She must have forgotten what he was like. She must by now be so enchanted by him that any meeting would be a traumatic experience. Robert could not resist the thought.

He had, he fancied, no illusions about his mother or about himself. He knew quite well her good points and her bad points. He knew she had what everyone called a hard life with his boisterous, violent father, and that this had made her resentful, if not disbelieving, of anyone else's happiness. Quite why she had set off on her travels Robert was not as yet sure. He expected to be able to decide after the first hour with her. It might just be, her husband having finally left her, at this ludicrously late date, she wanted to get away from everything. It might be some long-buried wanderlust. It might be a search for the affection she had been so long starved of. Or it might, and this Robert felt was nearest the mark, be an attempt to establish her claim to them all. He could imagine her thinking 'Now is the time for them to pay me back: now is the time for me to draw my dividend.'

Robert had given long and serious thought to this question of whether children owed gratitude, either material or emotional. He had come to the predictable conclusion that they didn't, but not by the usual channels. He was not so childish that he said 'I never asked to be born so I owe you nothing.' He considered this had very little to do with it. What he thought important was the recognition of natural bonds between parent and child. This was the true test: if you felt any bonds, however resented, however undeserved, did exist then there was no doubt that they must be openly accepted and responsibility acknowledged. If you felt none, then you had nothing to worry about. The interesting thing was that Robert felt some.

The realisation that he could not regard his mother as he did Mrs A. or Mrs B. came as a shock to him. He had always thought he merely used his mother for his own limited purposes. Certainly, he had never felt any obligation to support her, or be concerned in her life in any way. He had never worried about her, or felt it was up to him to look after her. He did not love her. He did not admire her. He did not, as far as he could remember, even like her. But sitting there, thinking about it, he also found he had an interest in her. It was amazing, but it was true—he was definitely sufficiently connected with her not to be able to say, even in the recesses of his own mind, that he did not feel she was any part of him. She was, not just biologically, but mentally.

Preparing a camp bed for Maudie—which he put in the store room—it occurred to Robert, for the first time, that the situation he was letting himself into might just be dangerous. He knew well enough that though he could regard the arrival of his mother with equanimity, ready to stand back and observe the scene, she might be incapable of doing so. He did not think she was prone to nervous hysteria. As a child, he could only remember her crying in a calculated sort of way. She had a contempt for what she called whining. But that was a long time ago, and she was now quite old. She might be incapable of restraining her emotions. Yet somehow he felt a lifetime's habit would die hard.

He was meeting Maudie on Malta at the airport. She would have done well enough to get herself that far without facing the journey across the island by car and then by boat to Comino on her own. It was really, Robert thought, rather splendid to think of her making all the arrangements and getting herself on a plane and so forth. It showed her will power and determination had not deteriorated. She might well still be a match for him.

They were still willing to let him on the hotel boat, which was just as well as there was really no other regular way of getting to and from Malta. The Gozo boat was much more infrequent and did not always call at Comino. Robert went to the front of the craft and sat on the ropes, ignoring the greetings of the Maltese and the hotel proprietor's son. He sat watching the rocky bays slip past to his right. The boat chugged along very slowly, although the sea was quite calm. Sometimes the island was cut off for weeks, the sea in the strait between Malta and Comino a heaving mass more like the winter Channel than a Mediterranean bay. It was always possible for anyone really determined to get across, but at the first sign of difficulty both sets of islands gave up readily. Robert was toying with the idea of buying a small boat of his own to make himself really independent of their whims. There seemed little point in living on an island without a boat, and yet always there was the thought that he might not go on living on an island for much longer.

The boat, the sea, the slowness of the journey kept further analysis of Maudie out of his mind. It was not until he had crossed Malta and was waiting at the airport that he bothered to think of her again—and even then he thought more of Jean and Sally and how they had got on with her than of his mother. It amused him to think she had been so careful to visit them in order of seniority. It would really have been much simpler to fly from Glasgow or London instead of trailing from Sally's outlandish village to Manchester. But fair was fair, no matter what the inconvenience, and he must come last. Well, it suited him.

He sat in the small, cool waiting area watching a Maltese family bidding farewell to what was obviously an elder son going off to England to seek his fortune. There were about twenty of them, all clustered round the departing hero, full of tearful last words, all excited, half-proud and half-fearful. It went on at all the small airports in the world. Robert remembered particularly the almost frenetic emotion of Shannon, where aspiring Kennedys flew off daily by the score, borne into the air on a rising tide of wails. He could not help smiling at the thought of his own silent departure from Glasgow. It would never have entered his head to let anyone but his mother know that he was going, for if he had only just discovered that she had some meaning for him, he had known all his life that his sisters had none.

The plane landed on time. He stood up and moved towards the exit. He wanted to see his mother enter the hall and walk across it. First in were the usual business men, followed by the holiday makers, all immediately claimed by hotel representatives. Last through the door was a stewardess, holding by the arm his mother. Robert drew back even further into the corridor and looked at her. Physically, she had only aged. He thought this surprising. Her face, her walk, even her expressions were exactly the same, merely older. As he watched her firmly remove the stewardess's arm, push her glasses back on to her nose, where they were already securely anchored, and look around her sharply, accusingly, he was confused to find that he actually experienced tenderness for her. It made him smile furtively to himself. Then, very slowly, he walked towards his mother.

CHAPTER TWO

The anti-climax was, for Maudie, quite physically painful. Meeting Jean and Sally she had expected so little and dreaded so much that the reality had been a relief. They had both had husbands and children and what with these distractions and the additional worry over her luggage on both arrivals, it had really been easy getting over the first hurdles. But with Robert it was bound to be different. She had become so confused by his letters that she had almost forgotten what he looked like and how he spoke. Then he was on his own. It was a face to face encounter, smack on, with nothing and nobody to help.

He didn't speak. She saw him coming towards her, smiling slightly, and she was ready with a rather choky sounding 'Robert' and a kiss if he wanted one. But he didn't say anything, just went on smiling, and patted her on the shoulder, and began to lead her very gently towards the door. She was numbed. Almost frightened, she allowed herself to be led to a car, where her son seated her courteously in the front with the driver, saying she would get fewer bumps there, while he himself sat in the back. The car started and Robert began to describe Malta as they drove through it, but she did not hear a word. She sat, instead, thinking wildly inconsequential things like 'hasn't he got thin', 'isn't his shirt clean for a man who looks after himself', and 'how short his fingernails are'.

On the boat, they sat together at the front. The two men and the boy who were the crew were all in the cabin. They sat prominently isolated, Robert with one ankle neatly crossed over the other, and his arms folded.

'It's a twenty-minute sail,' he said

'Oh yes,' Maudie said.

'Quite pleasant when it is calm.'

'I expect so,' Maudie said.

'When it's rough we don't leave the island.'

'No, I expect not,' Maudie said.

'But it isn't often very rough.'

'That's a good thing.'

'Over there, you can just see Gozo.' Robert unfolded one of his arms to point. Maudie strained to see, but, unaccountably, her spectacles were misted over and she had to spend such a long time cleaning them that Gozo had disappeared on the horizon before her vision was clear.

'Very soon,' Robert said, 'we will get our first glimpse of Comino. To the south of the island . . .'

Maudie could not concentrate. His slow, Scots voice droned on telling her, she was sure, millions of fascinating things, but she simply could not take it in. She wondered why she did not tell him to shut up and let an old body have some peace instead of lecturing her like a professor. She would have told Jean. She would have told Sally. But she could not even interrupt Robert, never mind actually raise her voice to be angry with him. She sat slumped beside him, feeling humble and useless, and not wanting him to see how she was failing him.

She wanted to look at him properly. For a few seconds, as he had walked towards her at the airport, she had had a chance to meet his eyes, but she had not taken it. Now, as the need to do this became more urgent, she was awkwardly placed. They were sitting side by side and she could not think how to look at him properly without standing up and facing him, as though to ask him to dance. That was too silly to even contemplate. So she went on stealing furtive looks at him, and all the time longing to see if her own embarrassment and tenderness were mirrored in his eyes.

It would explain everything. Her heart, she told herself, had gone out to him when he had separated them in the car. It was a device she well understood. His carefully chosen conversations about the weather and the geography of the islands were just such as she would have picked herself in the circumstances. Jean would have mucked everything up with foolish endearments, but not Robert. His restraint and tact, while they made her ache, were what she would most want to see in her son.

Then, quite suddenly, the boat turned slightly and, finding herself off balance, Maudie put out an arm to steady herself at the same time as Robert reached to do just that. They met in an embrace so complete that for a moment Maudie's nose was pushed right up against Robert's chest. Instantly, they both recoiled, with the effect of holding each other at arm's length. They could do nothing but stare at each other.

'I should have warned you,' Robert said.

Maudie could only gasp, and search shakily for her handkerchief.

'We're nearly there,' Robert said, and returned to his previous position.

Maudie never read anything into other people's expressions. She kept such a careful guard on her own, she thought, that she knew people could not be interpreted by their looks. She always criticised scathingly those who professed to be able to tell when others were offended or sad or angry. It was all too likely folk were wide of the mark when they began labelling a nose and eyes and mouth, all quite silent, as saying something. But nevertheless, Robert's face, so closely scrutinised in those minutes they confronted each other, quite plainly said something to Maudie. It said something because it said nothing. His eyes were blank. She knew for shattering certainty that he was hiding nothing of value. There was no disturbance going on in his head. Any unease must have been transitory, for there was none there now. He didn't need to flinch from looking at her because he had nothing to conceal.

Maudie thought for one thunderstruck minute that the Comino hotel was Robert's home. There was the long, low, glittering white building as they rounded the point into the wide bay, but then Robert was at her elbow saying quietly that that was the hotel and he lived round the corner, and she was instantly cross with herself for being so silly.

Her legs, when she stepped on to the jetty, felt very weak indeed. On the water, she had not noticed the heat, but now it struck her and she gasped and felt giddy. Robert took her cases and they began to walk very slowly up the path.

Robert stopped and looked at his mother. She was very white. Her spectacles looked as though they were going to mist over any minute. It was mid afternoon and the rough cart track over the hill to his hut was going to be in the full glare of the sun. He went ahead with the cases into the hotel.

The lounge of the hotel was a large, square patio, with a tiled floor and a fountain playing in the middle. It was cool and dark and Maudie sighed with relief. They sat on a sofa, and presently someone brought them long, sparkling drinks with ice floating on the top and Maudie was too grateful to ask what it was. She drank and felt better.

'The heat's terrible at this time of day,' Robert said, 'yet in another hour it starts getting cool and by supper-time you'll need a jacket outside.'

They sat quietly drinking, and the minute they had finished Robert led the way outside.

The track to his hut was made of roughly broken stones, covered with layers of thick white dust. It began near the hotel, as a fairly broad and regular road, but within twenty yards, where it forked left to the village and right to Robert's bay, it had shrunk to a footpath. In spite of its width, the first stretch was the worst. It went steeply uphill and faced directly into the sun. Once they had turned right, there was the breeze from the sea to help, always there however hot the day, and it was flat, quickly becoming downhill. Robert had no patience with people who had to point out the beauties of the scenery to others. If they didn't notice it for themseves, they would probably be oblivious to any prodding. And there was always the chance that, like him, they were noticing but saw no need to advertise the fact.

Robert's silence kept Maudie's amazement at the island in check. The awfulness of Comino only just began to strike her towards the end of their walk. It gradually dawned on her that they had not passed a single shop. One did not expect anything like a supermarket in a place like this—she wasn't stupid—but there wasn't even a corner shop. Did they have vans, then? She searched hopefully for a mobile butcher's or suchlike, but nothing passed them. Then an even greater truth penetrated: there were no houses, either. Since that hotel they hadn't seen or passed a single building of any kind. No shops, no houses, and lastly no people. Nobody on their way to or from anything. Not only no English people but no foreigners either, not one.

A deep unease began to stir in Maudie. What kind of place had she been lured to? It was like the island that man was always talking about in 'Desert Island Discs' on the Light Programme, where you were a castaway and had to fend for yourself. Perhaps only Robert lived here. This thought, instead of giving her pleasure, terrified her, and she had a wretched five minutes before she remembered the hotel. There was a guarantee that humanity was not far off. The perspiration flowed faster with the comfort of it.

All this while, Maudie peered eagerly ahead at every twist and turn waiting to see Robert's house. She vaguely expected it to be some sort of white bungalow with, perhaps, coloured shutters and a flat roof like the prefabs. She wasn't expecting anything grand. After all, he was a bachelor and not likely to care much about houses. But she was sure it would be a decent enough wee place.

'Isn't it,' Robert suddenly said, 'the most perfect situation imaginable? Can you think of a better background for a house than that sea?'

Maudie saw before her what might have been a Highland cattle pen. A small, an unbelievably small, square, squat stone

181

shed, perched on a rock in the middle of nowhere with all that nasty wet water only feet away. She shuddered. She felt physically sick. She could not even manage a 'Dear God'.

Miserable, Maudie allowed herself to be led forward. She stood silently on the threshold and looked at the bare and primitive interior. No wallpaper. No proper carpet. No chairs. No glass in the windows. No electric light. To think a son of hers, used to such comfort and all mod. cons., could have been reduced to this! Maudie tottered towards the bed and sat down heavily upon it, pretending to be overcome with the heat. She busied herself mopping her face with Kleenex tissues until her horror had subsided a little, and all the time she held her tongue for she must not let Robert—poor, poor Robert—see how much she minded for him.

She clutched the tea Robert had thrust into her hand and evaded his eyes. She sipped the tea gratefully, and shot sidelong looks about her, trying to work out where she was going to sleep and where there could possibly be room for a lavatory. She thought the place could not take much looking after—there was nothing to dust, nothing to polish, no fires to spread dirt. The minute she had realised this, she suddenly wondered what on earth she was going to do. If cleaning Robert's house would not take five minutes, what else would there be left in the day to do? She could not sit idle. She had hardly any knitting wool left and there was nowhere to buy any more. Outside, the loathsome sun would keep her from going for walks, even if walking on that rough path had held any prospect of pleasure. She would not be able to chat or make calls, for there was no one to do either with. She would quite definitely go raving mad. Carefully, so the hawk-eyed Robert would not notice her shaking hand, Maudie replaced the cup on its saucer.

The first evening was not, after all, quite so shatteringly dreadful as Maudie had spent the whole afternoon thinking it would be. There were people to ask after, conditions of health and wealth to be described, details of her trip to go into. It was, in many ways, easier than the awkward arrivals at her daughters' households. Robert made her a very creditable meal on his primus stove, and then the darkness seemed to come quite quickly and she could justifiably go to bed, with the comfortable feeling that they would manage after all.

It was the strangest bedroom Maudie had ever slept in. She could find nowhere to hang her clothes except on the back of canvasses, which did not seem right, nor were there any drawers or cupboards whatsoever. All she could see was one long shelf running along the wall the length of the bed. Upon this she arranged her most important possessions, and had to leave her other belongings inside their cases. She was upset to realise there was nothing on the floor, not even a small rug. It was bare stone, hideously cold even through her nylon plush slippers. If she got up during the night, as she would most certainly be called upon to, she would have to swing her legs over the side of the bed and negotiate her shoes with great precision. The thought of going outside to that dark and primitive lavatory gave her the shakes.

Somehow, Maudie got settled in the narrow camp bed after several vain attempts. The first time she got in, she knew immediately that she would have to put something between the sheet and the canvas of the bed, even if it meant sacrificing warmth above. So she clambered out and completely re-made the bed, putting the thickest blanket below, doubled over, to act as a mattress. But then she had overlooked the fact that, with nothing to tuck them into, the bedclothes let in terrible draughts at the bottom. Gamely, Maudie applied herself to this problem and concluded that her shoes would weight the bed at the bottom if she kept her feet very still. Her last discomfort was lack of pillows. Robert had provided one small cushion which was no good at all. Maudie needed three plump, substantial pillows before she could face a night with any confidence. She made do with all her woollies pushed into her nightdress case.

After all this labouring, she felt very exhausted, but knew that would not necessarily mean that she would sleep well. For one thing, she was still not really comfortable, and for another she was *too* tired, which was almost as bad as not being tired at all. She tried to console herself with the reflection that first nights were always disastrous wherever she went, so this one was going to be no worse than it would have been anywhere else. Except that of course it was worse because in addition to everything else she was frightened. Not badly frightened, but undeniably fearful.

It was a strange, unreasonable fear that gently washed over her, as the sea was washing the sand outside. She knew Robert was next door, but he was only one against what could be wild tribes sweeping upon them from all sides. Maudie hated the lack of locks and bolts. Anyone could walk in and there was nothing to stop them. Robert had said the island was practically unpopulated, but who knew what bandits lurked behind that hill? Then there was the water, so horribly near, so silent and deep. Robert said there was only a slight tide, but supposing there was a storm in the night and they were engulfed by giant breakers? Or even without a storm, which would after all wake her, smugglers could come upon this little bay and just fancy it for their hideout. It would be the work of five minutes to tie Robert up and dump herself in the sea.

Frowning, Maudie smoothed the sheets with her already sweaty hands. The perspiration was breaking out all over her. She heard scratchings outside and her mind leapt from people to animals. There must be countless wild beasts roaming around, ravenous with hunger, ready to slip into this hut in search of food. Even if they did not attack her, the very sound and sight of them would cause a stroke. It occurred to her that the camp bed was very near to the ground—an agile snake could scale that metal support with no trouble at all. Robert would find her in the morning quite dead with only a small black swelling on her neck to show where the bite had been.

Maudie began to say the Lord's Prayer over and over again.

She had always resorted to this when she was frightened in the middle of the night. She knew she had never not been frightened since Joseph left. However much she loathed him, his huge snoring presence had been enough to quieten any qualms at noises she heard. Since she had been on her own, she had started taking sensible precautions early in the evening so that by the time it was really dark and eerie she did not need to stir to see that doors were locked and windows tightly secure. In the buildings, she knew all the night sounds so well that she was half-ashamed to lie awake worrying at all. It was just a recent development she could not help.

Now, in Robert's flimsy shelter, she longed for the security of her own home. If only she could be there, she would sleep with all the doors and windows wide open, for there, she now felt, there was nothing at all to fear. With the Lord's Prayer on its sixth airing, Maudie was still rigid with a terror that was growing, not abating—she started to have waking nightmares in which she distrusted even Robert. She wished passionately there was another woman in the place, any woman, instead of just a man. She did not like to have the company of one male, even if he was her son. She was so much more at ease with women.

As the sweating and trembling began to make her praying wildly inaccurate, Maudie suddenly heard Robert whistling next door, very softly but clearly. He must be going to bed when she had thought him long since there. The tune was the Road to the Isles and every now and again he sang the refrain before going back to the whistling. When he got to the end, he went through the whole thing twice more, and then he stopped, whistled a couple of odd lines and lapsed into silence.

Maudie found she had automatically relaxed even before he had finished. She joined in the song in her head, and hummed the chorus aloud, and cursed herself for being a silly old fool. It was disgraceful to act like a child and be so frightened of senseless, imaginary things. To have lived all her life, only to end it unable to get a night's sleep, even with her own son next door, because she was afraid of the dark! Maudie felt she ought to be smacked, and so delighted herself with her verdict that she lay awake quite happily for a good while before falling into a light doze.

'Dear God,' Maudie complained, 'I've hardly set foot in your home and you're already suggesting we leave it.'

'I thought you wouldn't feel like settling down right away,' Robert said blandly.

'How many hundred miles did I come yesterday?' Maudie shouted. 'All that way and we're off on day trips already.'

'It isn't a day trip,' Robert explained, pleasantly, 'it's only a few minutes on the boat. It's like someone showing you round the neighbourhood.'

'Some neighbourhood,' Maudie said.

'There's no need to go if you don't want to.'

'Oh, I do what I'm told,' Maudie said. 'I'm just a guest.'

Grumbling and muttering, she began to make tea to fill her thermos. Robert packed his knapsack and smiled secretly into it. He knew quite well that she was dying to go out for the day, and that this protest was to conceal her pleasure. She had always been like that. The more she wanted a thing the more she had to pretend that she didn't want it at all. Recognising this trait all over again, he felt indulgent towards her, and took her arm tenderly as they set out.

'Why in heaven's name don't they tarmac this road?' Maudie asked.

'Because nobody uses it except me,' Robert said, and then, to tease her: 'Anyway, tarmac would look awful.'

'Who cares about looks?' Maudie snapped. 'It's folk's shoe leather I'm thinking of. You want to get on to the council about it.'

'I'll do that,' Robert promised, solemnly.

As they neared the hotel jetty, two bikini clad girls came out of the building and began to walk towards the beach. They smiled at Robert and Maudie.

'God in Heaven,' Maudie hissed.

'They're going swimming,' Robert said.

'Going what?' Maudie barked. 'They're going to tempt decent young men into wrong doing.'

'I don't know where they're going to find them, then,' Robert murmured, but his mother's attention had already been diverted to the three young waiters sitting at a table, whistling and combing their hair.

'I could never eat or drink in that place again,' Maudie said vehemently. 'Never. Not after seeing that contamination.'

'What was being contaminated?' Robert asked, mildly. 'The table wasn't set.'

'Germs breed everywhere,' Maudie said. 'You could almost see them breeding on that filthy comb.'

It went on like that throughout the long and gruelling day. By eleven in the morning Robert was heartily sick of his mother's endless sermonising and her deliberate distortion of events. It was no joke. She seemed incapable of accepting anything at its face value, incapable of removing from her mind a load of prejudices so restricting that they amounted to a way of life. He told himself that in her own sick and peculiar fashion she was enjoying herself, that the more things went wrong, the more highlights she would have to remember. But this conviction waned with the day. He became instead quite sure that her sniping was all part of a deep and undying war against everyone and everything.

At first, he played the idiot, always appearing not to understand the nastier of her implications. He was carefully and unfailingly amiable, refusing to fight over the principles she was forever dragging up. He saw his role as a passive one. He would be sponge-like, the better to absorb her venom. When she tore into the natives of Gozo as filthy, illiterate scum, just typical of foreigners, he let her continue and only fractionally edged her towards a group of fishermen mending nets with a nimble dexterity she could never have seen before. When she sneered at the food they had for lunch, and wailed for fresh

187

tea, he reminisced loudly about the boarding house in Rothesay where they had once been given half a kipper each for high
tea, and one margarined scone.

But the effect of her miserable intolerance was exhausting.
Robert felt crushed by her almost militant criticisms. Soon,
without really intending to, he was attacking her, with disastrous effect.

'That's right,' Maudie said. 'Side with them against your
own mother.'

'I'm not siding with anybody,' Robert said. 'I merely pointed
out to you that if you live on a hot, Mediterranean island you
cannot be expected to behave and dress as if you lived in
Glasgow.'

'And why not?' Maudie asked. 'Isn't Glasgow good enough
for you now?'

'You're not being logical,' Robert said.

'Why should I be?' Maudie said.

Robert stared at her. She looked so ridiculous, tensed and
glowering like an angry pekinese dog, that he had to laugh.

'You're marvellous,' he said.

He did not think she was marvellous at all. He thought she
was an irritating old woman. He was bored with her sharp
little voice and her sour expression. As they boarded the boat
home, he was mentally preparing himself to go into an emotional coma for the rest of her stay. She could go to hell. He
refused to upset himself over her. She was a silly, cussed old
fool who had deliberately rejected the friendliness with which
he had prepared himself to greet her. If she didn't want to
know him, she needn't. If she wanted to keep the stiff and
distant relationship of former years, let her. He had tried,
whatever Eleanor said. Immediately, having thought of
Eleanor, he wanted to argue the point with her. It annoyed
and infuriated him that he wouldn't be able to, for Eleanor
had enforced her own abolition from the scene until Robert
could gently break the news of her existence to his mother.
Originally, Robert had intended to tell Maudie about Eleanor

188

over a period of a week or so, gradually preparing the way. After one day, he now could not wait to do it like that. It would all have to come out in one piece and Eleanor be sent for at once. He needed his mistress to help him get over his mother.

When it came to telling his mother about Eleanor, Robert handled the situation even more ineptly than Eleanor had forecast. 'Don't,' she had begged, 'use the word mistress.'

'O.K.,' he had said. 'Whore will do.'

'Don't be cruel, Robert,' she had begged again, 'let her down easily. Say I'm your girlfriend. Say I sometimes pop over. Say I'm married already, happily. Say I'm more of a business acquaintance.'

'I'll say I love you,' Robert had said.

'No, no,' Eleanor screamed, 'don't say you love me. She would hate you using that word. You're her son. You must just like me.'

Robert remembered all her instructions.

'What a day,' Maudie was saying, as they entered the hut. 'And then only this to come back to. Really, Robert.'

'Eleanor likes it,' Robert said.

His mother made no pretence not to have heard. She took off her hat, stuck the hat pin carefully through it and carried it through to what was now her room. Then she came slowly back.

'It was quite a nice day, in the end,' she said.

Oh no, Robert thought, you don't catch me like that.

'I'm sorry you hated it,' he said. 'It was Eleanor's idea.'

'It made a change,' Maudie said.

Come on, come on, ask about Eleanor, Robert wanted to shout.

'That's what Eleanor thought,' he said.

'Well then,' Maudie said, 'you may as well tell me about her, if I can be bothered to listen. She must be a foolish young lady any road.'

'She's very beautiful and I love her,' Robert said, surprised at himself.

Maudie laughed, and snorted, and, apparently, could hardly conceal her derision. Eleanor, Robert thought, would have wept for her.

CHAPTER THREE

Eleanor was not an immediately attractive girl. She was small and thin, rather sallow skinned, with large nose and mouth and teeth, but also large and very compelling eyes of a grey-green colour which were beautiful and made you forget her other features. Her hair was ordinary brown, dull and strawy-looking, and she wore it coiled on top of her head in an old-fashioned, untidy bun. She was always complaining about her hair, but if it was suggested that if it was as awful as she maintained it might be a good idea to have it cut off, she immediately leapt to its defence. It would look terrible short. Its one hope, apparently, lay in letting it have 'shape'. So she kept it long and it always looked a mess.

Eleanor's large, faintly discoloured teeth protruded slightly, giving her a gawkish look. Her clothes added to that impression. She hated dresses, and wore either trousers or skirts and long, loose, striped sweaters. She went bare-legged or wore three-quarter-length white cotton socks, and denim sneakers. She had an interesting collection of bags, all huge, all with shoulder straps. Some were wide and made of straw, some long and narrow and made of hessian. They were all decorative and an inescapable part of her personality.

Eleanor was very frank. She prided herself on never pretending to like anyone or anything if this was not the case. Her main passion in life was health, both physical and mental. She was a devoted amateur student of psychology and could explain everything in terms of 'periods of equilibrium and disequilibrium'. In this, she was very American, but in her snobbishness she was very English. It was difficult to define exactly how she was a snob. Certainly not in the class or money sense—not precisely. It was more a matter of intellect. Some people were intelligent and some were not. Her highest mark of praise was to say that someone had turned out to be 'quite intelligent', or that she had had an 'intelligent' conversation with them.

Like most frank, confident, overpowering people, Eleanor was fond of describing herself as shy, retiring, hesitant and so forth. Nobody ever noticed these traits. Eleanor said she had difficulty making social contacts. To any observer, she seemed to have no difficulty at all. She also said she was a 'depressive worrier' which always struck any listener as very amusing indeed. It was impossible to imagine that Eleanor left any area of her existence private enough to be worried over. She seemed to tell her all to all and be incapable of brooding. But as she got very upset at any refusal to believe this claim, people tried to hide their amusement and pretend they believed her.

Eleanor lied about her age at all times and both ways. She was twenty-nine but operated a sliding scale covering the decade from twenty to thirty. Sometimes, she even attempted to try the teens—late teens, nineteen or eighteen and a half— and noticed with pleasure, but also with some contempt, that this was accepted unquestioningly. Why she did it, she did not know. She liked to think that it had begun as a genuine mistake on her part, but that seemed a bit feeble. It was a game, that was all, just a game she played with people's gullibility, and to show too what an arbitrary and silly thing age was.

Another point Eleanor habitually lied about was her financial position. Usually, she claimed to be a student, eking out a precarious grant by selling the odd painting. If anyone questioned the source of a grant that enabled her to roam the world at will, it became a travelling scholarship, or a prize, or a part of a most off-beat course at a little-known off-beat university. Sometimes, she didn't bother with the grant part. Since she had met Robert, she had fancied the idea of having saved like him, and she now used this explanation quite a lot. But in fact, Eleanor was very rich and supported by her father, or rather by the independent income she got as a member of her father's company. This company was a shoe manufacturing company and had dealings in twenty American states. Eleanor never told anyone this, and they never guessed because she neither talked nor dressed nor behaved like someone who was rich and independent. She was smart enough to know that, in the circles in which she wished to move, it would have been a very dangerous confession. As no one else was rich, it would have made her an easy, obvious touch. And material, shoe-manufactured wealth would have been thought rather disreputable.

Currently, Eleanor was working at a hotel in Malta. She was a receptionist/guide there, taken on to cope with the increasing number of American tourists. She nearly always had some job because it was a good cover, and anyway she liked working at menial jobs, as most people do who know they don't have to. She could rattle off a long list of things she had been, from waitress to mortuary attendant to postman. You name it, the adventurous Eleanor had been it.

No one could imagine Eleanor making a success of any of her jobs. She was too cheeky. She lacked application. As receptionist/guide of a Maltese hotel she was a disaster. She was supposed to be helpful and kind, to know what her fellow countrymen would want, to be a tactful liaison officer between hotel and customer. She was none of these things. On the very first day, she nearly lost her job for not being respectful enough. They only kept her on because she was satisfied with so little money, and was always willing.

Eleanor had come across Robert quite by accident. She had visited Comino, as a thing one did, and had wandered around the place as she was used to doing on her own. She had seen Robert's hut and Robert outside painting and they had fallen quite naturally into conversation. It had seemed a very short time before they were having a most satisfactory affair. The most marvellous thing about this affair was the placid approach of both of them to it. They were almost smug in their casualness. Neither ever made arrangements to meet again, neither took it upon themselves to make any plans at all. This, for two highly organised people, was quite an achievement.

When Robert had told Eleanor his mother was coming her concern had been immediate. His mother must not know about their affair. It would hurt her cruelly. She, Eleanor, could predict exactly what would happen. So she had painstakingly moved out of Robert's hut all the belongings she had accumulated there over the six months period she had known him. She was prepared not to see him again for the whole four months Maudie was staying. This Robert thought ridiculous. He could not bring himself to admit that the thought of four months without Eleanor appalled him. Instead, he kept insisting on it being ridiculous. Eleanor, who knew he meant not ridiculous but unbearable, was happy and proud and said alright, she would visit. She would creep in, the soul of tact, and creep out again, just whenever Robert thought the time suitable.

Eleanor was very alarmed to get Robert's message saying she must come at once a mere two days after his mother had arrived. She worried about what had gone wrong all the way over on the boat, and by the time she landed in Comino she had worked herself into a state of acute anxiety. It was such a bad way to meet Robert's mother—assuming, that is, that something *had* gone wrong and she had been sent for to ease the situation. Mrs Tipstaff would resent and hate her, Eleanor could quite see that. Whatever time they had met, she, Eleanor, was bound to have difficulties, belonging as she did to an entirely different generation and race. She knew she would look and sound all wrong, and that the great goodwill, even love, she felt for Mrs Tipstaff would never come through.

Almost trembling with worry, Eleanor walked down to the path leading to Robert's hut, realising as she did that her timing was bad. Robert would be out walking. He always was at that time of day. She would be bursting in on his mother and confronting her alone. She hesitated at the thought, and began walking even more quickly down the hill.

Eleanor met Maudie on the doorstep. Neither spoke. Maudie frowned, and Eleanor blushed and said, 'I'm Eleanor——'

'Robert isn't in,' Maudie snapped.

'Oh, I know,' Eleanor said, 'he always goes walking around now. He has this great need for silent communication with nature. Now I'm the opposite—I need to communicate with people. I'd just go mad on my own. Are you like that, Mrs Tipstaff?'

Maudie glared. 'I don't know, I'm sure,' she said, tight-lipped. 'Are you coming in or not? This is no place to blather.'

Eleanor followed her inside. Maudie turned, still standing, and seemed prepared for a long, unto-the-death, staring match.

'What a lovely word "blather" is,' Eleanor said, nervously. 'I love being a blatherer.' She smoothed her pink trousers with her hands and sighed. 'You're quite right. I talk too much. I'm going to stop right now.' Dutifully, she pressed her lips together and hugged her knees and stared at the disapproving Maudie intently. Every now and again she turned away, then back came her enormous eyes to rest on Maudie again.

'It's very hot,' Maudie said. Someone had to show this American how to converse properly. Eleanor nodded, but put her finger to her lips to show she wasn't speaking, which made Maudie tut with impatience.

'There's no need to be childish,' Maudie scolded her. 'A big, grown girl like you should be able to talk nicely without being silly.'

'I don't know what you want to talk about,' Eleanor said. 'You go ahead and tell me. I'm dying to talk to you.'

'I said it was hot,' Maudie said.

'Yes, it is,' Eleanor agreed. 'You want to talk about the weather?'

'I just said it was hot,' Maudie said crossly. 'That doesn't mean I wanted to talk about the weather.'

'What does it mean, then?' Eleanor asked.

Maudie snorted, and getting up began to look for something to do.

'You're trying to keep yourself occupied,' Eleanor said suddenly, watching Maudie rearrange the books. 'I can tell you've done that before this morning. Oh dear, it's so sad—you must have this terrible feeling of inadequacy. Here you are, with your son at last and nothing at all to do but enjoy him, and you're so unsure you have to keep thinking of jobs to do. Do you know it's very common to feel like that, Mrs Tipstaff? My own mother feels just like that when she comes to stay with me. I've discussed it with her, and we both agree it's a failure to function as separate beings when the other is around. We each feel kind of rejected, and we worry about it, and it makes it worse. It's inevitable, Mrs Tipstaff, that's why I was so worried about you. With a son it's so much worse, and with a son like Robert—I mean, he has such a big disorientation problem already—well, it's practically insuperable. You know, Mrs Tipstaff, I almost wrote to tell you not to come, it just upset me so much to think how upset you were going to be. But then I thought I don't know her. I knew about you from what Robert had told me, but I thought that isn't really knowing her. So I didn't do anything, and now——'

Maudie had gone out. She detested the hard bright sun outside, but she could not bear to stay in and listen to such gibberish. Half of what the American said she did not understand at all, and the other half was impertinent. How Robert had come to be involved with anyone so unladylike she could not imagine and she must ask him straight out, when he came back, just who Eleanor was and whether she was his fiancée or what.

Walking a little way from the house, Maudie was imediately stifled by the heat. She looked around, but there was no shade anywhere, no doorways, no shop blinds to dodge between, no trees. At her feet she could see lizards darting in and out of the rocks and she envied them the few inches of coolness they found there. Gasping, Maudie came to a halt where the rocks sloped down to the beach. Here, there was a slight breeze which she faced thankfully. There was nowhere she could possibly trust as a seat. Standing there, she gradually became calmer. She turned to see if that girl was following her, but she hadn't. Perhaps at last she had been shown her place and would stay there.

Alone in the house, Eleanor bit her nails with annoyance. The old lady had shown her the way, with her inane remark about the weather, and she had ignored this lead and crashed ahead blindly. She ought to have said yes it was hot but not so hot as yesterday or tomorrow or last week or next week, and wasn't there a pleasant breeze by the sea, and didn't the dark come quickly. A week of that sort of chat and they would have been ready, perhaps, to progress by degrees to more interesting matters. She knew quite well Maudie was the sort of person who would pass the time of day with a neighbour for five years and still think her a stranger. That, Eleanor decided for the hundredth time, was her own personal tragedy: she understood people absolutely, but she still treated them all wrong so that they never guessed she understood them.

She couldn't decide whether to wait for Robert or not. Hesitant, she looked out of the window and saw the stiff, unyielding figure of Maudie on the rock edge. She smiled. She could not leave the poor dear there. It was impossible to apologise, so all she could do was vacate the house before the old lady died of sunstroke. She would go to the hotel and have her lunch and a swim and decide afterwards whether to come back. As she left the house, she waved and shouted goodbye to Maudie, so that there would be no mistaking her going.

Being a lady of principle, Maudie stood another five minutes on the rock after Eleanor's pink-legged figure had disappeared up the track. Then she walked briskly back to the house as though she had been out for her constitutional. The comparative darkness of the inside made her determined never to go out again before the sun had begun to go down. She sat for a while recovering her energy, and then she set about making herself a cup of tea.

Tea in hand, she wandered round the small rooms unhappily. How could anyone like being idle? There was no pleasure in sitting when there was no load of work behind you or ahead of you. Sighing, she looked at Robert's books again. She had never been a great reader. *The People's Friend* and *The Sunday Post* were her only addictions. Somehow, all that small print in books had never attracted her, quite apart from never having the time to try this reading. She remembered Robert had always been a great one for it. It had driven her wild seeing him reading in front of the fire and not even hearing what she had shouted at him five times or more. She had stormed and scolded at all the books collecting dust and the time he was wasting, and yet at the same time she was also proud of him. She did not quite know why, except that reading was an accomplishment she associated with ministers and schoolmasters and other respected persons. It was better he should be reading—a nice, quiet, clean occupation—than covering himself with filth on a football pitch. That was what she always said to his father when he taunted the boy with being a little sissy.

But Robert's books in his house made no sense. She picked out one or two but there were no nice stories. So she put them back. She suddenly wondered, seeing the backs of the canvasses stacked on the far wall, what his paintings were like. He had never painted at home. It was a new craze, and she could not think how he had got on to it. She liked a good painting. Annie McAllister had one of a little girl in a crinoline dress, all blues and whites, which she had always admired. She had never bought one herself because it seemed such a useless thing to spend good money on. Perhaps Robert would paint her a picture. She wondered if he would mind if she turned his canvasses round and looked at them.

Maudie put down her tea. Feeling excited and curious, she

carefully undid the thin rope slotting the paintings together, and tipped back the first one, very gently, on to the floor. She stood back and twisted her neck round to look properly. There, staring up at her, was Eleanor, totally naked, sitting astride a chair with her chin resting on the back and her arms wrapped round it. All the hair was painted in between her legs and under her arms and the nipples of her breasts were sploshed with pink paint. Shaking, Maudie bent to pick the horrible object up to hide it, and as she took her hand off the rest, they all tipped over, the balance destroyed, and fell with a loud clatter in a heap on the floor. Distraught, Maudie struggled to put them back. She tried not to look at the seemingly endless sequence of Eleanor's nude portraits. Robert had painted her lying down and standing up, kneeling, sitting in the most awful positions, all in thick white paint which emphasised her nakedness.

When all the pictures were safely stacked up against each other again, Maudie tied the rope with fingers so rigid with disapproval that they could hardly make the knots fast. She felt she wanted to take them all outside, to that rock she had been standing on, and throw them one by one into the sea. If she had not slept last night, how could she hope to sleep any other night with those revolting things only feet from her bed? Oh, that she had ever spoken to the brazen huzzy at all! Coming here and stripping her clothes off and cavorting around in her indecency to tempt young men beyond endurance! It was girls like her who kept the wickedness in the world going. The worst part was, you could tell from the smirk on her face in all of them that she had enjoyed doing it. She probably touted herself round the world showing off her horrible body to all and sundry when no one even wanted to see it.

Nakedness was something Maudie had a lifetime horror of. It was not just that she was a prude—though she certainly was—but also because she could see no beauty in the human body whatsoever, male or female. She had never, during her entire married life, allowed herself to be seen without her nightdress. She hated looking at herself in the bath, or when she was dressing or undressing. It seemed to her that she had grown steadily uglier for as long as she could remember, but that in any case she had never been beautiful with nothing on. And she did not think Eleanor the slightest bit beautiful. Even those quick glimpses had shown her that the girl was all skin and bone, her breasts nearly flat, her bottom shapeless, her tummy plump. It made Maudie feel sick.

She was still trying to cope with the nausea when Robert came back. She immediately felt guilt replace her sense of outrage, and desperately wanted to conceal the fact that she had discovered the paintings at all.

'That American came,' she said, 'when you were out.'

'Damn,' Robert said.

'She's gone now,' Maudie said. Robert busied himself making some coffee and said nothing.

'Was it a nice walk?' Maudie asked.

'Yes.'

'Don't you get tired of it?'

'No.'

'Isn't it hot for walking?'

'Yes, it is a bit.'

He sat down, waiting for the water to boil. Maudie fidgeted. She remembered he used to sit like that sometimes in the evenings and give her the creeps. If she had ever asked him what he was thinking about, he had just said 'things' and gone on being silent, scrutinising her minutely, till she had to get up and go away. Now, there was nowhere to go. Petulant, she pulled at the cuff of her sleeve.

'I wish,' she said, sulkily, 'that American was a nice girl. She isn't beautiful, anyway.'

'I think she is,' Robert said.

'She talks a lot of silly rubbish,' Maudie said, eager to get into an argument of any sort.

'Yes,' Robert said, 'she does.'

Determined not to be foiled, Maudie said, 'Why do you put up with her?'

'I love her, at the moment,' Robert said, quietly.

Aghast, Maudie automatically looked towards the canvasses, and then as quickly away again, but Robert had seen and interpreted her glance. Mercifully, he said nothing. The water boiled and he finished making his coffee. He drank two cups in complete silence, while his mother squirmed in front of him.

'Well,' he said, 'time for my swim.'

'In that sea?' Maudie queried. 'Not in that sea!'

'Where else?' Robert asked, smiling. He walked towards the door.

'Where's your costume—and your towel?' Maudie snapped.

'You don't need either here,' Robert said, blandly. 'There's not a soul on this side of the island, and when I've had my swim the sun dries me in five minutes. It's not Rothesay, you know, Mother.' He laughed at his own wit. 'Come and watch me,' he invited, 'I'm a good swimmer.'

'Dear God,' Maudie said, 'as if I would do any such thing,' and turned her back on him.

She sat, hunched up on the bed, while Robert had his swim. She could not believe that any child of hers could behave in such a way in broad daylight and have the insolence to ask her to watch. Clearly, she had been wrong to blame Eleanor alone. Robert was equally wanton. They were both doubtless steeped in irretrievable sin, far worse than any that had beset Sally. Maudie cried with disappointment and vexation. She had banked on Robert most of all and he was turning out the worst of the lot. She curled herself up on the bed and sniffed to herself and experimented with wishing she had never had any children at all, while outside Robert dived in and out of the waves, still choking with mirth at the memory of her scandalised face.

After lunch, Robert went to the hotel where he knew he would find Eleanor. She was lying beside the swimming pool, fully clothed, as she did not believe in getting brown and exposed as little as possible of herself to the sun. Before Robert could speak, she said 'Poor old soul'.

'Why didn't you wait?' Robert asked.

'It would have been wicked,' Eleanor said. 'Your mother was going through agonies because of me.'

'Do her good,' Robert said.

'Oh Robert.'

'She is more of an old bitch,' Robert said, 'than I ever remembered her. Yesterday was hell. I took her to Gozo and she never stopped moaning and complaining the whole time.'

'Poor old soul,' Eleanor said again.

'I can't stand it,' Robert said. 'You'll have to come and stay.'

'Impossible,' Eleanor said.

'Then I'll have to tell her I can't stand her.'

'Robert!'

'I will, really. You have no idea how awful she is.'

'She is not awful,' Eleanor said. 'She's lonely and miserable and you've failed her. She's heartbroken with disappointment. She comes all this way, and you reject her in a day.'

'She rejected me,' Robert said.

'She loves you,' Eleanor stated, 'it's just that she doesn't know how to show it.'

'Thank you, Dr Freud,' Robert said.

Together, they walked back to meet Maudie, still deeply arguing the whole situation, with Eleanor gradually being brought to agree that she might come over most days. Maudie was looking out for them. She saw them from the window a long way off. They were arm in arm. Every now and again, they would stop and face each other, and then continue on their way. Maudie went into the back room so she could not see, and sat down on her bed.

They had had one day together, one brief but blissful day, just the two of them. He shepherded her with such care off and on the boats, he ordered their lunch with such consideration, he talked all the while on such a variety of subjects. She could never remember being so contented. She had always loved days out, even with Joseph. The time could be depended upon to go so quickly and there would be so many things afterwards to talk over. Her memories of her day with Robert were already crystallising into perfection, even while she yet remembered her own odd flashes of temper. She was ashamed of them. They had shamed her at the time, but she had consoled herself by thinking that Robert understood she did not mean to be like that. There was no need to explain or apologise. He understood. They could be forgotten, eradicated from her memory of the day.

Sitting in the semi-dark of the back room, waiting for them to come, Maudie felt that for the first time for many a year she had been made a fool of. She had never suspected there might be a woman in her son's life. They must all have been laughing at her, especially that American, thinking that she and Robert were going to be alone. What conceit! What stupidity! She was just the old mother, to be pushed into the background after one day.

'Mrs Tipstaff? Oh, Mrs Tipstaff, might I come in?'

Maudie could have spat in Eleanor's eager face as she put her head round the door.

'I can hardly stop you,' she growled.

'Robert would have me come back,' Eleanor said, shyly. 'But if you'd rather I went...'

'I couldn't care less what you do, I'm sure,' Maudie said.

'Good. I just wanted to say I'm sorry I kind of upset you this morning.'

'I don't know what you're talking about,' Maudie said, enraged.

'Well, anyway, I hope you're going to have a perfectly marvellous time, Mrs Tipstaff. You'll just love this island. Everyone kind of falls for it. I know Bobbie is just hoping and hoping you'll stay on here with him, and I am too. I'm hoping we'll see a lot of each other, Mrs Tipstaff, and that maybe I can be of help smoothing out any problems. You know the kind of thing I mean? Anything I can do, or tell you, that Rob can't help with—I mean, sometimes a man just doesn't think of the things a woman wants to know. I'll be right here to help, most days. I do hope we're going to be real friends, Mrs Tipstaff. I'm most anxious about that.'

Robert smiled, openly, and when Eleanor asked what he was smiling at, he turned the other way and went on smiling even more broadly. It was always such a joy to watch Eleanor, the student of psychology, alienating people with a deftness he could only admire. She opened her mouth and mowed them down with a warmth and sincerity so overpowering that they were immediately suspect. The more she wanted to make friends with someone, the more she irritated them. It was, Robert reflected, such a shame, for Eleanor was no hypocrite.

'Eleanor might stay the night,' Robert said.

'No, no—I never said that,' Eleanor said, crossly.

'I expect she's done that before,' Maudie said, but nobody seemed to take up what she had meant as a very insulting remark.

'But I want you to,' Robert insisted. 'I can sleep outside. It's a warm enough night.'

'No,' Eleanor insisted, furious with him. 'I must go back.'

After that, they stood in awkward silence for a minute or two. Maudie could not bear the sympathetic looks Eleanor kept so meaningfully giving her. Even more, she could not bear the closeness of the two of them, the endless little looks, the slight changes of expressions between them that were more obvious than the most flamboyant signals. She cursed them both, and longed to let them know that she despised their cloying intimacy.

Eleanor left very soon, when it became clear that Maudie was not going to speak. Maudie heard the pair of them whispering outside. She thought they giggled once. She thought she heard the faintest sound of lips meeting lips. They seemed to take a long time saying goodbye. Then, when Robert came in, she noticed immediately that he started to be kind to her. 'Be kind to your mother' she could hear that American saying, and she wanted to scream. Confused as she was over what she had exactly come all this way for, she knew it was not for kindness.

CHAPTER FOUR

Robert, during the next few weeks, made few concessions to his mother's presence.

He knew, of course, that Maudie was bored to tears, but he didn't see that anything could, or ought, to be done about this. If a grown person could not enjoy endless leisure, that was their misfortune. He considered he was doing her a service by providing her with free board and lodging and requiring nothing of her in return. He did not even want her to clean or cook for him: he had his own ways of doing both and preferred to stick to them.

Eleanor annoyed him with her endless nagging about his mother being miserable. He was sure she was not miserable. She had always been a grumpy sort of person, not given to great displays of happiness. You couldn't expect her to go around beaming and laughing. Nor, he believed, could you tell anything from her outward appearance. She believed you got on with the business of living and whether you were happy or not was irrelevant. All this he explained to Eleanor, brusquely and without resort to what he called psychological claptrap, and when she maintained he was wrong and Maudie was in fact suffering dreadfully and it was his fault, he shut her up quickly.

He knew his mother had seen the paintings of Eleanor, and he knew she wanted to know what his relationship with her was, but that she would never ask outright. He was tempted to volunteer the information, but decided against it out of a desire to keep the peace. Her antagonism towards Eleanor was so fierce that he suspected she would never believe he had initiated the affair himself.

When Eleanor did not reappear after the first visit, the days yawned on without interruption and Robert, observing his mother's boredom, waited for her to say that she was packing her bags and going. But she didn't. She managed to carve out for herself the bare bones of an occupied, if not a busy day with remarkable originality. She cleaned the house when Robert was out for his walk. She washed clothes while he painted. She rested on her bed when he went for his swim. She helped him cook the evening meal, and insisted on clearing it up herself. She went to bed very early and got up rather late. Through sheer persistence, she created a timetable of the monotonous variety she liked.

In the evenings, when he was writing, Robert sometimes broke off to indulge her with questions about the past. He knew she enjoyed answering the right sort of question, and he liked watching her response. Unlike Eleanor, he never ventured on the personal or abstract, but confined himself to factual inquiries such as 'How did we come to live in the buildings?' or 'How many jobs did Dad have?' and from there she was sure to wander on to the topics that, if directly brought up, would have shut her up immediately. When she really got going, he fancied she forgot he was in the room at all. Usually, it was just as darkness engulfed the house, before he had lit the lamps, with only a glimmer of light still coming in from the sea to show him her small erect figure pulling at the knitting wool on her needles in an absent-minded way, as her voice droned on, punctuated by short, unconvincing laughs from time to time.

There would, all the same, come a point each evening when Maudie of her own accord would put an end to what was an apparently successful session. She seemed able to go just so far, and no further, and would often break off in the middle of an anecdote with 'Oh well, I'm blathering on again, I must be off to my bed,' and then nothing Robert could say could dissuade her. It was never that she had reached a particularly revealing passage—it was impossible for him to see what had made her stop. But when she had, she wanted to get away from him as quickly as possible, as though his presence was somehow unbearable, or the atmosphere of the room contaminated by what she had been saying.

Intrigued as he was by this, Robert began to look forward to the evenings, and when he thought his mother about due to suddenly interrupt herself, he sought ways of prolonging her narration. She was like an interesting specimen to him. He viewed her almost in the same way that he did Eleanor's body when she was posing for him—clinically, with no feelings except those of a workman. He forgot she was his mother in order to find out more about her, sometimes asking her to tell him things he knew quite well as a test to see how well her memory functioned. From it all emerged a strange, contorted picture of himself which he found fascinating, and another of his mother which was both touching and disturbing.

He had tried for some time to get her, unwittingly, on to the subject of his conception and birth because, wanting to know everything about himself, he must begin at the beginning. But somehow she always evaded those particular events, whether by design or not he could not be sure. Then one evening, when he had gently led her through his father's unemployment in the 'thirties back to her inter-war memories, she suddenly said 'That was when Robert came along' as though he was not Robert, and he held his breath.

'That was a bad time,' she said, 'oh dear, it was. I'd prayed not to have any more children with the doctor's bills from all my trouble with the two I lost still not paid, and the two I had eating me out of house and home. I worried myself sick about it. I said to Joseph it would be the end of me if I fell wrong again and it must all stop, surely he could see it must, but all he did was swear about women and their insides and I knew the next night he'd had something to drink it would be no good trying to hold him off. I went near distracted waiting for it. I even took to sleeping with Jean and Sally to keep him off. Then one night he came home and he was so nice I never suspected a thing and asked after my bad back and how I was feeling and didn't I want an early night and I was fool enough to say yes and was in bed with him before I smelled his breath. He was away before I could do a thing. I fought and scratched him, but it was no good. I knew the minute he'd stopped his beastliness that that was that. And it was. Oh God, I near lost my reason. I tried everything to make it come on, though it was wicked of me, but this one wouldn't budge, it wouldn't. I wept the whole nine months, I'm sure I did. Then it was the worst birth of them all, though they say it gets easier. The pains began on the Friday and Robert wasn't born until the Monday forenoon and I thought I was dying. The doctor came and went six times and in the end he pulled and tugged Robert out with the forceps and I bled so much we had to throw the mattress away. I remember he said to Joseph that he was to stay in the room, and he did and passed clean out and when he came round doctor said "Now perhaps you will leave this poor woman alone, Mr Tipstaff, for the next one will kill her" and from that day on he never touched me. If it ever looked as if he would, I had only to mention what the doctor had said for him to mind it all and leave me be. He always seemed to dislike Robert, though it was the son he had always wanted, and I put it down to him blaming Robert for the doctor telling him to leave me alone. With Jean and Sally he was good when they were babies—never seemed to mind their crying the way some men do, I'll say that for him. He held them real tender, and he would even bath them if I wanted him to. That was curious, for he was rough with everyone else. But Robert he wouldn't touch. He didn't seem able to look at him without remembering the sight of him being pulled out. When the poor baby cried, he yelled at him something awful. Oh, we had more fights over Robert than anything else. I used to say he was taking it out on that child for his own sins, and it wasn't right for he was a good little boy once he got over the feeding trouble. I had my teeth out when he was three months old and the milk just went and I had to go on to a bottle and nothing agreed with him. He threw everything up. I went down to the doctor's with him and the doctor took one look and said "That child is dying of malnutrition." Malnutrition! It was true, too. He was all skin and bone and his tummy was all blown out—oh, it was dreadful to see him. Then someone told me to try this new Cow and Gate and I did and he took it and never looked back. After that, he was the best behaved baby you ever saw, sleeping the whole night through without any trouble and sitting so contented in his pram in the day. "You've got an angel there, Mrs Tipstaff" they used to say to me, and they were right. I had.'

Robert heard her stop. He had not been looking at her, but out of the window at the sky. He turned, but she was already rising stiffly to her feet and fumbling to gather up her knitting. She made little snorts of protest at her own inefficiency, followed by groans every time she had to bend to pick up a ball of wool or a needle. She was all alarm and confusion. He felt he really ought to set her mind at rest, but did not know how to do it, so instead he went over and picked up the rest of the odd assortment of objects she had had on her lap.

'You shouldn't let me go on so,' Maudie muttered. 'I'm wandering in my head when I get going.'

'There's going to be rain,' Robert said wisely. 'I've been watching the sky.'

'That'll make a change,' Maudie said, eagerly.

'It will all be over by morning,' Robert said, still seeking to soothe her. 'You'll wake up and it will be as fresh as ever.'

'Fresh? It's never fresh. Stifling, it's always stifling here,' Maudie said. 'Ah well, I must go to my bed.'

When she had gone, Robert walked over to the lamp and put it on and carried it across to his easel, which was set up in the corner. The canvas on it was turned inwards. Maudie never watched him when he painted, nor made any attempt to even peep at what he was doing, doubtless fearing the worst. But he did not want her to know what he was doing, for it was already hard enough trying to paint her without the additional complication of either her objection or self-consciousness. He wished he dared to get her to sit for him properly instead of carrying in his head the image of how she had looked the night before, but the risk of spoiling everything was too great. He must just go on doing it from memory.

He turned the canvas over and looked at it critically. The outline of the body and face were definitely fixed. He had caught, to his own satisfaction, both her frailty and her indomitable spirit. She looked old and weak but you could tell she was tough. The face he had hardly begun in detail. There was so much to convey. He wanted to have her staring straight out, but every time he painted her features he made her too fierce, too angry. There was, in actual fact, nothing soft or gentle there that he was failing to capture, but there was a weariness that gave her a less harsh look. This was what he could not get.

That night, her face had been more placid than he had ever seen it. Retelling the story of his birth, she had forgotten to tighten her features into their habitual watchful expression. Unguarded, they had slid into a looseness which drastically changed her whole appearance. She looked helpless, defenceless, she looked as though she had suffered all kinds of pain, instead, as she usually did, as though she was going to bite, like a snappy dog. He must get that in his portrait. He wasn't interested in the typical, but in the hidden.

It rained all night, but as Robert had said, the morning was as bright as ever. With the morning, very early, when they were having their silent breakfast, came Eleanor. Robert dropped a knife as he leapt up, and Maudie immediately took refuge in picking it up and washing and drying it.

Eleanor had kept well away. It seemed to her only sensible to leave Maudie to discover that life with Robert was very bleak when she had him all to herself. She had resisted Robert's reiterated pleas, made on his unexpected trips to see her, to move in with them. She did not want to be blamed, or made a scapegoat. Now, as she came in, and saw Robert alight with a rare enthusiasm, she felt Maudie's pain as her own. So she frowned at Robert, and showed she did not want him to kiss her.

'How are you, Mrs Tipstaff?' she asked, formally.

Maudie did not reply.

'Eleanor asked you a question, Mother,' Robert said.

'It wasn't a question, only a pleasantry,' Eleanor said quickly. 'I didn't expect a reply.'

'That's just as well, for you won't get one,' Maudie snapped.

'There's no need to be rude, Mother,' Robert said.

'And there's no need to be pompous, Robert,' Eleanor said. 'He really is terrible, isn't he, Mrs Tipstaff?'

But Maudie was not to be won over.

'Is there any tea left in that pot?' Eleanor asked.

'I'll make some fresh,' Maudie said.

'Please don't trouble,' Eleanor pleaded.

'If it was any trouble, young lady, I wouldn't do it,' Maudie said.

When she turned her back to put the kettle on the tiny primus stove, Robert lunged and caught Eleanor in his arms. Before she could push him away, Maudie had turned and seen.

'Is it tea you were wanting?' she asked, with contempt so magnificently stamped on her face that it was laughable.

Miserably, Eleanor drank the tea. There was nothing to be done but go. Maudie was incapable of understanding Eleanor's motives. Nor could she bring herself to find fault with Robert and not Eleanor. Eleanor saw quite clearly that Maudie resented what she meant to Robert, and not what she herself was. She could stand having an awful time with her son, get over the disappointment, tell herself it was bound to be that way—but she could not bear Robert's love to be given to someone else. She could not stand by and see that the love she so craved was there, but not for her. Far, far better to have believed it was not there at all.

Eleanor left, quickly. As soon as she had gone, Maudie said 'Good riddance.'

'I don't know how you can be so unjust,' Robert said.

'Coming here, gloating in my face,' Maudie said.

'Gloating? Over what? You must be mad.'

'I might be mad, but I'm not blind,' Maudie said. 'I can see what she's up to.'

'She isn't up to anything,' Robert said. 'If you'd only give her a chance, you'd find she's a good, kind girl only concerned with your happiness.'

'Dear God!' Maudie said. 'She's taken you in all right. I'm amazed she hasn't hooked you good and proper.'

'She won't have me,' Robert said.

'Clever monkey,' Maudie sneered.

'It's the truth,' Robert said. 'I'd marry her tomorrow if she'd have me.'

'You've no pride,' Maudie said.

'Do I need it?' Robert asked.

'And why won't she have you? What makes her think she's too good for you?'

'She just isn't sure we'd be happy,' Robert said.

'A likely story,' Maudie said. 'Have you given her any money?'

Robert stared at her. The whole of her thinking was so warped and deranged that it made him doubt her sanity. Yet, with her final insult, he suddenly realised that she did not mean a word she said. He had an absolute conviction that she was being carried along on a wave of spite she could neither control nor halt. She was that sort of person. Any upset released an automatic crudity that amounted to a defence so complete no one could penetrate it. Gibe led to gibe, until a full scale row was in progress, obliterating the hurt from which it had sprung.

'I'm not going to mention Eleanor again,' Robert said, quietly.

Maudie was left, as she put it to herself, to stew in her own juice. Robert was barely civil to her, Eleanor did not come again. She thought of going home, but that would be giving in.

Instead, she nearly drove herself dotty going over and over what had been said, and struggling with her conscience to admit that she had been in the wrong. She was still in this hideous state of self doubt when Eleanor came again, in the same way and at the same time as before.

'Hi,' she said, looking in at the window. 'I'm the early bird.'

'Oh dear God,' Maudie said in the time it took for Eleanor to get from window to door, but looked immediately ashamed of herself.

'You look so funny, the two of you,' Eleanor said, delightedly, 'sitting there, munching away like a couple of tortoises.'

'And what should we be doing but munching when we're eating our breakfast?' Maudie asked.

'Quite right,' Robert said. 'Sit down and munch too, Eleanor, or go away.' He was resolved to be as helpful to the good cause as possible.

'That is a fine welcome,' Eleanor said, 'when I've come all this way at this hour to invite you to my house for my birthday lunch. I'm thirty. I'm so depressed I'll go insane if I have to spend the day on my own. Will you come?'

'No,' Robert said, 'I'm busy. You know I'm busy.'

'Liar,' Eleanor said. 'Why don't you just say, straight out, that you don't want to come?'

'I don't want to come, straight out,' Robert said.

'In fact, you'd hate to come,' Eleanor insisted, happily.

'In fact, I'd hate to come.'

'I knew you would. But I hoped your mother might. Will you do me the favour, Mrs Tipstaff? We could go on the ten o'clock boat and I'd have time to show you some of Malta and then we'd eat and maybe do the shops in Valetta. Can I persuade you?'

Though Maudie could hardly bear the thought of having to refuse the promise of such an outing, for a moment she felt she might have to in the interests of keeping Eleanor at bay. But oh, the thought of getting away from this horrible island where the hours dragged so dismally! And above all, the thought of shops, of things to look at and people to elbow past and the bustle and activity of it all. Her feet ached with the desire to be tired, to feel the heat and hardness of a real pavement. But would agreeing to go be taken as a sign of defeat? Hesitant, dying to say yes, she fiddled with her butter knife and sucked her lower lip.

Robert smiled over her at Eleanor, and winked.

'Mother will go with you,' he said, 'won't you?'

'Well, I don't know,' Maudie said, tremulously.

'I'd like you to go,' Robert said, emphatically.

'Would you?' Maudie asked, happily.

'I would. There are things you could get me.'

'Shopping?' asked Maudie, ecstatic.

'Shopping. Get some paper and a pencil and we'll make a list.'

Oh the joy of it! Maudie flew around dressing herself in her best, unearthing her beloved best shopping bag—maroon leather with black handles—writing out Robert's list, and gathering together all the equipment she considered necessary for such an excursion: umbrella, gloves, smelling salts, purse, handbag, cough sweets, watch. It upset her that Robert didn't have a long mirror so that she could check she was neat and proper all over. It was no good asking either him or Eleanor as they had no standards at all.

Before they set out to get the boat, it was arranged that Robert should meet the 7 p.m. boat coming back. Maudie was most anxious to extract a promise that he would be there, without fail, for she dreaded walking back on her own through that heathen country. Robert duly promised, and walked with them to the headland. When he left them, Maudie was already sweating in best coat and dress and laced shoes, while beside her Eleanor looked even more cool and casual than usual. He watched them go towards the hotel bay, Eleanor swinging her bag and ruffling her hair now and again, Maudie stepping out smartly, her left arm at right-angles so that her handbag could hang properly suspended from it. He wondered exactly how many hours their strange alliance would last and prophesied to himself the return of Maudie on the midday boat in a towering rage. Poor Eleanor would never win.

Maudie herself privately wondered too, as they set out, how much of Eleanor she would be able to stand, even for the sake of shops. But Eleanor was rigidly well-behaved. She discussed the heat very solemnly, was silent the whole boat journey, shepherded Maudie on and off with careful but not insulting gallantry, and suggested a cup of tea the minute they arrived in Valetta. She sat very quietly in the café, paid for the tea, whispered where the ladies was, and in all left nothing to be desired as a companion.

They spent the morning alternately drinking tea and sight-seeing in exactly the sort of quick, speedy, no-nonsense fashion Maudie liked. She did not like standing gaping at things and she did not like hearing about their history. She liked to do a once over, find out what everything cost and then move on. At precisely the right moment, Eleanor suggested they went to her flat for lunch, and hailed a taxi to take them, for which Maudie was very grateful as she was more tired than she would ever have admitted.

In the taxi, Maudie steeled herself to tolerate Eleanor's flat and not say nasty things. She was sure she would want to say nasty things. One look at Eleanor, and she had known in what sort of arty squalor she was bound to live. Maudie prepared herself for dust and dirty ashtrays and dishes everywhere, for an unmade bed and a smell of unwashed clothes. As for the lunch—well, Robert probably had his reasons for refusing. It would be rubbish out of tins and no tablecloth.

It was, in fact, nothing at all like that. As an interior decorator, Eleanor could have earned her living anywhere. Where furnishings were concerned, her taste was flawless. No house-wife could ever have been quite so fastidious as she, and no cook more imaginative. She showed Maudie into a cool, pale green room, seated her on a spotlessly clean beige linen covered chair, drew her towards a table set with the prettiest primrose china and put before her chicken such as Maudie had never tasted, followed by a chocolate mousse that melted in her mouth and coffee that persuaded even tea-worshipper Maudie to a second cup. Everything was done neatly and efficiently with no fuss or bother at all, and when they had finished, Eleanor dealt with the dishes so rapidly and unobtrusively that Maudie hardly noticed they were being done.

'Well,' Maudie said, 'praise where praise is due, Eleanor.' It was the first time she had used the girl's name. 'Did you do all that yourself?'

'I did,' said Eleanor. 'I like cooking.'

'And this room and kitchen—was it like this when you came?'

'No. I decorated it and furnished it all myself. Home-making's my best subject.'

'Well,' said Maudie, 'it's all a credit to you, a real credit. You'll make some young man a lovely wife. Now, if Robert had a nice place like this . . .' and she tailed off, aware that the two statements were much too close together.

Maudie was happy. A visit to the bathroom had her in raptures, a tour of the kitchen—a most scrupulous tour—made it plain that Eleanor was a gem. She could hardly tear herself away from such perfection to go to the shops at all, but Eleanor had their route all planned so they went. Maudie was no dawdler, but she liked to look and Eleanor liked to look too, so there was no friction. They bought the few things Robert wanted, then they had tea and then it was time to go for the boat, to Maudie's barely concealed regret.

She was utterly miserable as Eleanor left her, safely installed on a seat inside the cabin. It was not just that she had had a lovely day, that it had been a lovely break. It was a positive dread of facing another two months on Comino, two months of boring days, two months of living alone side by side with

Robert. She did not want to live with Robert. She did not want to live how and where he lived. Standing on the deck for the last few yards of her journey, already seeing Robert waving, she knew she did not want to live with anyone. She wanted to live, like Eleanor, in her own home. By herself, she was lonely, but with her children she was isolated.

CHAPTER FIVE

Maudie went to spend another day with Eleanor the following Thursday, and again the Thursday after that. It seemed only a very short step from there to staying the weekend, and from staying the weekend on two occasions it became pointless troubling to go back to Comino midweek, so she stayed a whole week. Once the break had been made, the tradition established, there was no going back. No one quite knew where Maudie was supposed to be in residence.

Robert had no objections to this state of affairs at all. He had not realised, until she went, that Maudie interfered with his way of life to any serious degree. But she had interfered. He wanted calm and Maudie spoiled it. Simply by sitting around, long-suffering, bored, she ruffled the placid flow of thought he was trying to keep going.

It was a pity about her portrait. She was now with him so rarely that he kept forgetting her expressions. They no longer had the same endless evenings stretching ahead, and when she was there, her mind seemed to be occupied and her tongue never stopped and somehow her face lost all the range of emotions he had been trying to interpret. So he destroyed the canvas and started instead on a portrait of himself. He did not get on very well with it, and came to the conclusion that the sooner his mother stopped popping in and out the better. He wished she would realise her visit was an experiment that had failed, and get back to Glasgow, where he would be quite happy to send her a great number of exemplary loving letters.

But Maudie had no intention of going before the date that had been set before she came. She was, in fact, beginning to enjoy herself thoroughly. To start with, she hadn't liked to

impose on Eleanor, but the girl had been so insistent—
Maudie was sure she had never heard anyone so insistent—
that she had to give in and come again. And then it had been
so obvious that Eleanor had a lot for her to do that it had
seemed silly to go back to Robert, who never had anything for
her to do. Eleanor was dying to talk, whereas Robert hardly
opened his mouth.

Maudie's indispensability was founded on Eleanor's desire
to have her flat spring-cleaned, even though it was autumn and
not spring. Now Maudie could understand that feeling. She
did not tut-tut and say Eleanor's place was immaculate: she
knew just what was meant. Accordingly, Maudie took on the
role of Spring Cleaner. When Eleanor was at work, she
scrubbed and washed and polished, and when Eleanor came
home they went shopping for material to make a new bed-
spread and kitchen curtains and so forth. Oh, it was a busy
time alright. Yet Maudie was not allowed to get tired. Each
morning, Eleanor brought her a nice cup of tea in bed, and she
always made the meals, and insisted Maudie rested in the
evenings.

Eleanor watched Maudie quietly and was amazed at herself.
Three times she had had her own mother to stay, and each
time had been more disastrous than the last. Yet her mother
was very like Maudie. She ought to have got on well with her.
She ought to have been able to make her equally happy. When
she had thought of having Robert's mother to stay, it had been
almost for the sake of entertainment value. Partly, too, because
it made her feel good to think she was succeeding where
Robert and his sisters had failed. But once the old lady was
installed, the pleasure Eleanor experienced was as genuine as
Maudie's own.

She naturally wanted to discuss all this with Maudie, but a
sort of understanding had sprung up, based on the success of
that first day together, that they would keep off any topic that
was liable to send Eleanor off into what Maudie called 'fits of
nonsense'. Eleanor chafed under the restriction, but honoured

it until she felt she would go insane with all the conclusions and counter-conclusions that were busy forming in her head. It was a relief when Maudie unwittingly gave her an opening as they sat sewing one evening.

'This reminds me,' Maudie said, 'of when my mother was alive. She used to like to have us all sitting round a lamp sewing, though what we sewed, I can't for the life of me remember.'

'Why should you?' Eleanor said. 'It's the closeness you want to remember, not what you were sewing. Can you just feel the intimacy your mother shared?'

'Hum,' Maudie said, and cleared her throat.

'What did you like your daughters doing?' Eleanor asked. 'What's your closest memory?'

'Oh dear me,' Maudie said, crossly, 'I don't know, I'm sure. We never all sat still for five minutes doing anything that I can remember.'

'There must be something,' Eleanor probed.

'Well, there isn't,' Maudie snapped, 'so there.'

Eleanor was determined not to be baulked. 'If I ever have any children,' she said, 'I hope they are all boys.'

'Boys are nice when they're little,' Maudie said, 'but you get nothing out of them when they grow up.'

'Do you get anything out of daughters?' Eleanor asked quickly.

'Maybe not,' Maudie said, guardedly, 'but you're more likely to. It stands to reason.'

'It doesn't,' Eleanor said, promptly, 'it doesn't stand to reason. All the time, mothers are really competing with daughters and that's why they're uncomfortable together. They don't need to compete with sons.'

'Oh!' Maudie said, exasperated. 'Oh, you go on something dreadful. I don't understand a word you're saying when you go on like this.'

'Were you happy,' Eleanor asked, 'with your daughters when you stayed with them?'

221

'No,' Maudie said, driven against her wishes into a truthful reply. 'No, but I'm no more happy or whatever you call it with my son.'

'Maybe nobody should have children,' Eleanor said, 'nobody is ever happy with them.'

'I didn't say that,' Maudie said, crossly. 'There you go, putting words into my mouth. Of course people should have children. What else would they do if they didn't have children?' She pointed a triumphant finger at Eleanor, and nodded her head to emphasise her victory.

'But it's all such a disappointment,' Eleanor said. 'You can't deny it. You brought up these three children, devoted your life to them and then you go and visit them and they're all like strangers. It's so cruelly disappointing.'

'I never said I was disappointed,' Maudie said.

'But you are. You're getting old and you look to them for comfort and companionship and there just isn't any.'

'I never said I was disappointed,' Maudie said stubbornly. 'And I'm not. It was just the way things turned out. They could have turned out differently.'

'They couldn't,' Eleanor said, gloomily, 'not basically.'

'They could so,' Maudie said. 'Now, if one of my girls had had a job and a nice place like this——'

'It wouldn't have made any difference,' Eleanor said, 'you would still have been disillusioned.'

'We would have got on lovely,' Maudie asserted, 'just the way we're doing ow.'

'My mother didn't "get on lovely",' Eleanor said.

'Then she must be a very funny lady, with all due respect,' Maudie said, firmly.

'No, she isn't funny, she's just my mother.'

'Oh, stop it,' Maudie said, 'no one could help having a nice time here. If it had been like this at Jean's or Sally's I'd never have been able to go.'

'And Robert's?' Eleanor asked.

'I don't know about Robert,' Maudie said, 'but then he's

turned peculiar. Don't you think so? Don't you think he's a little peculiar sticking himself away on that island?'

'A little,' Eleanor said, smiling.

'Well, there you are then,' Maudie said, satisfied. 'You couldn't expect me or any other mother to enjoy being stuck there. I never imagined anything like that. Now, if he'd kept to his schoolteachering and had a nice little home in Glasgow, it would have been different.'

'It would have been exactly the same,' Eleanor said, but was ready to give up.

'Oh, you,' Maudie said. 'Anyway, I've had my run-a-round. I'll be home soon. Thank God I've a home to go to. I don't need any of them and I can't think why I ever thought I did.'

'Next time——' Eleanor began.

'There won't be any next time,' Maudie said.

'But I hope you'll come and stay with me often,' Eleanor said, and then, experimentally, 'with Robert and me, that is.'

Maudie knitted furiously for a few minutes, and Eleanor thought she was not going to be taken up on her insinuation.

'Are you intending to marry Robert, then?' Maudie finally asked, frowning very hard.

'I don't know,' Eleanor said, 'I really don't know.'

'If in doubt, don't,' Maudie said, quickly.

'Would you rather I didn't?' Eleanor asked.

'Nothing to do with me,' Maudie snapped.

'I just wanted your advice.'

'You seem very nicely set up here on your own,' Maudie said. 'What do you want to go spoiling it for?'

'Would it spoil it?'

'Men spoil everything,' Maudie said, firmly, 'they're a pest.'

'I certainly love Robert,' Eleanor said, and then, watching Maudie's expression: 'What's the matter, Mrs Tipstaff, don't you believe in love?'

'No, I do not. It's all a lot of nonsense.'

'Then why did you get married, Mrs Tipstaff? Honestly, now?'

'Dear God, how can you expect me to remember that?' Maudie asked, crossly.

'It's not the sort of thing I'd have thought you would forget,' Eleanor challenged.

'Well, young lady, if you expect me to tell you a lot of sloppy nonsense you'll be disappointed. I got married because I wanted a home and children of my own. You can't get those without a man, more's the pity.'

'Then why Mr Tipstaff and not someone else?'

'Because he was persistent, and because I thought I could make something of him.'

'Did you?'

'No, I did not. I regretted marrying him every day of my life.'

'It's only what you deserved for marrying him without loving him,' Eleanor said, daringly.

'Then marry your precious Robert and see if you can do any better,' Maudie said, childishly. She was instantly furious with herself and returned to her knitting with redoubled vigour.

'I didn't mean to upset you,' Eleanor said. 'It's just I'm so afraid of marriage. Yet I can't do without Robert and if I'm going to spend the rest of my life with him, I might as well marry him, and make everything more convenient.'

'Do what you like,' Maudie said. 'You're welcome to him.'

'Oh, Mrs Tipstaff, don't say it like that. You love Robert, don't you? You might not have loved your husband, but surely you loved your children? Why, you said you married to have them.'

'Of course I loved my chidren,' Maudie said, sticking over the word 'loved' even in that chaste context. 'I'd be a strange woman not to. But that was when they were children.'

'Have you stopped loving them?' Eleanor asked.

'Oh dear, be quiet,' Maudie said.

She felt hopelessly confused. She was not used to talking

about her emotions, and doing so gave her a shivery feeling. She was startled at some of her own answers and felt she must stop before it was too late. Closing her eyes, she could still see quite clearly Eleanor on the carpet in front of her, somehow so very young and soft with her endless earnest talk about love. She had never been like that, she knew. She had always been tight and secretive and distrusting. If, like Eleanor, she had loved someone. she would never have dared breathe a word of it. She did not understand this shameless avowal of passion. Whenever Jean had said she loved Edward, she had felt enraged; when she saw Sally clinging to William, she had been furious. She felt so cheated when she saw love returned by love. Why had no one loved her? Why had she never had this blissful confidence, this delicious comfort of giving and being given to?

Then there were children: she had loved them unreservedly, and it had done her no good. As soon as she had seen that they no longer loved her completely, she had started concealing her own love so that she would not be rejected. Till they were seven or eight she was lavish with her affection, but then, when they began to spurn her endearments, she had called a sharp halt. From then, they had grown rapidly away from her. She went on loving her children, who were hardly connected at all in her mind with the three she had been visiting.

'I won't be stirring from my own fireplace again,' she said, suddenly. 'They'll have to come and see me, not that they will.'

'Oh, they will,' Eleanor said, not at all convincingly.

'They won't,' Maudie said, 'not if the last ten years is anything to go by. They'll never come near the pläce unless I ask them, and I wouldn't do that. I can manage.'

She said this very firmly, but listening to her Eleanor felt sick with depression. She could see Maudie in her little room, lonely, perhaps ill, watching for the post and nothing else, and it was all so tragic and corny and yet inevitable that she could have wept. Maudie would never, of course, go into a home.

That would be utter degradation. She would stagger on until they had to take her into some geriatric ward, where she would quickly die. But then that was what happened to all old people. Perhaps it was as much part of life as growing old itself.

Maudie was sitting placidly sewing again. Eleanor watched her and wondered why she hadn't burst into tears at the thought of the years ahead. She didn't even seem to be particularly worried, or frightened, and she certainly wasn't resigned. She must, Eleanor decided, have simply come to the conclusion that it was never going to happen. It would be cruel to prove to her that it would.

As the day for Maudie's departure began to near, she grew perkier and more animated by the minute, a state of affairs Eleanor could not understand. Privately, she had thought Maudie might break down and need comforting for the first time ever. She had planned several little outings to tide the old lady over the worst days, but they were not needed. It became quickly obvious that Maudie was dying to get back to Glasgow and to the loneliness Eleanor suffered such anguish over, on her behalf.

'Oh, it will be nice to be back,' Maudie kept saying, over and over again.

'East west, home is best,' Robert said, pleasantly. They were sitting, the three of them, on the bench outside his house. For once, his mother was not objecting to flies, heat or dark.

'You may mock,' Maudie said, 'but it's true. I haven't had a good night's sleep since I left my own bed in my own home.'

'I thought you never ever had such a thing as a good night's sleep,' Robert said, drily.

'Well, I don't,' Maudie snapped, 'but it's been far worse since I left home. That in there no one but a humped backed beggar would call a bed.'

'It's bad manners to criticise other people's furniture,' Robert said. He was feeling very light-hearted at the thought of his mother going and never having to see her again. To

226

suffer occasional melancholic pangs for her was infinitely pre-ferable.

'I can't help that,' Maudie said, and sighed. 'I wonder how everybody is keeping?' she asked. 'They'll all complain about me not writing, I daresay, but postcards and stamps to all of them would have cost a fortune. And I'm not taking any presents, that's flat. It's ridiculous. That Annie McAllister will expect something, but she'll be disappointed. She made a fool of herself, in my opinion, carting back all those bottles of shampoo and potato peelers the time she went to the Isle of Man. The way she went on about it—you would have thought the Isle of Man was abroad. Why, it isn't even on the con-tinent, let alone properly abroad.'

'Oh to have been abroad!' Robert murmured. Eleanor smiled, very tenderly, and stroked his hand.

'I daresay,' Maudie said, 'the minister will want me to give a talk at the women's meeting, but I won't, not even to oblige him. Mr Cooper, I shall say, Mr Cooper I could not do it. The soonest forgotten about the better, I shall say—otherwise, I know the kind of talk there will be about me being above myself.'

'Did Annie McAllister give a talk on the Isle of Man?' Robert asked.

'She did,' Maudie said, scornfully. 'It was the most embarras-sing thing I've ever heard in all my days, it was really—most embarrassing. If I'd been Annie I'd have been plain humili-ated. She hadn't said more than two words before she forgot what she was going to say, and then her photographs—dear God!—all of herself with a silly smile on her face. I didn't speak to her for a week. No, there'll be no exhibitions like that from Maudie Tipstaff. If anyone asks me what it was like, I shall say "quite nice thank you for asking" and that will be that.'

'Just think,' Robert said, leaning back, 'it will be warm and quiet and beautiful here when you're back in cold, wet, grey, noisy Glasgow.'

'And what is wrong with that?' Maudie challenged. ''Tis a climate more suited to God-fearing, hard-working folk than this lazy place. Ugh, it makes me feel ill to think of living forever in a muggy atmosphere like this. You can keep it. And as for the quiet—I can hear plenty of noises and I don't like any of them. When you hear a bus, you know it's a bus, but here you don't know what it might be.'

'Definitely not a bus,' Robert said.

'Well, mind you don't come back then,' Maudie said. 'I notice all these folk that run down Scotland and go gallivanting off to other places are only too glad to come back when they've had enough.'

'I won't go back,' Robert said.

'Then you don't know when you're well off,' Maudie said, sharply. 'I won't come back here, either, thank you very much.'

'Then you don't know when *you're* well off,' Robert countered.

'That's as may be,' Maudie said, and shut her lips to show she had retired from the argument with dignity. Eleanor laughed to herself, and thought how alike they looked, outlined in what remained of the sunset. They were both so cross that the other spurned their ideal. Really, she thought, they had a lot in common, which made it all a wicked shame.

Robert walked with Eleanor to the boat, not that she needed him to, but Maudie insisted on the chivalrous act being performed as it was so very dark by then. There were, she pointed out, no street lamps like there were in Glasgow. Eleanor might walk slap bang into the sea and no one would be any the wiser. So Robert went with her and Maudie steeled herself to wait for him.

They walked in silence all the way to the bay, and then, when they could see the last boat had not yet arrived, they sat at the side of the path on top of the hill, instead of going down to the hotel.

'You'd better get back,' Eleanor said, 'she'll be terrified on her own.'

'I know she will,' Robert said, 'but she enjoys it.'

'She certainly doesn't,' Eleanor said, indignantly, 'how can you say such a thing? She's a poor, feeble little old lady and it's just ridiculous to say she enjoys being made to feel frightened.'

'She's deadened your usual acute psychological observation,' Robert said, 'she's not at all feeble. She'd scare the living daylights out of anything that came along. And she does enjoy being scared—or she enjoys the relief afterwards which is the same thing.'

'You don't know her,' Eleanor said.

'Ho-ho, so now we're boasting! What makes you think you know her better than I do?'

'We've got very close these last few weeks.'

'That's a lie, for a start,' Robert said, equably, 'no one ever gets close to Maudie. She doesn't believe in it. What you mean is that you had some nice chats together.'

'They were more than chats,' Eleanor said, proudly, 'we discussed the whole framework of the maternal relationship.' Robert laughed and plucked the grass on either side of him, and hurled it in her face. 'You can laugh,' she said, 'but it happens to be true. You're just jealous that I succeeded where you failed. It's natural.'

'It's rubbish,' Robert said, 'I didn't fail at anything. We were just bored to death with each other and there's no reason why we shouldn't have been. Most people bore me.'

'You said, before she came, that you felt a kind of strange affinity with her,' Eleanor reminded him.

'If ever,' Robert said, 'I want to hear how stupid I sound, I only have to get you to play something back to me. I deny it, anyway.'

'It's absolutely verbatim,' Eleanor protested.

'Then I was teasing you.'

'You were deadly serious.'

'Exactly. Well, now I'm not. I'm sensible enough to be casual and flippant about the whole thing. For my sainted mum, I feel nothing but irritation. When she's gone, I'll feel the way I do about the starving hordes of India.'

'You mean—a kind of remote compassion?' Eleanor asked, earnestly.

'Oh, Eleanor, my love, what a way you have with words,' Robert said, gravely. 'Look, there's the boat. I trust you will meet madam and convey her to the plane with all due dispatch and care on Friday, for which I shall be truly grateful. 'Tis better her memories of her son should be happy ones.'

'They won't be happy,' Eleanor said, sadly, 'but at least she won't expect anything ever again.'

'Good,' Robert said.

'Is it good?' Eleanor asked, 'I don't think it's good. I think it's absolutely terrible. There she's been, your mother, all her life wanting to be loved and told she's loved, and no one has ever done it for her.'

'She's never done it for anyone herself,' Robert said. 'She didn't even like my father.'

'I know. But she loved her children.'

'Her babies, you mean. Once we were individuals she didn't even want to know us, never mind love us.'

'Oh, you're wrong,' Eleanor wailed. 'You're so wrong, but it's always like that. Are there any happy families, do you think?'

'Yes,' Robert said decisively.

'Name one.'

'Ours. Yours and mine. We'll love our children and understand them and they'll love us and understand us.'

'That's cheating,' Eleanor protested. 'But even supposing we had children, it wouldn't be like that.'

'But it would.'

'How can you be so sure?'

'Because we love each other, and we'd have children because we wanted them and expected nothing from them.'

'Is that all it takes?'

'It is. You'll miss the boat.'

'I will, I must run.'

'See you on Friday night.'

'You take a lot for grantd.'

'All people in love do.'

'Friday,' Eleanor said, and ran down to catch the boat, waving without looking back.

When Robert got back to his hut, Maudie was sitting waiting for him, very composed and expectant looking.

'Did she get the boat?' Maudie asked.

'She did.' Robert whistled cheerfully as he sat down and took his shoes off.

'She isn't a bad girl, really,' Maudie said, and sniffed. 'Needs a lot of silly nonsense knocked out of her, but her heart's in the right place.'

'I'm glad you think so,' Robert said, sweetly.

'You ought to marry her,' Maudie said. When Robert didn't reply, she added, with a great effort, 'I'd like you to marry her.'

'I told you,' Robert said. 'I'd marry her tomorrow if she'd agree.'

'Why won't she?' Maudie asked. 'She cares for you.'

'She's frightened of marriage.'

'Silly thing.'

'I'm not worried,' Robert said, 'marriage is only a ceremony, after all. If I can have Eleanor without marrying her, it comes to the same thing.'

'It does not,' Maudie shouted. 'It does not come to the same thing at all. Two people are not made one unless they are joined in holy matrimony before a minister of the church.'

'Two people,' Robert said, quietly, 'are never made one. Two people are always two people. Eleanor is on her own and I'm on my own and you, Mother, are on your own. Holy matrimony, nor anything else, can alter that.'

Maudie stared at him. Without seeming to realise what an impact he had made, Robert went on doing the things he always did before he went to bed. In the middle of the heavy silence, he rattled tea cups and refilled the lamp and pulled his bed slightly away from the wall. Maudie left him and went next door, and sat on the bed in the darkness. Everyone was on their own, that was what he had said. Even people truly in love were on their own. Even when you had been physically joined to someone you were on your own, and even when you had created someone they were not an extension of yourself but someone separate, on their own. Robert saying that made such a difference. It made it more bearable to realise that her search had been fruitless before it began, because everyone was on their own.

'I am on my own,' she said in her head. 'They are on their own,' she said.

Maudie's last few days were a halcyon period. She had so many last things to do that she did not need to upset Robert's house. She even condescended to spend the earlier part of the mornings sitting stoically on the beach to make the most of the sunshine she had loathed, though she made her escape in plenty of time to avoid Robert's swim. In the evenings, she would not be drawn into any garrulous sagas, but busied herself furiously finishing a sweater for her indifferent son, only opening her mouth to repeat some admonition about what she thought generally and in particular of his way of life. It was worse, she claimed, than giving him up to be a missionary in darkest Africa.

They said goodbye brusquely and with ease. Maudie sarcastically thanked Robert for putting himself out on her behalf, and said she hoped he would dress himself decently when he came to her funeral, as that would doubtless be the next time she would see him. Robert just smiled, and bowed his assent, and left Eleanor to do the honours.

Eleanor tried, but was hurt to find Maudie seemed to have forgotten the new depth and harmony between them. She brushed off Eleanor's emotion with something akin to her old disgust, and was barely civil to her. She told her twice she ought to wear a skirt like a proper lady, that she was too old to have her hair cut like a boy's, and that she ought to learn to

232

speak proper English. All in all, Eleanor was glad to see her charge on to the plane, and even more glad that Robert was not there to witness her treatment. She could hardly bring herself to think 'poor old lady' as the plane took off and she waved hard at its disappearing outline.

Meanwhile, Maudie had settled herself in, an immense satisfaction already sweeping over her to be going home and to be shot of the lot of them. A satisfaction so deep that it soon sent her to sleep, which only went to show what a seasoned traveller she had become.

EPILOGUE

The rain rattled against the front door and dripped steadily through the leak in the skylight of the back kitchen roof. It only did that if it had rained solidly for a very long time. As an indulgence to herself, seeing it was her first morning back, Maudie had got out of bed, lit the fire, made a pot of tea and got back in again. She lay now with the covers up to her chin, watching the fire, experimenting with how bad her arthritis was and thinking how busy her day was going to be.

She had arrived back quite late the night before, which was as she would have wished it even if the plane had not been late. There had, of course, been no one to meet her, but with so little of her spending money spent, she had treated herself to a taxi from the terminal, a wicked, shocking waste only justified by the awful weight of that blessed case. She had got the man to drop her at the end of the street, and drop her case further up at the door, just so she could savour the joy of coming home to the full.

There had been nobody about to recognise her and pester her with embarrassing questions. Annie McAllister had been warned to light the fire and then get herself right out, which Maudie was hoping she had done. She walked very slowly down the street, trying to pretend she was coming back from shopping in the town. Her legs felt stiff with all the sitting. She counted the doors as she walked along, a silly habit she had always had because she liked the neatness of her door being bang in the middle. They were good, solid doors, nearly all painted brown or black or dark green. The colour of the stone to either side of them seemed a mixture of the same drabness.

Maudie had paused to look through her own front window

234

before turning into the yard and going in at the back, just so she could see everything was all right out there. She had always been glad to be one of the seventeen people to have a front door and a front window. Most of the buildings only had a hall door at the end of their particular passage. The front room had looked satisfyingly calm and tidy to her eagle eye. Nobody had been taking liberties, mentioning no names.

Climbing the back stairs, her excitement had made her short of breath. She would have murdered anyone who hailed her at that point, so she tiptoed as quietly as possible past the bottom window. Her key slid easily into the lock and the minute she opened the door and stepped in, she knew Annie had done her job well. There was no mustiness. The window had been opened regularly. There was just a pleasant, close, intimate smell which she recognised as a rabbit must its burrow.

The place looked lovely, a proper treat. Each little thing she did brought her more pleasure than the last. She talked to herself cheerfully while she made her rounds, and even hummed as she wound the clock and put a bottle in her bed. She hadn't unpacked her case—best save that for tomorrow. Instead, she aired an old nightie she'd left behind and put that on after trying the mirror test—pressed it against a mirror where it would leave a faint film if it was damp—and slipped into bed. She said her prayers lying down, asking to be excused.

But she had that busy day ahead. Her long holidays had made her idle. She had shopping, such a shopping, to do and cleaning and baking—there was no hope of getting even a five minutes' sit down till midnight. Taking a deep breath, she got up and as she did so, remembered it was Tuesday. Jean's letter always came on Tuesdays. But their routine had suffered a long interruption: Tuesdays might not be Tuesdays any more. All the same, she opened the door and looked down the passage before she got dressed, and when she saw the letter on the mat she was delighted. Robert's came on Wednesdays, and Jean's on Tuesdays, and that was how it was still going to be.

The first month after her travels was Maudie's most enjoyable part. She never felt lonely or fed up once. It took her days, as she had known it would, to even feel time hanging a little heavily on her hands. There was so much in the immediate past to feed on that she never found herself getting upset by anything further back. She was so thankful to have her precious routine back that she did not get depressed at the few things she had to look forward to.

Now and again, Annie would say slyly to her, 'I don't know why you came back at all if you had such a fine time.'

'You wouldn't,' Maudie said, 'you'd be like a leech to get off if anyone invited you to stay.'

'I haven't anyone to ask me,' Annie said. 'I haven't any children welcoming me in my old age.'

'Oh shut up,' Maudie said.

'Which one will you go and live with in the end?' Annie asked.

'In the end I'll live in a box six feet under ground till my Maker sees fit to take me up,' Maudie snapped.

'I meant——' Annie began.

'I know what you meant,' Maudie said, 'and you've got more of a silly old fool than I remembered you were.'

That sufficed for the occasion, but weeks later Maudie found herself thinking about whether she would ever go to see them again. The summer was here, so nothing was so bad, but after that stretched the winter and there was nothing at all in it. Nothing would happen. Nothing would change. All she would do all the time would be think about her children and what they were doing, and had done and would do.

So when Annie started again on the same tack with 'Don't your dear bairns want you back with them again?' Maudie said 'Yes, they do.'

'And will you be going?'

'I might. I can't very well *not* go again, can I?' grumbled Maudie.

'Oh, you're so lucky having them,' Annie wailed.

'Dear God,' Maudie said, thinking she would write to Jean that night, 'dear God, Annie McAllister, if I go off again it'll be to get away from your endless whining, and that's the truth. Just to get a bit of peace, that's all.'

Humbly, Annie smiled. 'Oh it must be lovely living with them,' she said.

'It isn't lovely at all,' Maudie said, more to herself than Annie. 'It has its drawbacks, same as everything else. If I had any fancy notions about how it would be, Annie McAllister, I got rid of them last time. But it's better than staying here.'

'Oh yes,' Annie breathed. 'Oh, it must be lovely not to be on your own.'

'Rubbish,' Maudie said, emphatically. 'Everyone is on their own and the sooner you learnt that and stopped moaning the better, Annie. Everyone—is—on—their—own.' And so saying, Maudie got up and flung open her kitchen door to show the lowly Annie that the audience was terminated.